The Temple of the Blind

Book Five

Secret of the Labyrinth

Brian Harmon

Secret of the Labyrinth

Published by Brian Harmon

Cover Image and Design by Brian Harmon

ISBN: 1477690387

ISBN-13: 9781477690383

Also by Brian Harmon

The Box
(Book One of The Temple of the Blind)

Gilbert House
(Book Two of The Temple of the Blind)

The Temple of the Blind
(Book Three of The Temple of the Blind)

Road Beneath the Wood
(Book Four of The Temple of the Blind)

For Mom & Dad

Chapter 1

Nicole stopped and looked back the way she'd come. She was beginning to wonder whether this tunnel would ever end. It had been well over an hour since she, Brandy and Albert stepped through the north gate of the hive-like City of the Blind and yet the walls of this passage continued to unfold from the darkness before them, threatening to go on forever.

Her feet hurt. Her legs were sore. She could feel the cool air upon her naked skin, but the sheer exertion of pushing ever forward was adequate to fend off the chill.

"Tired," Brandy sighed as she stopped walking and leaned against the wall of the tunnel. It was the first thing any of them had said in a while.

Nicole turned and looked forward again, her eyes washing over her friends. All three of them were still filthy from entering that awful, mud-filled chamber. The drying, putrid sludge had hardened into a malodorous crust that covered their flesh and hair. The stench of it still filled her nostrils, refusing to fade away and let her forget that it was there. She could even taste it on her lips. It was foul. And it was a constant reminder of what she and her friends had already endured within this strange labyrinth, this "Temple of the Blind," as Albert called it.

And it was not done with them yet. They had only begun to explore the corridors beyond the city. How much longer would they have to endure? And what unpleasant things still remained in store for them?

Brandy pressed her back to the wall and then let herself slide down the cool stone until she was sitting on the floor and resting her aching feet and legs in front of her.

Albert had gone several steps farther before stopping. Now he stood silently in the beam of Nicole's flashlight, staring into the endless darkness that constantly filled the passage ahead. She stared at his bare back, wondering what he was thinking.

There was no lack of troubling things to weigh on his mind. So much had happened in such a short amount of time. It seemed like days ago that she stood in the bathroom at Albert and Brandy's apartment, listening to the ringing phone that no one wanted to answer. It seemed almost silly now, after all they'd been through, that those silent messages had filled them with such dread. They had no way of knowing then that the real nightmares were waiting for them in the dark corridors of

Gilbert House and this temple.

Was he contemplating the numbing reality of Beverly Bridger's horrific death? The disturbing memory of that moment was still vividly fresh in Nicole's mind, and unlike her, Albert actually *saw* what became of the poor woman. He had actually seen her body. She was sure that it must weigh even greater on him. And now that she thought about it, she remembered that Albert was also the only one who saw the bodies in Gilbert House…

She did not envy the things his eyes had seen.

Or was it instead the heavy words of the Sentinel Queen that occupied his thoughts? She had burdened them with a mysterious task, a quest vital to the very future of humanity, if she could be believed, and yet she refused to tell them how to get there or even what it was that they sought. She had mentioned only a doorway of some sort. However, she'd had no problem thrusting that whole psychic thing onto Albert and Brandy. Nicole had no idea how she would feel if she were in their place, but she suspected it would bother her considerably.

Or maybe Albert was merely worrying about Wayne, all alone in some other ungodly passageway, trying to rescue poor Olivia from that nightmare forest.

Nicole stared at Albert, her light illuminating his dirty back, tiredly admiring his build, barely aware of her eyes lingering on his mud-caked buttocks.

"I've got to rest for a while," Brandy said. "My feet are killing me."

Albert stood where he was for a moment longer, still staring into the darkness ahead, not speaking. Then, finally, he slowly turned and faced them.

Nicole looked away from him, embarrassed, and stared back the way they came. She had become perfectly comfortable with her own nudity by now, accepting that Albert was her friend and that it was okay if he saw her naked. In fact, it was much easier to stand naked in front of him than she would ever have imagined. But it still made her feel strange to look at *him* like that. It felt so wrong. She envied Brandy. As his girlfriend, Brandy had no need to feel embarrassed by the sight of him unclothed.

But then again, she rather envied Brandy for a lot of reasons…

"I think that's a good idea," Albert agreed. He walked back to where Brandy had stopped and sat down beside her. Immediately, she seized his left arm and pressed herself against him, resting her head on his shoulder.

"You're stinky," she told him.

"I know."

Brandy smiled tiredly and closed her eyes.

Nicole lingered for another moment, looking back and forth into the looming darkness that filled the passage on either side of them, and then she joined them, sitting down on Brandy's other side and scooting close to her.

"How much farther?" Brandy asked, not opening her eyes.

Albert did not respond. He merely shook his head wearily.

"We haven't even got to the labyrinth yet, have we?"

Albert kissed her head. The lovely, apple scent of her shampoo was gone. A deep, vulgar stench clung about her from the crust of stagnant mud that clung to every surface of her body. "I don't think so," he admitted.

There were no branches in the road, no decisions, no wrong ways. There were not even any turns in the path. There was nothing here that even remotely resembled a labyrinth. This was all merely one single passage.

Immediately after they passed through the north gate, they found a set of steps leading up a short distance, exactly like those leading away from the south gate, except that there was only one flight. At the top was a small, oval-shaped room with two sentinels.

Albert had stopped at the top of the steps and studied these statues for a moment. They seemed different than the others, warmer somehow. The one on the right was reaching toward them with its long left arm, its deformed hand open and inviting. Its right arm was stretched out in the other direction, its freakishly long index finger pointing the way forward. The blank surface where its face should have been was fixed on them. There were no eyes or mouth or other features to suggest emotions of any kind, but it was clearly urging them forward.

The statue on the left was identical, but facing the other way, as if inviting someone coming from the other direction to venture forward into the Sentinel Queen's city. Albert passed between the statues and turned to view them from the opposite side of the room. It was eerie to see the same view from both sides. It was easy to imagine forgetting which way was out. But of course, there was nowhere to go but back to the north gate should they get so turned around.

Brandy had stood between the two sentinels for a moment, looking at them. She commented that they were contradicting each other, but Albert knew better. "Don't forget what the Sentinel Queen said," he reminded her. "She was talking about fourteen women who entered the city from the north gate."

"Could that be true?" Nicole asked. She found it very difficult to imagine that humanity somehow migrated into the world through this very room.

"I don't know if it is or not," Albert replied. "But it doesn't matter. If *anyone* ever came through here, from wherever this leads, these guys would have greeted them exactly like they greeted us just now. It's a two-way door, of sorts. A welcome mat that points both ways." He stared up at the statues for a moment, wondering. "If it *is* true, if those women were real…we could be standing in a very important place. It's like a crossroads in time. Thousands of years apart, but seeing it exactly the same way they did... Even if those women weren't all the Sentinel Queen said they were, even if they weren't carrying the entire human race in their wombs, they might still be significantly important to our history."

They said no more about it. Silently, thoughtfully, the three of them moved on past the room with the two welcoming sentinels, ready to get started on their long (and likely very unpleasant) journey into the labyrinth. But there had been nothing beyond that room but these same four stone surfaces. The passage had merely stretched on and on.

The three of them sat together for a while, listening to the eerily empty silence, thinking about all the things they had seen and done in the hours that led them to this quiet moment.

"Do you think we'll ever see him again?" Nicole asked.

Albert and Brandy both lifted their faces and looked at her. It was a question that had troubled them all since the Sentinel Queen tore Wayne away from them. It seemed so cruel after all they'd been through. They faced the monster in Gilbert House with him. They suffered together. They journeyed together into this insane temple. He became their friend in the midst of all the horror and wonder. And then he was simply taken away, as suddenly as Beverly Bridger, if not as gruesomely.

But they had to let him go. They had to believe that Olivia might really still be out there. They had to believe that death was not the only inevitability of this insane adventure.

Brandy wanted to say yes. Of course they would see him again. He was big and strong and brave. He would certainly endure whatever silly trials awaited him in his quest to find Olivia. But she didn't know that. Not really. For all she knew, he was already dead. After all, what did they really know about the Sentinel Queen? What reason did they have to trust her? For all they knew, she could have lied to them and led him away simply to shove him into another pit of spikes or feed him to a pack of hounds.

And even if he *did* survive, even if he *did* manage to rescue Olivia and find his way home, who was to say they would ever cross paths with him again? Either way, they may never know what became of him after the Sentinel Queen took him from them.

She simply didn't know.

"I think we will," Albert said after a moment.

Brandy and Nicole both looked up at him, their eyes hopeful.

"Everything that's happened down here… It's so far beyond ordinary. It has to mean something, right? It can't all just be cruel chance. Whatever the reason for us all being down here, I'm sure he's as much a part of it as we are."

"You really think so?" Brandy asked.

"I do."

"Is that your psychic sense telling you that?" Nicole

wondered.

Albert smiled. “I have no idea. Maybe.” It was still so weird to imagine that he was actually psychic. He was still getting over the shock of such a profound idea. He certainly didn’t know how to use it. “I just feel like we’ll see him again sometime.”

Brandy squeezed his arm a little tighter and rested her head against his shoulder again.

“I hope so,” said Nicole. She watched them for a moment, her two closest friends in the world, then lowered her eyes to her flashlight and wondered what Wayne was doing at that very moment.

It was embarrassing to think about, but she’d actually been nurturing a little bit of a crush for Wayne. After all, he had appeared out of nowhere, seemingly for no other reason than to keep them safe as they wandered blindly into the dangerous hallways of Gilbert House. It was not so very unlike the way Brandy and Albert were brought together. And she couldn’t help but feel a small pang of jealousy whenever she thought about Brandy’s amazing story of how she fell in love with the man of her dreams. She’d give anything to have made such a powerful connection with someone half as wonderful as Albert.

All she’d had was Earl…

Of course, Wayne hadn’t really been *quite* as impressive as Albert. He was handsome, sure, and brave. He was *bigger* than Albert. Stronger. But it was clear that he didn’t have nearly the patience or the even-temperedness that Albert possessed. The anger he displayed toward Beverly certainly didn't win her affection, even if she *was* sympathetic of the emotions beneath his temper.

Wayne also hadn't seemed to be as keenly intelligent as Albert, either, but that had since proven to be a gross misperception. Wayne may not have been the impressive mystery-solver that Albert was, but he was definitely very smart.

He was full of surprises. Just like Albert…

But Wayne wasn't bravely charging into that terrifying forest to rescue Nicole. He was doing it for Olivia.

She looked again at Albert, who was tiredly staring past her into the darkness that led back to the City of the Blind and the mysterious Sentinel Queen. She considered asking him if he really thought they could do this, if he really believed they had what it took to survive down here. She considered asking him how they expected to navigate a labyrinth this size when they didn't even know what they were looking for. She considered asking him how long he thought they could continue to keep away from the hounds. But she didn't get to ask him anything. The tired thoughtfulness on his face suddenly vanished. He sat up and aimed his flashlight into the darkness where he'd been staring.

Startled, Brandy and Nicole both swung their flashlights in the same direction.

There was nothing there.

"What is it?" asked Brandy. There was an unmistakable edge to her voice.

Albert continued to stare into the darkness, his expression puzzled. Finally, after a moment, he shook his head. "Nothing, I guess. Imagining things."

"I'm sorry, Sweetie," Brandy retorted nervously, still searching the empty tunnel for whatever compelled him to shine his light toward it, "but you're not the most *imaginative* person I know."

Albert glanced at her, amused. "Maybe." Again his eyes returned to the empty passageway. "But there's nothing there."

But something *did* seem to be there a moment ago, some indefinite shape in the darkness, something that was gone now.

"Maybe it was that blind guy," Nicole suggested. "The Sentinel Queen's son. Maybe he was checking up on us."

"Maybe," Albert agreed. Although the last time they saw the man with no eyes, he didn't seem to be in the best condition for stalking.

Nicole hugged herself tightly and shivered as a sudden chill gripped her. She wished this place had lights. It was unnerving to see nothing but darkness at the end of these tunnels for so very long.

"We'll rest a little longer," Albert decided. "Then we'll move on."

Brandy squeezed his arm again and nuzzled a little closer.

Nicole rested her head on Brandy's shoulder and stared back into the darkness, watching.

Chapter 2

The passage continued on. The relentless darkness refused to give up anything more than the same two walls, the same floor and ceiling, the same gray stone. Albert was beginning to feel trapped. Claustrophobia was creeping in, wrapping its cruel fingers around him, slowly squeezing the very breath from him. It had become far too easy to imagine that this tunnel had no end at all, that the three of them would merely walk and walk and walk, never to find anything more than the same endless stone. It was as if they were going nowhere at all, as if they could turn around right now, only to find the two sentinel statues standing just beyond the veil of darkness at their backs. Or perhaps they would walk for hours, only to find that the tunnel was as endless backward as it was forward. The sheer hell of such a merciless eternity was more than he could hope to comprehend, yet his thoughts were mired in the idea, like a car spinning in the mud, and he could not pull them free. How long before they collapsed from exhaustion? How long would it take to die down here?

He forced these awful thoughts from his mind. That was a ridiculous thing to think. The passage could not really go on forever. That was nonsense. Even after all that he'd seen, even after the impossible things inside Gilbert House, he couldn't really believe that they were suddenly trapped inside a magical, endless loop of passage. Hard logic told him that it must have an end as surely as it had a beginning. And yet, that logic only allowed him to more clearly see the enormity of the task before him. How big was the Temple of the Blind? How massive was this labyrinth they were expected to navigate? He supposed they could be going in a circle rather than a straight line. They could only see for a short distance in either direction, after all. A subtle-enough curve in the path would be imperceptible. But even so, the sheer size of this place remained overwhelming. How could the Sentinel Queen possibly expect them to succeed? Psychic or not, they were only human.

He glanced at Brandy as she walked beside him. She looked tired, of course. The rest they had taken was not enough. She needed more than a few minutes off her feet. She needed a meal and a night's sleep in her own bed. She wasn't cut out for such an exhausting trek. Neither was Nicole. Neither was he. They'd undergone no kind of endurance training. They were not soldiers or athletes. They were just ordinary college students. They were in good shape. They were healthy. They were neither overweight nor malnourished. But they weren't used to this sort of exertion.

"How you doing?" he asked.

Brandy looked at him, her eyes weary. "I'm okay," she replied. "Feet still hurt."

"Mine too." He glanced back at Nicole, who was keeping pace behind them. "You okay?"

"I'm fine." And she *did* sound fine, if a little tired. Of all of them, she was probably the most capable. She was the one who worked out. She was the one who spent her spare time in the college gym, the one who actually jogged in the mornings. She was not simply handed that ideal body, after all. She worked for it.

Brandy frequently went with her to the gym. She was no stranger to the treadmill. But she didn't go religiously. And she wasn't very fond of jogging. It wasn't about looking her best. For her it was merely a way to get out and enjoy some girl-time with her best friend.

Albert, on the other hand, hardly ever set foot inside the gym. He grew bored working out. It left his thoughts frustratingly idle. He'd rather spend his spare time engaging his mind with a good mystery novel, or perhaps challenging himself with a puzzle, even if it was only the daily Sudoku.

Did that mean it would ultimately be *he* who collapsed first from exhaustion? Would the girls be forced to look after him in their final hours should the darkness refuse to relinquish anything more than this same maddening passageway?

Again, he turned his eyes to his girlfriend. He couldn't bear the thought of something happening to Brandy. Maybe he should turn back. Maybe he should tell the Sentinel Queen to forget it, to find someone else to seek out her mysterious doorway. After all, each step they took was one more step they'd presumably have to take to get home. The farther they went, the farther they were from the warmth and comfort of their own beds.

But it would only be that much farther he'd have to travel when he came back. And he knew damn well that he *would* come back. His maddening curiosity would never allow him to stay away. The mystery of this place would haunt him for the rest of his life.

The tunnel stretched on. The darkness relinquished nothing, step after step, and Albert began to understand how easily the human mind could be plunged into madness.

With claustrophobia crushing down on him, and a mounting, irrational fear that they were not actually moving at all, he was about to stop and attempt to gather his wits when something finally emerged from the relentless darkness.

For a moment, he thought he was imagining it. For so long there had been nothing there. But it was real. It was a stone archway, exactly like the one they passed through when they first entered this maddening passageway, back when they departed the City of the Blind. It was also identical (or as identical as Albert had the capacity to discern) to the two archways that stood on either end of the much shorter passage that led them from the mud-filled chamber to the south gate of the city.

His eyes washed over the carvings on the stone surface of the arch. All those naked bodies, writhing together in a strange amalgamation of emotions, screaming, moaning, sobbing, laughing, filled him with a strange sense of self-awareness. He was suddenly very eager to see what lay beyond…yet he was afraid of what may await him. He felt the soreness of his feet and legs more than ever, and yet he felt a powerful urge to run ahead. He was newly embarrassed by his nudity…and freshly aroused by the nudity of his companions.

Beyond the archway was nothing. The walls and ceiling and floor simply ceased beyond the intricately carved stone. An enormous chamber lay on the other side, shrouded in the same eternal darkness that crowded the long passageway at their backs.

Albert shined his light into this cavernous space. He could see no solid surface for as far as his light reached.

A few inches from his bare toes, where the floor abruptly dropped into black oblivion, was the still surface of a vast pool of crystal-clear water.

It appeared that they would again have to swim.

Brandy swore bitterly at the sight. She had not felt warm all night, not since leaving her home early that evening. It wasn't fair. Why did they have to keep suffering like this? What was the point in it? More and more, she hated this insane temple. It seemed that it was designed for no other purpose than to torture anyone unfortunate enough to enter it.

"On the bright side, it should wash off some of this stink," Albert offered.

"I'd rather stink," Brandy retorted.

"I don't think *anything* can ever wash it off," Nicole grumbled.

Albert shrugged. "Okay, then. As long as we're all staying positive." He peered down into the water. There was no gradual descent in this room, only a sheer drop with no visible bottom. In a way, this should be easier than the first time. He could simply jump into the water and get it over with quickly. It would be far easier than the gradual torture of the slow descent he'd endured in the last pool.

"Where does all this water come from?" Nicole asked.

"I'm guessing the whole temple is fed by an underground river somewhere, piped through a sort of reservoir system built right into the stone. There's probably an inlet and an outlet somewhere in this room to keep the water level. Or maybe just gravity. I doubt it's even all that complicated."

"Why *wouldn't* it be complicated?" Brandy asked. "They

haven't made anything else simple."

"True." He removed the backpack and handed it and his flashlight to Brandy. "Might as well get it over with."

Neither Brandy nor Nicole objected. There was no alternative. It wasn't as if a boat was going to pull up and ferry them across.

Albert stepped into the archway and took a deep breath. He desperately did not want to do this. No amount of psyching himself up was going to make it any easier. But there was no other choice. Going back was no better an option and he knew it.

He braced himself for the worst and leapt out over the water.

He was wrong. There was no easy way to face the water inside the temple. It was cold. Much colder than the stone, colder than it should have been, it seemed, as if it sprang from some unfathomable, frozen depth. In an instant, his body was enveloped in a blanket of brutal cold that gripped every square inch of his flesh. It did not numb him, but rather stung him, almost burning him with its icy touch, as if he had not leapt into water at all, but a great sea of flesh-eating acid. For a moment, he could not even move. His muscles were locked, his heart seemingly frozen in his chest. He couldn't even open his eyes.

He realized he was sinking. His breath gone, sucked from his lungs in a great fury of bubbles in that first, agonizing instant, he was no longer buoyant enough to stay afloat. Slowly, he was slipping deeper and deeper into the darkness beneath him, as though he were encased in heavy, crushing stone. Panic welled up within him as the seconds ticked by. He was paralyzed by the cold, unable to tell if his heart was even beating. He doubted suddenly that it would feel any different if he had leapt into liquid nitrogen, his body literally frozen, trapped helplessly within himself as death closed its frigid hands around him.

He had just enough time to wonder if he was going to die like this before his heart exploded back to life and he burst free of his paralysis.

Desperately, he scrambled upward, thrashing and kicking until his face broke from the surface and he gasped for air.

"*Fucking damn it!*" he screamed, his voice echoing throughout the enormous chamber.

"Well that's encouraging," mumbled Nicole.

"Are you okay?" asked Brandy.

Albert tried to gather himself, tried to calm the shaking and the chattering of his teeth, but it was overwhelming. He felt chilled all the way to his bones. "It's damn cold," he told her. "Colder than before, I think."

The concern on Brandy's face was overshadowed by dread. She did not want to go in there. She did not want to be cold again. It was a miserable feeling knowing that she would have to face that kind of discomfort all over again.

"I'm going to get so sick," Nicole sighed.

Around Albert, the water had grown murky from the mud that had been caked on his skin. It wafted off him in a foul black cloud as he swam back to the archway and held his hand out for his flashlight.

Brandy knelt down and handed it to him, then dipped her fingers in the water. Albert was right. It felt even colder than the last pool, if that was possible. The very thought of submerging herself in that frigid water made her teeth begin to chatter.

"Good thing we all know how to swim," Nicole observed, staring down into the black depths.

Albert nodded. It was true. If any one of them had been unable to swim, or worse, suffered an aquatic phobia, this might have proven to be an impassible barrier. He had a cousin who was afraid of water. He refused to go aboard boats and could not even be convinced to put his feet into a pool. Growing up, Albert never understood. It was just water. Surely he could see that it was not dangerous. It was utterly irrational. But as he grew older, Albert began to understand that it was the nature of phobias to be illogical. By their very definition, they were irrational.

Now that he was thinking about it, there were a great number of fears that the temple of the blind encouraged. Water, darkness, small spaces…bloodthirsty hounds…

In fact, he decided it was best not to think too much about

any of those things. To say the least, this would be a lousy time to develop an inconvenient phobia.

"Come on," he urged, taking the backpack and slipping it over his shoulders.

Brandy looked at Nicole and held out her hand. "Go in with me?"

The pitiful look in her eyes told Brandy that she did not want to, that she would rather do almost anything but go in there, but she knew that she had no choice. They had to go forward. Even if they went back, they would eventually have to get wet again.

Albert swam back to give them room. Even shivering so hard he could barely breathe, even with his teeth hammering together with the violence of the cold, he could not help but appreciate how lovely the two of them were as they stood before him, their lean bodies dirty and bare. The sight would have been tremendously arousing if the biting cold hadn't severed his body's ability to react to such a thing.

Well… Mostly.

Brandy and Nicole squeezed each other's hand and then stepped forward and plunged into the water. Brandy pinched her nose with her free hand as her feet left the stone floor. Nicole threw her free arm up instead, as though changing her mind at the last second and reaching for a safety line that wasn't there. For a brief instant they were in the air, their bodies rigid against the unpleasant shock they knew was imminent, and then they splashed into the water and vanished beneath the chopping surface.

Brandy shot back up like a bobber on a fishing line, a shrill scream on her lips. Nicole remained under for a few brief seconds, possibly having suffered the same paralyzing jolt that Albert experienced, and when her head broke the surface she, too, screamed.

Already, the water around them had become murky with the filth that had washed from their skin and hair. A dark cloud blossomed around their bodies as they struggled to stay afloat.

"*Fuck that's cold!*" Nicole exclaimed, her body already racked with shivers.

Brandy screamed a second time, short and shrill, then a third time and a fourth, her arms splashing at the water, fighting the biting cold.

"Oh my god!" Nicole went on. "Oh my fucking god!"

"Oh god!" Brandy agreed.

Albert would have laughed if he hadn't been fighting the same gnawing cold himself. "Come on," he said. "Let's get to the other side before we freeze."

Shivering violently, the three of them made their way across the water, their flashlights in constant motion so that the chopping waves became a disorienting kaleidoscope of light and shadow through which they struggled, barely keeping their heads above the surface. The room itself was at least a hundred yards across. Perhaps more. It was difficult for Albert to estimate it while battling the cold. It *felt* at least as long as a football field. And there was no knowing how wide it might be. By the time the far end of the chamber came into view, a real fear that they might get turned around and lost had begun to pervade his thoughts.

But somehow they had only veered a few degrees off course. Albert wondered if they were merely lucky or if the psychic abilities the Sentinel Queen claimed he possessed gave him some kind of guidance system down here. He rather doubted that he had such abilities, but he dared to hope. It would certainly come in handy.

The three of them climbed out of the water and into the next passageway. It was identical to the one they just left, and it wasn't difficult to imagine that they had done nothing more than circle back to where they began. But somehow Albert did not think that was the case.

"Oh god!" Brandy cried as shivers raced through her naked body.

Albert turned around and embraced her, pressing his body against hers, trying to pass what little warmth he had into her. When Nicole approached them, her body trembling with the cold, he took her by the arm and pulled her toward him as well. She did not refuse him. Perhaps she didn't have the strength.

The cold was draining. It overwhelmed them.

Albert wondered how real the danger of hypothermia was down here. Was the water cold enough? It sure *felt* cold enough. It was agonizing. And yet, they'd survived an extended swim through it, their skin numb but otherwise unharmed. In the arctic seas, exposure to the water for more than a few minutes meant certain death. This water had felt cold as hell, but it wasn't frozen. It likely wasn't anywhere *near* freezing. In fact, it was probably at least ten or twenty degrees warmer than that, making it a laughable choice for a polar bear club, which he was now convinced that he would never join. Not for any amount of money.

For a long time, the three of them stood this way, huddled together in the darkness, naked and dripping, quivering in the cold, their bare flesh pressed together. It was an intimate moment, but it was not at all erotic. There was a bond between them now that was akin to that of a close family. Just hours ago they might have felt uncomfortable huddled together like this, even with their clothes on. But now it was as natural to each of them as a conversation.

"We should get moving again," Albert suggested after a while. "It'll warm us up faster."

"I hope so," Nicole said with a sniffle. They were all sniffling now. Perhaps she had been right about them getting sick. "I feel like I'm freezing to death."

“Me too,” agreed Brandy.

But the three of them remained a moment longer, their shivering bodies pressed intimately together.

Chapter 3

Though they were not precisely clean, the swim across the frigid pool had washed the majority of the mud and muck from their skin and hair. In the backlight of their flashlights, their bodies again glowed softly pink in the gloom.

They walked close together, their arms interlocked, their thighs brushing, still attempting to share their warmth. The cold continued to envelope them long after the water had stopped dripping from their naked skin. They shivered hard and deep, as if their very bones were frozen.

This tunnel was not as long as the last. They followed it only a few hundred yards before they stepped into a chamber that was larger than most, but still considerably smaller than many that they had found. Sentinel statues stood tall and alert along the walls, but not as they had in the rooms that preceded the emotion rooms. These were closer together, their elbows nearly touching. Each one was the same. Their feet were together, their legs and backs straight, arms at their sides, penises limp. They did not appear to convey any sort of message. They were merely silent sentinels. Nothing more.

At the far end of the room, a short set of steps led up to a large, square opening. Still shivering, Albert moved toward it as he examined the statues on either side of them. They were all identical, and no different from the others they'd seen scattered throughout the temple. There were forty-two of them in all. He wondered if the number was in any way significant.

Inside the opening, the stone surfaces of the next tunnel were carved with strange, incomprehensible markings. They completely covered the walls, ceiling and floor.

"What *is* all this?" Brandy asked.

But Albert had no idea. He felt as if he were constantly saying, "I don't know." But the fact was, he simply *did not know.* Everything down here was so far beyond his comprehension.

These markings were different from the intricate carvings on the archways leading in and out of the City of the Blind. Those carvings had been of people. These weren't of anything he recognized. It didn't even look like language, exactly, just an obscure randomness of shapes and curves. There was no pattern, no flow, suggesting anything as intelligible as words or letters. There were no lines. The eye was not drawn in any discernable direction. If it was meant to be read, he could not tell where he was expected to even begin.

This carved passage stretched several yards and then ended in a T-shaped intersection where the carvings abruptly ended, leaving the stone surfaces smooth and featureless again. From this intersection, they would have to choose left or right, and Albert had no idea how they were supposed to know which way to go.

He examined the two choices. Both tunnels ran as far as he could see without branching, and neither gave anything away. They were empty. They were identical.

"So where do we go?" Nicole asked. She stood beside him, rubbing her shoulders for warmth, her teeth still chattering from the cold of their swim.

Albert did not know. There had always been something before, a clue of some sort, either inside the box or from a statue. But now there was nothing. He turned and looked back the way they'd come, thinking of the forty-two sentinel statues that stood against the walls of the last room, wondering if he'd missed something, and for the second time, he became aware of something standing just at the edge of the darkness, something that wasn't there before, something darker than the shadows that surrounded it.

And then it was gone.

He squeezed his eyes shut and then opened them again.

Nothing. But there was *something* there. He'd been sure of it.

He began to walk toward the place where he saw the figure, his eyes searching the shadows.

"Albert?" Brandy turned and followed him, Nicole close behind her.

Albert walked all the way back to the opening of the previous tunnel and peered into it. Whatever it was had apparently retreated. Assuming that it was ever really there at all.

He stood there for a moment, still shivering, staring into the darkness that had so long been to his back.

"What is it?" Nicole asked as she and Brandy approached him. "Did you see something?"

"I don't know," he confessed. "I thought I did…but…" But he couldn't have. There was nothing there. "Forget it. Come on."

He began walking back to the intersection, back to the decision they would have to make without any help from the box or the sentinels. But Brandy and Nicole lingered for a moment.

"I don't like it," said Nicole. She was staring into the darkness of that previous tunnel, wishing she could see all the way to its end.

Brandy did not like it either. She and Albert had experienced the same thing when they first entered the Temple of the Blind thirteen months ago. Something kept appearing in the shadows at the edge of their vision and then vanishing before they could investigate. They assumed later that it must have been the man with no eyes. And maybe this was him again, perhaps keeping an eye on them for his mother, the Sentinel Queen. But back in the City of the Blind, he hadn't appeared to be in ideal shape for such stealthy stalking.

Albert took another look at the forty-two sentinels as he passed them, trying to find some kind of clue hidden among them, but there seemed to be nothing to find. There were no messengers among them. They were only sentinels. Nothing more.

He climbed the steps and approached the tunnel…and then he saw it there.

It was standing in the middle of the intersection, right where he had been standing mere moments before. It was a dark figure, almost black, much smaller than the sentinels. Its shape was hard to see. It was hunched forward. It did not move. He would have dismissed it as another statue had it not simply appeared there while his back was turned.

Was this what he had seen in the passage behind him? If so, how had it gotten ahead of them?

Brandy and Nicole had been following him up the steps, several paces behind him. Now they stopped and stared, startled by the thing they saw waiting for them.

Albert took a cautious step forward, trying to get a closer look at it. He had seen a lot of strange things already. The man with no eyes. The monster inside Gilbert House. The Sentinel Queen. But this was unlike any of them. It was small, little more than four feet in height, and skinny, almost skeletal. It was more like a corpse than any living creature he had ever seen.

He took another step and the creature's head moved just a little, almost a twitch, and he stopped.

"What is it?" Brandy asked, her voice barely a whisper.

Nicole reached out and took her hand.

It slowly turned its head to the side, not on a vertical axis in the manner of a man or a woman, but on a horizontal one, rotating it clockwise as if its spine was connected at the back of its skull instead of at its base, until its chin was almost straight up and the crown of its head was pointed at the floor. As it did so, something on its face shifted grotesquely. After holding this curious pose for a few seconds, it slowly returned its head to its upright position and again there was that strange motion on its face. It did not appear to be violent. Instead, it had a look of great age, as though it might be as old as the stone walls in which it stood. But Albert was nonetheless cautious.

He took a couple more reluctant steps forward and his view of the creature improved. But it only became even more bizarre as he neared it. Its skin was dry and cracked, like old leather left out in the weather. It was loose and sagging, hanging off its body in dangling folds. Like the blind man and the Sentinel Queen, it wore not a stitch of clothing, but its flesh drooped around its waist like a skirt. It had likewise pooled around its small hands, so that it looked like the sleeves of a coat that was much too big.

"Hello?" Albert said hesitantly.

"I've been expecting you," the skinny creature said. Its voice was so coarse that its throat might have been filled with gravel and broken glass, but its words were perfectly clear.

Albert turned and looked at Brandy and Nicole, startled to hear the creature speak.

"Come closer."

Albert hesitated, not sure if he should trust this creature, but there was little else he could do. He could not simply turn back after all they'd been through and this thing blocked the road forward. While it looked small enough to do them no harm, he underestimated nothing in this place. He braced himself, ready for the worst, and stepped forward.

The creature's face was horrid. The skin on its forehead and cheeks was excessively loose and hung over several of its features like empty, fleshy sacks. Those parts that could be seen were narrow and pointed. The nose was tiny and sharp. The mouth was a small slit, similar to the mouth of the Sentinel Queen, but it hung slightly open and he could see tiny black teeth just behind its fine, almost nonexistent lips. A wrinkled mass of flesh hung from its chin almost to the middle of its naked chest.

It sniffed the air, just as the blind man had done before instructing them to disrobe. The dangling flesh of its face jiggled grotesquely as it did so. "Mmm," it said, as though it had discovered something deeply intriguing about their scent.

Albert stood there, watching the strange little creature.

"Interesting." The thing began to rotate its head again, still sniffing at the air. "You're not alone." It was not a question.

Nicole and Brandy stepped up behind Albert and studied the creature. Each of them gripped one of Albert's arms as though they feared they might suddenly fly away. He could feel their breasts pressed against his skin, but his attention was entirely focused on the creature that stood before him.

The thing had turned its head almost upside down again and Albert saw what it was that had shifted before. The flesh of its face fell away, drooping from its cheeks and forehead to reveal dull, black eyes that studied them intently.

Now it changed direction and was slowly turning its chin back toward the floor.

"Who are you," Albert asked.

"I am the Keeper," it said.

"The keeper of what?" Albert pushed.

For a moment it did not seem that the creature would reply, but then it said, "Of lots of things."

Albert looked at Brandy, then back at the creature. "I saw you behind us a minute ago, didn't I?"

"Yes."

"How did you get around us?"

"I didn't."

Albert didn't understand. He opened his mouth to ask, but before he could do so the creature said, "You would not understand if I told you. It is beyond your ability to comprehend."

He had no doubt that it was. Almost everything down here was.

"So you've been following us down these past few tunnels?"

"I've been following you the whole time."

"The whole time?"

"Since the very beginning."

The very beginning? He wondered what the beginning was. Did it begin with the trip to Gilbert House? With his finding of the box? Or had it begun long before that, a series of events leading up to this day of which he had always been ignorant.

The Keeper did not elaborate. It lifted both its hands and held them out to its sides, pointing down both passageways. "The labyrinth begins here," it said. "It does not matter which way you go. There are many ways to get there."

"To get where?" Nicole asked. "What are we looking for?"

"You will know it when you get there."

"Do you know the way?" Albert asked.

"I know all the ways."

"Can you tell us how to find it?"

"No."

Albert would have been lying if he said he was surprised. Somehow he had not expected this strange little creature, this "Keeper," to help them any more than it had to.

"You must find it on your own. It is the way it has to be."

"Like the way we had to be naked?" Albert challenged.

"Yes."

"I see." Although he didn't.

"The path will be very dangerous."

Brandy squeezed Albert's arm.

"Since you have made it this far, I feel that you deserve something. Therefore, I will warn you of the guardian of this labyrinth. The beast is known as the Caggo. You must avoid him at all cost. He was put there long ago and is bound to these walls like the darkness. He will kill any who cross his path. It is his only joy."

Albert stood there for a moment, trying to grasp the idea of some sort of killer creature stalking the corridors. How the hell were they supposed to avoid something like that inside a giant maze?

"Go now," the Keeper said.

But still Albert did not move. "What about the hounds?" he asked. "I've heard them in other areas of the labyrinth."

"The hounds exist within their own labyrinth," the Keeper replied. "The two are separate, but they intersect frequently. You do not need me to tell you how dangerous those places are."

"No," Albert agreed. "I guess I don't."

"It is not an impossible journey. You need nothing more from me. Go now. I'll answer no more questions."

Albert hesitated. He had no reason to doubt this Keeper when he said he'd answer no more questions, but he felt he deserved considerably more than this. These…*people*, for lack of a better word…were expecting a lot out of them for no more than they were willing to give them. He was quickly becoming disenchanted with the whole "mysterious intention" thing. He just wanted a straight answer to all his questions. That was the whole reason he was here.

"You need nothing more," the Keeper said again, as if it had read the thoughts right from his mind.

Reluctantly, Albert began to walk. Brandy and Nicole followed closely, their eyes fixed on the eerie little creature. Albert wanted badly to ask more questions, wanted to learn all that it knew, but as with the Sentinel Queen, he somehow knew it would be pointless.

As Nicole passed by the Keeper, it put one bony hand out and softly grasped her arm. The feel of its hot, loose flesh sliding across its bones almost made her scream.

"You," said the Keeper. "You are different. For you, I'll offer one more piece of advice. Stay away from the meadow. If you see it at the end of a tunnel, turn around and go the other way. There is nothing for you there but pain and death."

Nicole pulled away from the little creature, afraid of it and its words. She did not know what it meant about being different. She was no different than her friends.

After they passed, the creature began to walk away from them, its movements slow and cautious, like those of a feeble old man. As they watched, it paused. "And one more thing," it said, not looking back at them. "If you find the secret of the labyrinth, do not linger. By finding the way out, you will unleash a terrible curse upon these walls, one that you cannot possibly survive. Its only weakness is that, like the Caggo, it will be bound to the walls of the labyrinth."

The Keeper hobbled away, down the steps and into the darkness, vanishing from their sight.

"A curse?" Nicole asked, her voice anxious.

"I don't doubt it," Albert said.

"Which tunnel do we take?" Brandy was staring down one of the passages, her thoughts lingering on the idea of a bloodthirsty beast roaming these scary tunnels.

Albert shook his head. "It doesn't matter." He took off the backpack and removed a piece of yellow sidewalk chalk from the plastic tube inside. They would mark the tunnels as they walked, leaving a trail to follow that would at least lead them back if they got utterly lost. There were twenty thick pieces of colorful chalk in the tube, four of each color, which had looked like a lot when he saw it sitting on the shelf in the store. But now, as he shined his flashlight into each of the two tunnels, trying to decide which way to begin, it seemed laughably inadequate to the task. Suddenly he wished that he'd bought as many tubes as he could cram into the backpack. But it was too late now.

Entirely at random, he chose the path on the right.

Chapter 4

Albert had a bad feeling about this place. Being inside the labyrinth was even worse than being inside Gilbert House. The wrongness of these walls was like the lingering stench of a corpse. Though he had never really believed in evil, in that persistent notion that "bad" could be a force of nature all by itself, he could almost believe that this was an evil place. It virtually stank of wickedness, like the eerie scene of some grizzly murder. He could tell by the way Brandy clung to his arm as they walked that she could feel it too.

Somewhere among these countless stone walls was a meadow through which they must not walk and something called the Caggo whose only joy was in slaughtering trespassers, yet these were not the things that made this place feel wicked. It felt wicked because it was a wicked place, built of blood and suffering for the exile of a world. Albert did not know how he knew this, but somehow he did. He could almost hear the weeping of the first souls to ever walk this path, the weeping of women, naked, cold and pregnant and carrying a terrible burden upon their shoulders.

Albert tried to force these thoughts away. That could be nothing more than his overactive imagination. He had no way of knowing any of these things. All he knew was what he'd been told by the Sentinel Queen. She told him that fourteen women entered the city of the blind through the north gate and that they were pregnant. He had no way of knowing that they were naked. He could not possibly know that they carried a burden or that they wept as they traveled. These were merely things in his imagination, assumptions he was making in his uneasy mind. Yet these things still felt real to him, as though he had reached into the very fabric of time, into unwritten history itself, and seen them with his own eyes.

About fifty yards from the labyrinth's entrance, they encountered a second intersection. Three choices faced them. In the tunnel that went left, they could see another choice they would have to make: a passage that branched off to the left again, essentially back the way they came. Back was not the way they wanted to go, but in a maze, backward was sometimes forward. Alternately, the passage to their right was curved to the left, promising to ultimately carry them forward, but sometimes mazes spiraled into nothing. Finally, the tunnel straight ahead led forward unimpeded, with no intersections or curves for as far as they could see in the limited reach of their three flashlights.

"Which way do we go?" Nicole asked.

Albert did not know. This was only the second in a long line of decisions they would have to make. They would have to choose paths entirely at random and their chances of choosing the correct path every time were virtually nonexistent. The Keeper revealed that there were many solutions to the maze, but even if there were hundreds of paths that would lead them to the end, there were probably thousands, maybe tens of thousands of paths that would not. They were likely to spend hours, if not the rest of their lives, wandering these corridors, walking in circles.

"It's definitely a good idea to mark the path," Nicole observed, glancing back the way they came. It was comforting to see the yellow line leading the way back.

Brandy nodded. "I hope we don't run out of chalk. I left my lipstick in my purse." The previous year, with nothing as convenient as sidewalk chalk at their disposal, she had marked one of the passages with an X in pink lipstick to identify the way home. The chalk was far more practical.

Nicole looked at her, curious. "Why *did* you bring your purse last time?"

"I always take my purse with me," Brandy replied, a little too defensively. They'd had this conversation before. She knew what Nicole wanted to hear. She wanted to hear her say that she'd brought her purse because she wanted to stay pretty for Albert, with whom she was already a little smitten. Admittedly, she *had* been a little interested in Albert before they entered that service tunnel all those months ago. She'd be lying if she said that her attraction to him had nothing to do with her decision to join him on that strange adventure, but that was not the reason she took her purse with her. She took her purse because she felt secure carrying it. Her money and identification were in there. So were her keys. So was her cell phone. So was a small can of pepper spray. Albert knew it was in there now, that she carried it for self-defense. He approved strongly of her carrying it. But she had a feeling that he still didn't realize that she'd kept it within easy reach during their first trip through the Temple of the Blind. She did not really know him back then, after all.

Albert ignored the girls. He did not care about Brandy's purse or why she took it into the tunnels with them thirteen months ago. What he cared about was the labyrinth. He looked at their three choices. Four, if he took into account the intersection he could see down the left passage. He considered his odds of picking the shortest path to the exit and found it overwhelming. He had less than one in four chances of getting it right, since he had only a one in two chance of picking the correct tunnel at the labyrinth's entrance. Even knowing there was more than one path to the exit didn't improve those odds by much.

"Should we split up?" asked Nicole. As soon as the words were out of her mouth, she regretted speaking them. That was the last thing she wanted. Splitting up would mean wandering off alone in this awful darkness.

"No," said Brandy quickly, grasping Albert's elbow as if fearing that he would leap at the idea.

But Albert did not like the thought any more than she. "No," he said. It was an emotional response. He couldn't stand the idea of sending Brandy and Nicole down these desperately dark tunnels all alone. There was a monster stalking these corridors, and they would probably be easy prey for such a beast. If they parted company now, he may never see them again. "Definitely not. Besides," he realized as he considered the idea more carefully, "if we split up, we may never find each other again. We need to stay together."

"Safety in numbers," Brandy agreed.

Albert nodded. "We leave the way we came in: *together*."

He picked the middle passage, as randomly as he'd chosen the path on the right the first time, and resumed walking.

A few minutes passed and the tunnel continued straight ahead with no intersections or obstructions. As he walked, he dragged the chalk along the wall with his left hand. He was careful to press lightly to conserve it. It was their only way of knowing where they'd been and when it was gone, they would have nothing to keep them from walking around in circles.

The tunnel began to slope upward, becoming a hill, and Albert felt a sick dread begin to creep into his stomach.

"Are we going up?" Brandy asked.

Albert nodded. "I don't think this is going to be as simple as we thought."

"Who thought it was going to be simple?" Nicole asked.

"If this thing turns out to be several stories deep," Albert continued, "there's no telling how long we could wander around down here. We could walk for days and never even find our own trail."

"That's it," Nicole said. "Keep on encouraging us."

"I'm sorry."

"Look," Brandy said, trying to be positive. "We're not completely in the dark down here. We know that Caggo thing is down here. With any luck, it doesn't know about us yet. That gives us *some* advantage. And we know we're going the wrong way if we see the meadow, thanks to Nicole."

"Thanks to me?"

"Yeah. I think that thing back there liked you."

Albert grinned. "I think you're right. He probably doesn't see many hot girls down here. Maybe if she goes back and flirts with him, he'll give us some more clues."

"Oh god!" Nicole exclaimed. The expression of disgust on her face was priceless.

"Come on," Brandy urged. "If you put out, he's *bound* to show us the way out!"

Nicole laughed. "Don't even joke about that! Did you *see* that thing?"

"So what?" Brandy replied. "He's got a better personality than Earl."

Nicole rolled her eyes. "No shit."

"He's a working guy," Albert offered. "He must get great benefits. You two could settle down in a nice cave somewhere. Have a bunch of freaky little mini-keepers."

"Oh, it would be such a lovely wedding, wouldn't it?" Brandy giggled.

Nicole shivered comically and mimicked a gag reflex. She could almost feel the little creature's hot hand upon her shoulder again, its skin sliding across its bones as if it were not actually attached to its flesh, but merely wrapped in it.

"It would be perfect," Albert agreed. "I can hear him now, asking, 'Who's your creepy daddy?'"

"Seriously, stop!" Nicole laughed.

Brandy had to stifle her laughter behind her hands. Tears sprang to her eyes.

"You guys are horrible! Gross!"

They reached the top of the incline and the floor leveled out again. A short distance beyond, they encountered a T-shaped intersection, leaving them with another left-or-right decision, neither one of which was likely to be the magical passage that would lead them out of these walls and out of reach of the Caggo.

As randomly as he'd selected the past two, Albert chose the right tunnel and tried not to think about the shrinking odds of finding a correct path before the resident monster caught their scent.

"Seriously, though," Brandy said after the humor had subsided, "what *was* that thing?"

Albert shrugged. "He definitely tops the list of weird things we've seen today."

"Do you think he really just hangs around the entrance to this place, waiting for people to happen by?"

"Has anybody but us *ever* 'happened by?'" Nicole asked.

"It would definitely take some serious dedication to your job," Albert agreed.

Brandy giggled. "He's like a Wal-Mart greeter in hell."

Albert grinned. "He is, isn't he?"

Another intersection appeared from the darkness ahead of them. They could go right or they could keep going straight. Trying not to think about all the wrong ways they could go, Albert chose right and kept moving.

A few minutes later, they turned a corner and found their first dead end. Immediately, claustrophobia and panic tried to fight through Albert's rationality, but he forced it back. "No problem," he said. "We knew we'd hit a few of these. We'll just back up to the last path we didn't take and try again."

The three of them turned and followed the yellow chalk line back to their most recent wrong turn. "If I keep the chalk in my left hand," Albert reasoned, "we'll always know which way we were going when we come back to our path. Plus, if both sides of a passage are marked, we'll know it was a dead end." Mindful of his concern about running out of chalk before they could finish navigating this enormous maze, however, Albert chose to conserve it by only marking the wall near the previous intersection as he made his way back. It served no purpose to use any more than that.

"Good," Brandy said. She was glad he had a plan because she certainly did not know how they were going to get out of this place. Without him, she was certain she would be trapped down here forever.

There was a possibility of erroneously marking a passage as a dead end when it was not, Albert realized. If they made a big circle, for example, they might return to a previous intersection, where they would have little choice but to follow a previously traveled path, possibly leaving behind unmarked and unexplored passages that could lead straight to the exit. He was counting on the Keeper's assertion that there were many solutions leading where they wanted to be to allow for that kind of mistake.

They turned right, down the passage that Albert decided

against the first time, and continued walking. A moment later, they entered into a small chamber where three separate tunnels intersected, giving them six passages from which to choose. Five, not counting the way they came.

"Are we lost yet?" Nicole asked.

"We're not lost as long as we have a way back," Albert assured her.

"Which way do we go?" asked Brandy.

"Doesn't really matter," Albert replied. "Straight ahead I guess." He pressed the chalk to the wall and began walking again.

After a few minutes, Nicole asked, "What do you suppose the Keeper meant when he said that I was different?"

"Maybe he meant that you're not psychic," Brandy suggested. "The Sentinel Queen told us that Albert and I were psychic, but not you and Wayne."

"That was what I thought he meant, too," Albert said. "But I really didn't know. He wasn't exactly talking my lingo."

"I don't feel very psychic," Brandy said.

"She said we were a lot less psychic than Beverly," Albert explained. "That's why we could get through that room between the spike room and the bridge and she couldn't."

"I guess so," Brandy said. "But I still don't know if I believe it."

"I guess it doesn't really matter if we believe it," Albert said. "We're kind of stuck with it."

“I don’t know,” Nicole said. “I think it would be cool. You guys could work on it, maybe go to Vegas.”

Brandy laughed. “Yeah. That would be cool.”

“I don’t know how this thing works,” Albert said. “Knowing my luck, I’d probably have a blind spot for aces.”

Ahead of them, the path that Albert had chosen from the six-way intersection forked into two separate passages. Albert chose the left branch and kept walking. This took them into a curve that became an ever-shrinking spiral, eventually leading them to a dead end. They retraced their steps to the fork and went right instead, only to eventually find themselves right back to the six-way intersection and their own yellow line.

“Okay then,” Albert said, considering the situation. They had explored half of the tunnels they were now looking at. “Let’s try this one,” he decided, choosing the passage to the left of the one that led them to the fork. He was glad he thought to keep the chalk in his left hand. Knowing which direction they had traveled might be useful later. And given that his first piece of chalk was already considerably smaller than when he started, he couldn’t afford to waste time on bad decisions.

Soon, Albert saw two more tunnels branching off of this one, one to the left and one to the right. As he drew closer, he saw that there were two more identical tunnels beyond those two and the tunnel they currently occupied continued on into the darkness.

More decisions.

More mistakes waiting to be made.

Chapter 5

For nearly an hour, Albert, Brandy and Nicole explored the labyrinth. The paths before them curved and diverged, twisted and intersected. Frequently, the passage ended in a solid wall or else circled back to their yellow chalk line, and each time it did, the three of them grew a little more anxious.

There had so far been no sign of the Caggo, but it was likely only a matter of time before it realized they were here. And Albert had no idea what they were supposed to do when it came for them. With no idea what sort of beast it might be, he could not even begin to formulate any kind of defense against it. With each second that passed, he became more certain that they could not possibly hope to escape it. They were, after all, lost within *its* labyrinth. It was inevitable that it would eventually catch their scent and it would either run them down or corner them against one of the countless dead ends. They had no weapons and no means of escape. He could not imagine why the Keeper would even bother to warn them of such a peril. It only served to panic them as they became more lost.

What was the Caggo, Albert wondered. How would it attack them? What would it do when it discovered them? Was it anything like the monster in Gilbert House? That thing had been a walking nightmare. Solid as stone, freakishly strong, like a great, bald ape, it had the ability to crush their bones with its bare hands. And it almost used that very talent on his and Wayne's skulls. Perhaps the Caggo was the same sort of creature. But on the other hand, it might be something far more carnal. Perhaps it slashed and tore instead of bludgeoned and crushed. Perhaps it was all teeth and claws. Or perhaps it was something even worse, something that did not kill so swiftly.

The first stick of chalk was gone and they were now using the second. After some consideration, Albert decided to stick with the color yellow until it was gone. He was anticipating being down here for a long time (assuming the Caggo didn't eat them in the next few minutes) and if he used each of the five colors in the tube only once, he'd be able to tell when they circled back to their path about how long ago they'd been there. He wasn't sure if this information would come in handy or not, but it couldn't hurt. If nothing else, it might potentially provide them a shortcut back to the beginning of the labyrinth if things turned nasty.

And, as it turned out, the potential for nastiness was considerable.

The passage ahead of them suddenly opened into a small, empty chamber. The floor of this room was set approximately six feet below that of the passage from which they approached, with no easy means of descending. It simply dropped straight down. Albert knew even before he shined his light onto it that the floor was covered with those mysterious, telltale scratches.

The hounds had their own passages, an entire labyrinth all their own, according to the Keeper, interwoven throughout the temple with the corridors he was attempting to navigate. This was one of the places where those two labyrinths intersected. And it was a terribly dangerous place to be.

Albert could see two passages leading out of the room a short distance ahead. Both of these tunnels were flush with the floor, and therefore accessible to the hounds. Beyond those passages, the darkness loomed. They had two choices. They could turn back now, or he could drop down and see if there was another raised passage on the other side.

On one hand, they should remain safe from the hounds as long as they stayed out of their territory. But on the other hand, they were not altogether safe anywhere. For all they knew, the only way to reach the exit and escape the Caggo was to take risks in places like this.

"I'm going to have a look down there," he decided.

"No!" Brandy snapped. "The hounds!"

"I know," he assured her. "But I don't hear any."

"That doesn't mean they're not here."

"I know that too."

"Then don't," she begged him.

"I'll be okay. I'm just going to see if there's a way across. For all we know, it could save us hours."

"Or take us right back to where we started," Nicole argued.

"I'll be fine." Without waiting for further protests, he dropped into the passage and cautiously crept out into the room, swinging his flashlight between the two tunnels.

"Be careful!" Brandy whispered after him.

Two more passageways appeared from the darkness beyond the first two, both of them belonging to the hounds. He probed each of them with his light, making sure there was nothing lurking there, and made his way toward the far side of the chamber.

Another raised passageway appeared at the opposite side of the room, just as he'd hoped. And when he approached it and shined his light into it, he saw that there were no scratches on the floor.

"Come on," he called, daring to raise his voice only enough to be heard across the chamber.

Brandy and Nicole did not hesitate. They dropped down and crossed the room at a near run, unwilling to spend any more time than necessary where the hounds could reach them.

Albert helped Brandy climb up into the higher passage and then Nicole. Then he paused as he glanced down at the scarred stone beneath his feet. Something was there, lying just a few inches from the toes of his left foot. He knelt down and picked up a small object. It was about the size of an arcade ticket, roughly rectangular, and a deep, reddish-brown color that faded into translucence on one side. He almost hadn't noticed it in the darkness. One of its long edges—the darker colored one—was rough, as if it had been broken from a larger object. The other edges were all extremely fine, like a blade.

"What is it?" Nicole asked, kneeling at the top of the ledge and lending her light to his as he stared at it.

"No idea," Albert replied. It was extremely thin, but also very strong. It flexed a little when he attempted to bend it, but did not break. He gently ran his thumb down its edge and found that it was as sharp as he'd suspected, leaving a shallow slit in the friction ridges of his thumb.

"Looks kind of like a razor blade," Nicole observed.

It did. Very much so. He held it up and looked at it again. "But it's not metal."

In fact, it looked organic. Was it some kind of tooth? Or claw? It was chipped in several places along its sharp edges. Albert looked down at the floor again, at the scratches that scarred the stone. He wondered if something like this could have made those marks.

"Sweetie?" Brandy interrupted as she stood beside Nicole, her empty hand resting on her bare hip while she pointed the flashlight at him with the other. "Think you could take a look at that up here where you're less likely to get eaten by a monster?"

"Sorry," Albert replied. He started to drop the mysterious object back onto the floor where he'd found it, but decided instead to take it with him. For all he knew, it was a clue of some sort. He slipped it into his backpack instead and then climbed up into the upper tunnel. Before turning away, he scanned the scarred floor of the chamber once more with his flashlight. There didn't seem to be any more, but their dark color probably made them difficult to see on the gray stone with just a flashlight.

As the three of them continued on, Albert contemplated the mysterious object, wondering if this night would finally give him his chance to see these strange creatures…and if he'd live to regret it if it did.

Chapter 6

Soon, Albert had come to the conclusion that the object was probably not a tooth or a claw. The texture and color suggested that it *was* probably composed of keratin, like fingernails and hair. But while it *could* be a broad and very sharp fingernail or a peculiarly shaped claw, he thought it was more likely that the object was a scale of some sort.

Did this mean the hounds were reptilian? That certainly added a new dynamic to his imagination. He remembered talking about the temple after their return the year before, at first with Brandy and later with Nicole as well. He had compared the unusual noise they made to that of an agitated rattlesnake, among other things. He had no idea what they could be. He never saw the creatures. That noise was the only clue he had. But earlier that evening, when the man with no eyes confronted them, he warned them to be wary of the beasts and referred to them as "hounds." Since then, he had been imagining some manner of fearsome canine, a mutant wolf perhaps. Now this scale was a reminder that he still had no idea what they really were, that the damn things could be anything at all.

But he didn't know for sure that the scale and the hounds were even related. For all he knew, the scale could belong to the Caggo instead. Or perhaps it belonged to some third creature of which they were not even aware. He certainly didn't trust the Sentinel Queen or the Keeper to tell them everything. They both seemed fairly determined to share as little information as possible with them before sending them unarmed into a deadly labyrinth.

If this thing *was* a scale, however, it suggested that the creature it belonged to might be formidable in size. And it would probably be well-armored. The last thing he wanted was to run into one of them…and yet he was still dying to see what one looked like.

They reached the end of the passage and had to choose left or right. Albert no longer took the time to consider the possible wrongs and rights of each decision. He paused only to flex his left hand, which had grown a little stiff from holding the chalk for so long, and then randomly turned left. When that path intersected another, he turned right and soon found another dead end. He returned to the previous intersection and took the left passage instead, then right, then left again.

For nearly half an hour, the labyrinth revealed nothing new. Only empty passages emerged from the darkness.

"This is hopeless," Brandy groaned. "How the hell are we supposed to find our way out of a maze this big?"

"It's not hopeless," Albert assured her. But he understood perfectly how she felt. The massiveness of the labyrinth was almost overwhelming. It weighed him down, sapping his very spirit. "The Keeper said there were lots of ways to get there. We're bound to find one of them if we just keep walking."

But he wondered how much more likely they were to find the Caggo than the exit.

They turned left at the next intersection and walked to the end of the next passage. But instead of another intersection, this one led them to a large chamber. A wide walkway ran along the wall to the right and left. Directly ahead of them was the softly rocking surface of a very large pool of water.

"Do we have to get wet again?" Nicole asked. "Because I still haven't warmed up after last time."

"I don't think so," Albert replied, shining his light around. The walkways leading away from them along the chamber walls offered a dry path that was never an option before. He doubted if they were meant to simply dive blindly into the water. The logical assumption would be to try to walk around it first.

"What is this place?" Brandy asked as she shined her light out over the wavering water.

Albert aimed his light down into it. It looked as bottomless as the last pool they encountered. "Some kind of reservoir system, I guess."

"Why's the water moving? You don't think there's something in it, do you?"

"Could be," he admitted. The idea wasn't particularly appealing. "But maybe it's a current. This system probably flows through the entire temple. It only makes sense that there'd be something like this. There's an entire city back there, remember. Plus the hounds and this Caggo thing. You've got to keep your guard dogs watered or they're not going to do their jobs very well."

"So glad they thought of that," Nicole retorted. "Wouldn't want anything bad happening to all the *monsters*, now would we?"

"We haven't met any yet," Albert reminded her. "You never know. You might like them."

"Excuse me if I won't get my hopes up for a new pet."

Albert could see no difference between going left and right, so he chose left for no other reason than to keep his chalk line on the same side. Before he could take more than a few steps, however, he was startled by the sound of splashing water.

All three of them turned, their flashlight beams racing out over the water to see what was there. But by now they could see nothing but the widening ring of ripples spreading out from where the surface had been broken.

“What the hell was that?” Brandy asked.

“The Caggo?” Nicole reasoned.

Albert said nothing. He hadn’t expected to find the Caggo in the water, but again, the Keeper gave him no information about the monster except that it was here and it was dangerous. Could the Caggo be an aquatic creature? Could it be right there, hiding beneath the surface, watching them from the depths? It was suddenly far too easy to imagine a great, kraken-like sea monster lurking down there, snaky tentacles slowly rising toward them, silently reaching to snatch them into the frigid depths to die.

He hated not being able to see anything.

They moved on, their lights constantly in motion, searching the room around them for any sign of an imminent attack.

The chamber was even larger than it first seemed. They followed the walkway along the water’s edge for several more minutes before another splash halted them. This one was much more distant than the last, far out in the water, well beyond the reach of their light.

“I don’t like this,” Nicole groaned.

Albert didn’t like it either. The openness of the room made him feel vulnerable. Suddenly, he craved the protection of the claustrophobic tunnels, where danger could only come from two directions.

They kept moving, pushing ever deeper into the gigantic

chamber. Soon, another walkway came into view, this one leading out over the water and into the darkness beyond. As they approached it, a loud splash rose from the same direction. The water's surface rippled out toward them, sloshing onto the walkway near their feet.

Something had jumped into the water.

Something large.

"Okay, I'm scared…" Nicole breathed.

Albert crept forward, his light fixed on the walkway that stretched out over the water. A moment later, a second splash rose from the walkway, followed quickly by a third.

"Lots of them," Brandy observed.

Albert nodded. Whatever was in here with them, there was definitely more than one.

"Hounds?" Nicole wondered.

"I don't think so." He was reminded of walking around the pond near his grandparents' farmhouse when he was growing up. This was very much like the way the frogs would leap into the water as he approached. It wasn't the behavior of bloodthirsty creatures. They seemed to be fleeing from their path.

"Something else?" Brandy asked.

"Nobody said anything about any other things living down here," Nicole recalled.

"We were only told to stay away from the hounds and the Caggo," Albert reminded them. "It's not exactly been a free exchange of information. If there's something down here that's not extremely dangerous, they probably wouldn't have bothered telling us."

"So you think they're harmless?" Brandy asked.

"I didn't say 'harmless,'" he returned. "I wouldn't bet on that. But they might leave us alone if we don't provoke them."

Another splash broke the stillness of the room as another unseen creature threw itself into the water.

"Don't worry about that," Nicole assured him. "*I* sure as hell don't intend to do any *provoking* down here."

"It makes sense, when you think about it," he explained. "There has to be some sort of renewable food source to sustain a population of hounds. There has to be something down here that they regularly feed on. And since there's no sign of vegetation, these reservoir systems probably sustain an aquatic food source. Whatever we're hearing could be prey for the hounds."

"I just assumed the blind people raised them," said Brandy. "The Sentinel Queen's children. Or whatever."

"Or maybe the Keeper," Nicole added. "Seems like something a keeper would do…"

"Maybe," agreed Albert. He stepped out onto the bridge and shined his light down on the stone surface. It was wet and slippery. Something that had been in the water was recently here and it was probably one of the things they heard dropping into the water. "Could be that these things have some other kind of purpose. Maybe they keep the water clean."

He shined his flashlight down into the water. It was as clear as crystal, but extremely deep. He could not nearly see the bottom. It faded to black in every direction, revealing nothing.

"Either way, there could be an entire ecosystem hidden down here." Somehow, he found this idea exciting. He could almost imagine finding creatures down here that no one had ever seen before.

Preferably of the non-lethal variety.

The path that ran along the wall continued on past this bridge, but Albert decided to cross the water instead, curious about the width of the pool.

Occasionally, they heard splashing. Usually it came from ahead of them, just beyond the reach of their light, but sometimes they heard the splashing from other areas of the chamber, some of them remarkably far away, making Albert wonder just how big this place could be.

Several minutes later, the three of them reached the other side and found a walkway along the far wall just like the one across from it. Albert turned left and continued exploring the enormous chamber.

Chapter 7

A deep channel, about twelve feet wide, carried water away from the large reservoir chamber. On the right side was a walkway, just wide enough for the three of them to walk side-by-side, but they chose to stay single file next to the wall and out of reach of anything that may decide to lunge out of the water at them.

Walking with the wall on his right side obviously made it impossible to keep the chalk line on his left, as Albert had reliably done until they crossed the bridge to the far side of the water. Therefore, rather than break his left-hand rule, he chose to conserve chalk during this time by simply drawing arrows on the wall to indicate where they were going.

Frequently, their flashlights gravitated toward the mysterious depths of the water where they watched for threatening shadows or mysterious bubbles or ominous dorsal fins or other signs of imminent doom.

Albert again considered the scale he'd found. Perhaps it belonged to some kind of fish. It didn't seem likely that any fish could crawl out of the water and wander freely about a dry labyrinth, but nothing else down here had ever seemed "likely" either.

But for all he knew, the scale might have absolutely nothing to do with the temple. Perhaps it had merely migrated down here the same way Wendell Gilbert's pocket watch did.

He hated not having all the information, especially when his and his two closest friends' lives might be at stake.

After a while, the channel led them into another chamber. Here, the water was distributed into a dozen openings in the walls, each one just large enough for a man to fit through, though Albert had very little doubt that the destination of any of those small tunnels emptied into the wave pool at Hurricane Harbor. If he were to fall into the water and be sucked into one of those tubes, there was no way to know where it might spit him back out, and probably very little chance it would do so in less time than he could do without air.

But then again, being swept away didn't really seem like much of a danger here. The water did not seem to be moving very fast. In fact, he could barely tell that the water was moving at all in these chambers. And perhaps that was intentional. After all, if the Sentinel Queen was right, and the Temple of the Blind had been here since ancient times, what kept all this water from eroding away the stone? Either the stone was very hard or the water's current very slow.

The walkway circled the distribution chamber to a passageway on the left side of the room. They left the water behind them and followed this passage for a short while until it intersected a long, wide corridor with a familiar drop-off between its floor and the one in which they stood.

Hounds.

"Smells bad," Brandy observed.

It did. There was a different odor to this chamber than any before it. It was more like the tunnels back in the Briar Hills sewers, musty and underlain with the subtle reek of decomposition.

Albert realized at once that they were far deeper into hound territory than they had ever been before. It had the potential to get very dangerous down here. But at least they always had the choice of turning back.

So far.

Like last time, the hounds themselves were nowhere to be seen or heard. Were they still sticking close to the pillar where the blind man hung their undergarments? Or had they converged on the areas where they and Wayne had crossed through their territory, hungrily sniffing the floor where their bare feet had passed, memorizing their scents?

Or perhaps it was nap time. There was simply no way to know.

Their passage continued forward on the other side. Other passages could be seen in either direction, but Albert did not press his luck. It was dangerous enough just crossing from one side to the other.

He knelt over the ledge and shined his light down into the passageway. Immediately, he saw several more broken scales littering this passage floor. This seemed to help confirm his theory that these were related to the hounds, but it also presented a number of new questions. Why hadn't he found any of these in the first two lowered passages? On the other side of the City of the Blind, there had been only scratches and a few scattered bone fragments.

"I feel like it's a dumb idea to cross these tunnels," Nicole said. "Maybe it's just me."

"It's definitely not just you," Albert agreed. This passage was worse than the little room they crossed last time. It was bigger and probably much more traveled. One of the beasts could wander by at any moment. "It just feels like we're covering more ground when we do," he explained. "We don't spend as much time backtracking."

"I guess so," Nicole admitted. He had a point. If they turned back now, they would have to retreat all the way to the reservoir. But then again, for all they knew, the next passage in the reservoir might take them right to the exit.

But so could that passage directly across from them. It did no good to second guess themselves. The best course of action was to simply keep moving and cover as much ground as possible.

"I'm with Nikki," Brandy announced. "I don't like taking the risk. Makes me nervous."

"We may not be able to take the risk later," Albert explained. "For all we know, once they catch our scent they might be waiting for us at every one of these."

Brandy and Nicole both shuddered at the idea of a swarm of man-eating monsters snapping and snarling at them at the end of dozens or even hundreds of passageways.

Albert scanned the passage carefully with his flashlight and then took a deep breath. "Here goes." He dropped onto the lower floor without another word, his eyes and ears wide open for any sign that they were not alone, his flashlight swinging back and forth in the darkness. He stepped across the path as Brandy and Nicole descended behind him and then helped both of them up into the next passage before climbing after them.

Once safely in the upper passage, he again almost wished one of the hounds *would* appear, just so he could see it.

"Now let's just hope this doesn't lead us right back here again," Albert said. "I definitely don't want to spend too much time spreading our scent in one area. Unless of course I know for a fact we're never going back to that spot."

But for the next hour, they encountered nothing but empty passageways and the occasional dead end.

Chapter 8

The late hour insured that Wayne had no trouble entering the steam tunnel between the Field House and Juggers Hall. The streets and sidewalks were completely deserted. Though the iron cover sounded as if it would alert the entire campus to their trespassing, no one came to investigate. And after he slid it noisily back into place, he had only to follow the faded markings that Albert pointed out to him the first time he came down here.

He still could not believe that he was starting all over again. It was a long trip through these tunnels before he even reached the Temple of the Blind. Once inside, he would then have to find his own way to the City of the Blind, navigating the three emotion rooms along the way. He'd have to swim through that cold water. He'd have to squeeze through the tiny passageway where he nearly became lodged last time. He'd have to make his way once more through that reeking mud. And after what the old man told him, who knew if the Sentinel Queen would even let him pass through her city. For all he knew, she might even try to kill him.

Assuming he made it that far, he would have to pass through the City of the Blind's north gate and somehow try to catch up with Albert, Brandy and Nicole, though they had a tremendous head start on him.

He had no idea how he was supposed to catch up to them. How would he even know where to begin? It was preposterous to think that he could locate a mere three people in a labyrinth that size. But he had to try. If nothing else, he needed to warn Albert of the old man's claims. Either he or the Sentinel Queen was lying to them. Perhaps both of them. He could not begin to say which one they should trust, but he felt confident that he could trust Albert to help sort it out.

He followed the florescent green markings into the next passageway and to the old, iron ladder that waited to carry them deeper into the earth. "Careful," he warned as he gripped the metal rung and began to climb down.

Olivia and Andrea followed close behind him. He still could not believe that these two lovely young ladies were both willing to wade through sewer tunnels, strip down to their birthday suits and risk life and limb to accompany not just him but each other, two complete strangers, on a frightening—and frankly *insane*—

adventure they knew almost nothing about. The very idea was unfathomable to him. Although he supposed that it was no more insane than his own actions. He had, himself, come here in the company of three strangers, with no idea what was in store for him. And now he was going back again, regardless of the horrors he had seen.

He had asked them many times before arriving at the tunnel entrance if they were certain of their decision, warning them that it was dangerous and reminding them that the trip required them to give up their clothes. Although he could see in their eyes that the thought of disrobing bothered them both greatly, they still refused to back down. They were both strong-willed and stubborn and, truthfully, he had to respect them for that.

And the company they gave him while traveling these dark and moldy tunnels was more than welcome.

Olivia had been mostly quiet since the three of them left the parking lot outside Wayne's apartment building. He wasn't surprised. A lot must weigh on her mind. After all she'd been through, it was astounding that she was still going. Now that she was inside the steam tunnels, she had the look of a frightened animal, her eyes twitching from shadow to shadow, her jaw clenched. If not for the determined way she kept meeting his eyes when he glanced back at her, he wouldn't have believed she was the same person who refused to even consider remaining in the safety of her dorm room.

Andrea, however, was an entirely different story.

"This is so cool!" she exclaimed, gazing wonderingly around at every new tunnel they entered, her blue eyes wide and bright, as if she were a child on Christmas morning. "How far do these tunnels go?"

"Can't say," Wayne replied. "But it's still a long way to the temple."

"So awesome! It's like a movie set down here!"

Each time they walked past an adjoining tunnel, she paused and poked her flashlight into it for a moment, exploring as much as she could get away with. Then she would hurry to catch up again.

"Be careful," he reminded her. "Remember, some of the machinery down here is dangerous. You can burn yourself on some of this stuff. Or cut yourself. This place isn't exactly approved for tours."

"I'll be careful. Do these tunnels go under the whole city?"

"Not sure. Maybe," he replied, although he wasn't entirely sure she was even listening to his answers.

"I used to hear stories about tunnels under the city, but I never knew if any of them were real."

The girl's eagerness was amusing, and her energetic personality was refreshing in such a gloomy place. Her chattiness was definitely a welcome distraction from the task ahead. He wondered if she always talked this much or if it was just how she dealt with scary situations.

"You're sure we're not going to get in trouble for being down here?" Andrea asked as she looked back the way they came. She half expected to see flashlights chasing after them.

"Nobody saw us," Wayne assured her.

"My dad would probably kill me if I got in trouble for something like this."

"Even if someone saw us, they'd never find us. It's a maze down here."

Wayne found it amusing that she was more afraid of getting caught trespassing than she was of spiders and rats.

Andrea returned her attention to where she was going and saw that she had lagged behind again. Hurriedly, she caught back up and then resumed scanning every surface with her flashlight. "My friends would never believe all this," she announced. "Never."

Wayne had to smile a little. She wasn't even out of the steam tunnels yet. Just wait until she saw the temple.

He glanced back at Olivia again, and again she met his eyes with that steely determination.

"There'll be some tunnels down here that are too small to walk in," he explained. "Some are pretty damp. We'll probably get a little wet and muddy."

"That's okay," assured Andrea cheerfully.

Olivia merely nodded.

Wayne focused his attention back on the tunnels ahead, careful not to miss any of the florescent green marks that would guide him back to the Temple of the Blind. He could not afford to get lost. Albert was already several hours ahead of him and still moving. That distance was only going to increase every moment he wasn't working to close it.

Andrea pulled her cell phone from her jeans pocket and examined the screen. "No signal down here," she reported. "Guess that's not really a surprise, huh?"

"Yeah, you can forget about your phone," Wayne warned. "Those things are pretty well useless where we're going."

Andrea returned it to her pocket. She didn't like not having her phone. She felt vulnerable. But it was hardly unexpected. She probably lost the signal almost as soon as she entered the tunnels.

They were utterly on their own down here.

Chapter 9

After wandering blindly through the empty passages for so long, it was almost comforting to come across another water chamber. Any end to the monotony of the blank, gray walls that didn't involve a vicious, drooling beast was a welcome one. This passage was almost identical to the one that led away from the reservoir and to the small distribution chamber, except that there was a walkway on both sides and many passageways leading away from it.

They were walking on the left side, passing by the openings that led back into the closed-in labyrinth in favor of the open space for a while.

"I think my batteries are going dead," said Nicole, giving her flashlight a shake. She realized a while ago that it had faded. It was already putting out noticeably less light than the other two.

Now it seemed to be struggling against the darkness, rapidly dying away. And there was something remarkably ominous about watching it dim to a dull glow like that. Even knowing that Albert had enough extra batteries in his backpack to replace them in all three flashlights at least four times, it was unnerving. What if they were stuck down here long enough to use them all up? What if they found themselves trapped down here in the dark? She found the very thought indescribably dreadful.

Albert stopped and took off the backpack.

Nicole handed him her flashlight and then sat down with her back against the wall and rested her weary feet. After a moment, Brandy joined her and the two of them sat and watched as Albert fumbled open the new package of batteries and replaced the spent ones.

After he had finished and handed back the newly invigorated light, Nicole and Brandy made no effort to rise from the floor and Albert made no effort to coax them up. Instead, he sat down with them and joined them in a long-overdue break.

Their feet and legs were beyond sore. But Nicole was still far from wishing she hadn't come. She'd always wanted to do something like this, something bold and adventurous. It was about being a part of something big, something that went far beyond the mundane world she was living in.

She would have given anything to have been the one to go on the adventure with Albert last year. She was so envious of

Brandy's incredible love story.

But she was not nearly as lucky as Brandy. She was just Nicole. There was nothing special about her. Sure, she was *pretty*. Her friends were always telling her so. They told her she was beautiful. But she didn't feel *beautiful*. She allowed herself to feel *pretty* because she worked hard to be that way. She jogged and she ate right and she went to the campus gym. And even *she* had to admit that genetics had dealt her a lucky card when she hit puberty. She could not have asked for more perfect breasts. But she would not use the word "beautiful." She did not think herself beautiful. She knew too many people who she honestly believed were far more beautiful than she. Brandy Rudman was one of those people. It was not beauty for which she worked so hard, anyway. It was for herself, because she simply did not believe that she was as good a person as she could be.

Earl Tannis was proof of that. A better woman would never have gotten involved with him. He was a pompous jerk. He was mean, rude, vulgar and about as romantic as a sledgehammer. She knew that neither Brandy nor Albert liked him. She'd always known that, though they'd done their best not to let her see it. They were so wonderful to her. She did not blame them for how they felt. In fact, she agreed with them. Earl Tannis was as much a man as any pile of garbage on the side of the street. But he was company. In a world where her best friend found the kind of man she'd always hoped to find, while stumbling into the kind of adventure she'd always dreamed of going on, she needed a little company.

Yes, she was a little jealous of Brandy. Her eyes washed over Albert as he sat resting, his whole body exposed to her. She was so lonely, so starved for the kind of romance that Brandy sometimes described to her when they were alone together. The relationship they shared was a perfect combination of romantic adoration and scorching passion, the latter of which she sometimes whispered about after a few drinks, incredible stories about steamy nights they'd spent together, intensely hot, erotic moments that she could not resist greedily soaking up, though they often left her aching long into the night with depressingly unattainable desires.

Albert Cross was everything Nicole had ever wished for. He was kind, loving, romantic and generous. He loved deeply and truly and passionately and he was both a boy and a man in all the right ways.

Of course he had no brothers, no friends to which he could introduce her. There was no one else on earth like Albert. Period. And she couldn't just clone him. There were laws about that sort of thing now. And she supposed that would just be kind of awkward anyway.

Nicole watched as Brandy reached over and took Albert's hand. Perhaps thinking about these things was healthy. Perhaps it wasn't. Either way, it took her mind off the labyrinth and her anxiousness for a few minutes. She supposed that she might have a small crush on Albert. Hell, she had a big crush on him, if she was going to be honest, but it changed nothing. Brandy was her best friend. Albert was Brandy's boyfriend. She would have to be the most hateful, malicious bitch on the planet to want it any other way. Besides, there was bound to be another Albert out there somewhere, right? One custom fit just for her. Maybe even one who liked romantic comedies.

She turned away and looked at the softly rocking surface of the water. She felt as though she were creeping onto thin ice on this subject. She did not want to think this way. Her love for Albert was not romantic. Not really. It was the love a sister felt for a very dear brother. It was the love of close friends. Those other things she felt were nothing more than projections of her unfulfilled desires, desires that her gorilla of an ex-boyfriend would never be capable of satisfying.

But she also did not want to think about the labyrinth. Specifically, she did not want to think about the Caggo. She did not want to be afraid. So her thoughts rolled around in her head, bouncing from one thing to the next until it was time to get up and carry on.

Chapter 10

"That is just so *wrong!*" Andrea giggled as she stood in front of one of the sentinels, her flashlight fixed on its enormous erection.

"It gets a lot more wrong," Wayne warned her with no amusement whatsoever in his voice. He and Olivia stood before the face of the moaning woman. It was still startling to look upon.

"It's so…*perfect*," Olivia marveled. "How did they make it so real?"

Andrea stepped up beside her and examined the face. "Can the statues in there really make you…do those things?" she asked, blushing a little.

"They made Albert and Brandy do those things the first time *they* came down here."

Olivia shuddered at the thought. How humiliating. She couldn't imagine such a thing.

"They really did that?" Andrea pressed. "Right in there?"

"Like a couple of animals," Wayne replied. Although Albert and Brandy had never explicitly described in steamy detail what happened to them inside the sex room, he made it a point to exaggerate his knowledge of the incident. He wanted to discourage any curiosity that might arise before reaching the other side.

"Wow."

"Yeah," Wayne agreed. "Wow. Just remember, we can't peek in here."

Andrea didn't know how mere statues could do something like that. She thought the statues out here looked ridiculous. But she had to admit there was something extremely creepy about the woman's face that framed the doorway. It was like Olivia said: it was just so perfect, so disturbingly real. She couldn't find anything funny about it. And she liked finding reasons to laugh at scary things. It made them easier to deal with.

"Let's get this over with," Wayne sighed. He lifted his glasses and rested them atop his head so that he wouldn't lose them. Then he carefully ducked into the moaning woman's mouth and peered into the sex room.

Immediately, he realized that his eyesight was considerably better than Brandy's. The shape on the floor in front of him was clearly a woman lying on her back with her feet spread in the air as a man mounted her.

He closed his eyes and waited for a moment as he tried to judge whether he was being affected or not. He didn't feel overly aroused. His body was not reacting to the sight of the dirty act he had just witnessed. But he felt something uncomfortable deep in the pit of his belly. Was that the first stirring of the sex room's mysterious power taking hold of his senses? Or was that simply his nerves? The task before him was dangerous and his confidence questionable. What if he wasn't strong enough to lead these girls through this room?

From behind him, Olivia reached out and grasped his hand. She didn't have a flashlight. She chose to let Wayne and Andrea carry the two that they brought, therefore she would be the link between them as they walked.

Wayne opened his eyes again, this time holding his flashlight so that it pointed back at his belly, illuminating the room ahead of him indirectly. This darkened the room considerably, and the extra dimness, combined with the shadows, helped to reduce his visibility. But it wasn't quite enough.

"Turn off your flashlight," he instructed. "I need it a little darker in here."

Andrea hesitated, but obeyed. She didn't need it anyway if she was going to have her eyes closed. But the very idea of turning off her light was a little unnerving.

"That's better." Now he could scarcely make out any details at all. "Brandy's eyes are better for this than mine."

"Funny way to say she's more blind," Olivia observed.

"True," Wayne agreed. "It's a funny thing. Not many instances where it's actually an *advantage* to have poor eyesight."

Olivia found it intriguing to think that being extremely nearsighted, of all things, was the key to safely navigating these bizarre chambers.

"Okay," Wayne announced. "I'm going to start moving now. Stay right behind me. There's a lot of places to bump your head in here. And remember to keep your eyes *closed*. No matter how bad you want to peek."

Olivia didn't need any encouragement. As Wayne started forward into the sex room, she found that she had no interest at all in seeing what was inside this room. He had already told them—multiple times—what would happen, what the statues in here could do, and that was enough for her. After all that she had seen at Gilbert House, she had no reason to doubt a single word that he said. Though she could hardly fathom the idea of losing control and turning into a sex-crazed slut just by looking at a few statues, she had been through quite enough these past few days to keep her from being the slightest bit tempted to test it. She could certainly do without humiliating herself down here.

Andrea, on the other hand, was terribly curious about this chamber. Could it really do the things Wayne said it could? She couldn't help but doubt. She couldn't imagine *anything* making her do the things he said it would. She simply wasn't like that.

"I can see the doorway already," Wayne announced. On one hand, it was a relief to be able to rely on his own nearsightedness. Without Brandy's glasses, he could indulge in glancing to the sides when something seemed to be reaching toward him in his peripheral vision. But he still could see a little too well for his liking. The details of the statues were shrouded in a shadowy haze, but he could see what most of them were doing, and he found that this alone turned him on a little. He could not imagine what he would feel if he put his glasses back on and actually looked at them. The idea of losing all control was so incredibly foreign to him that he almost wished he could do it, just for the experience. Just to know the feeling. But of course the consequences of doing that could be unimaginable.

"How are you doing back there?" he asked.

"I'm fine," Olivia replied.

"Me too," reported Andrea. But the truth was that she was dying of curiosity. All around her supposedly stood fantastic statues. *X-rated* statues. Statues that would make her throw herself shamelessly at any man with merely a glance.

They couldn't be real. Not the way he described them. She could buy a lot of what he had told her, but this was too much. Maybe if she were some kind of exhibitionist slut already. Maybe then she could believe it. She even knew a couple of girls who she suspected might be susceptible to such a place. But not *her*.

And now that Wayne had told them that they were already approaching the exit, she found herself even more tempted to peek. Just a little. Just a tiny glimpse. That was all. That couldn't hurt.

Could it?

"Almost there," Wayne assured them.

"Good," replied Olivia. She didn't like stumbling around with her eyes closed. It was too much like being in the dark. And she didn't care for the dark anymore. The dark reminded her of Gilbert House, of that horrible restroom, and the endless hours she spent waiting for someone to find her.

Andrea said nothing. They were almost out. It would soon all be behind them. Then she might never know what was in this room.

And what if there was nothing here? What if this was all an extravagant lie? What if this was her one chance to realize that she was the victim of an elaborate deception? If she opened her eyes now and found nothing more than an empty room…

But what if it was exactly what Wayne said it was?

She bit her lip as she struggled with the urge to take just that one little look. It couldn't do those things to her. It just couldn't. She was sure of it.

She opened her eyes.

Immediately, her attention was drawn to the left, to a tall, gray shape, and she found herself staring at the brazen image of a man and a woman in the midst of ferocious copulation. It was a startling sight. She was barely able to stifle her gasp. The details were so real it was difficult to believe they were nothing more than stone. They could have been real people, their bodies merely painted to match the surfaces around them, acting out their filthiest fantasies. In the brief instant before she turned away, she saw the frozen face of the man with perfect clarity, even in the gloom. His lips were peeled back in a terrible grimace as he cried out with an unmistakable mix of ecstasy and agony, caught at the very apex of a powerful orgasm. The woman had her arms around his neck, her legs locked around his waist, her head thrown all the way back, her eyes bulging, her long hair dangling toward the floor. Somehow she looked both furious and rapturous.

She tore her eyes away, only to be met by a second statue, a man, sneering with lecherous delight as he mounted a woman from behind. He was frightfully skinny, with lean, taut muscles, and the woman was much plumper, with huge, meaty breasts that hung toward the floor beneath her as she moaned with obscene pleasure.

She closed her eyes, but she could not block out the images she had seen. Even with her flashlight off, they had burned themselves onto her memory. They lingered in her mind, as vivid as if she were still staring at them, imprinted on her thoughts like a tattoo, utterly inescapable.

She felt a hot blush fill her cheeks.

She wouldn't lose control. She wasn't like that. No matter what Wayne said, she'd never do anything like what he described. But there was a hot feeling spreading deep in her gut. Her body began to betray her. She remembered the things Wayne had told her, about Albert and Brandy coming here and wandering into the room unaware. It was such a carnal image that he had painted. It was so dirty. It was so *wrong.*

And yet, it was strangely alluring… She found herself trying to imagine the two of them in here, forcing themselves on each other, tearing at each other's clothes. The thought was surprisingly sexy. She was suddenly dwelling on the idea of the two of them down here, naked and alone, furiously attacking each other. It was such an easy thing to visualize.

It was so *hot.*

She was suddenly curious about what other awful, fascinating scenes surrounded her, inviting her to look upon them. She wanted to see them, wanted to see what naughty things they were doing. It was intriguing.

She squeezed her eyes closed as tightly as she could. This was wrong. This wasn't who she was. This wasn't how she behaved. She didn't want to see the things that were in this room. These things were *disgusting.*

But the truth was that she was incredibly turned on by

them.

What was it doing to her? She'd never felt like this before.

She should have listened to Wayne. She should not have peeked. Now there were dirty thoughts in her mind. There were naughty ideas. And worst of all, she liked the way they made her feel.

"Here we go," Wayne called back to them. "Watch your head."

Olivia stepped out of the sex room behind him and opened her eyes, relieved to be free of the darkness again. In front of her, Wayne was returning the glasses he'd retrieved from his bedside earlier that night to his face. He looked good with them on. He looked gentler.

"Are you two okay?" he asked, blinking through the lenses as his eyes readjusted.

"I'm fine," Olivia replied. And she was.

Andrea merely nodded, her face lowered toward the floor.

"Andrea?" Wayne asked.

"Yeah," she replied quickly, nodding again. "I'm fine. No problem." She dared not meet his eyes. She studied her flashlight carefully instead, inspecting it, hoping he would just turn around and start walking. She didn't want to tell him she'd disobeyed him. She didn't want to acknowledge what she'd done. It was embarrassing.

She didn't even want to think about it, but it was right there at the front of her mind, tormenting her.

"You sure?"

"Yeah." She forced herself to lift her eyes from the flashlight and meet his gaze. He was remarkably handsome, with the dirt on his face and his hair all messed up like that. He looked *sexy*. "It's just…weird down here," she told him as her face flushed even hotter than before.

Wayne nodded. "It is." But his eyes lingered on her and she could meet them no longer. She looked down at the flashlight in her hands again, embarrassed. She was sure he could see the color in her cheeks, sure that he knew what she had done.

But he said nothing more. He turned away and started down the next passage with Olivia right behind him.

Andrea turned her flashlight on and followed, her eyes washing over Wayne's cloaked body as he led the way ahead of her.

Chapter 11

Shortly after leaving the last water chamber behind them, Albert noticed that the tunnel they were in had begun to spiral to the left. He almost turned around right then, not wanting to waste time, strength or chalk on a dead end. But a spiraling path did not necessarily have to go nowhere, and he soon found that this one did not. At the center was a small room into which three tunnels opened.

The three of them stepped out of the middle passage and considered the other two. They circled back out together, all of them wrapped around the same central point that was the room in which they now stood. Their choices were to spiral back out from this room on the inside of the tunnel they had just exited or on the outside.

Albert chose the outermost tunnel.

"I don't get it," Brandy said. "The Sentinel Queen brought us here. She sent us the box and showed us the way to the city. She even sent her son to make sure we were doing it right. She went to all that trouble and said it was because she was running out of time. So why didn't she tell us how to get through this?"

Albert could not even begin to speculate. "None of this makes much sense to me," he admitted.

"I mean, it was so important to her that we got to the labyrinth. Why? So we could die down here?"

Albert still had no idea.

They reached the end of the spiral and followed the tunnel around a sharp left turn. Ahead of them, it split into two separate passages. Albert chose the left one, marking it as he went with the same yellow line that had been following them since the labyrinth's entrance.

He was nearly out of yellow. He'd have to choose a new color soon.

"Do you think she knows what she's doing?" asked Brandy.

Albert looked at her, curious. "The Sentinel Queen?"

She nodded.

"Yeah. I think she must. She knew enough to know how to get both of us down here in the first place. She knew how to get us this far."

"Do you think she could be wrong?"

Albert shrugged. "Maybe. Everybody's wrong about

something, right? I mean, maybe the reason she didn't give us any help getting through the labyrinth is because she doesn't know the way."

The tunnel curved to the left and then turned sharply right, where it intersected another passage. They went straight across the intersection and in a few minutes they found themselves standing on another stone bridge, staring around them at the chasm they had crossed on the other side of the City of the Blind.

"We're back here again?" Nicole asked.

Albert stared up into the darkness above them, as amazed by the sight as he had been the first time he saw it.

"Which one of these bridges did we cross earlier?" wondered Brandy.

"Probably none that we can see from here," replied Albert. "There's no telling how far this thing could stretch."

There were a lot more bridges visible from this vantage point than there had been when they were last here. They spanned the chasm above, below and to either side, and to Albert the sight was abysmally discouraging. This place was enormous beyond comprehension. They stood over a veritable canyon with no visible bottom or top. There was no way to know how far or how high or how deep it went.

What was even the purpose of such a thing?

How were they supposed to get through a maze this size?

They would be lucky if they did not starve to death in here, much less get eaten by the Caggo.

Nicole stared out into the darkness. She could not help but wonder if a pair of eyes might be watching them from some distant bridge.

“I don’t like this place,” Brandy decided.

Albert continued forward without replying. He wished that he had not chosen this path, that he had gone a different way at the last intersection. It was overwhelming. It was impossible to look out over that vast space and not feel defeated by the magnitude of their task. Surely they would never find their way out of here. They were utterly lost.

The three of them walked on, each of them feeling more lost with each step they took.

Chapter 12

Andrea Prophett had done a lot of things in her young life. She'd always wanted to be different. She wanted to be *unpredictable.* She wanted to be held back by nothing, least of all by other people's meaningless expectations. She'd begged her mother for years to let her get her nose pierced and her mother, always understanding, always encouraging, had finally allowed her to do it for her seventeenth birthday. When she turned eighteen, only a few weeks ago, she'd surprised her mother by coming home with not just her eyebrow pierced but her navel as well, both of which she'd saved up and paid for herself. She liked surprising people. In ninth grade, she'd surprised her best friend, Rachel, by boldly asking out Greg Pobson, whom she'd had a crush on for some time. (He said yes, actually, but he turned out to be a very boring person and she broke up with him just a few days later.) Tonight, however, she was surprising even herself.

She hadn't really intended to take off her clothes down here. She was neither an exhibitionist nor a slut, and until this night, no one who hadn't changed her diapers had ever seen her naked. She was still a virgin, with the intention of saving herself for her wedding night. But here she stood, covered only by her trembling hands, wearing nothing but her jewelry.

She could not have said what it was that she planned to do when the time came to disrobe. Wayne warned her over and over again that she would have to do so and still she hadn't listened. Somehow, she just hadn't believed that it would actually happen. Perhaps he was lying to her for some reason. Or perhaps she thought they might find another way, a way that would not require them all to be nude. Or perhaps she merely thought that she and Olivia would simply refuse to do it.

Then they reached the pool of water. Five sets of clothes lay discarded on the floor. At the very sight, her stomach had rolled over. She actually thought she might vomit for a moment.

Jeans and shirts, shoes and even a backpack, all lay in little piles, waiting for their owners to return, but no socks, underwear or bras were to be seen. The man with no eyes had taken those, she remembered. It was a part of Wayne's fantastic story, a story that was vividly playing out before her eyes.

She recognized all of these clothes. Albert, Brandy, Nicole, Wayne and Beverly had all been wearing these items when she spied on them from her hiding spot in the trees near Gilbert House. It was odd to see them lying there like that. It was such a small detail, yet it felt incredibly profound.

She remembered the way Wayne's eyes lingered on the black shirt and khaki pants that had belonged to Beverly. She saw the deeply sad look of regret in his eyes. That was one pile of clothes whose owner would not be returning. She was gone forever, utterly lost to the madness of the temple.

But there was no time to feel sad. At that moment, Wayne turned away from the orphaned clothes and yelled into the silent darkness as loudly as he could, startling both her and Olivia. He called for the man with no eyes, telling him to come and get their undergarments, to clear the way for their passage as he had done before. In the empty corridors, his voice echoed like thunder, trampling the silence.

But the blind man did not come.

Wayne had stared out over the water, looking both puzzled and troubled, and Andrea understood why. This eyeless man of whom he had spoken was supposed to take their underwear into the maze, where their scents would distract the hounds and keep them from catching wind of the real prey. If he did not come…

But of course Wayne would not be stopped by the mere absence of the blind man. He unfastened his cloak and dropped it to the stone floor, leaving himself stark naked before her startled eyes.

"This is it," Wayne told them. "If you're not coming with me, I don't blame you. I really don't want to put either of you in danger." He kicked his sandals off next to the shoes he left here on his first trip and then turned to face them, his body utterly exposed. "This water's freezing. And if you don't turn back now, you may not be able to later."

Andrea had just stared at him, unable to believe that he was naked right there in front of her. She could actually see his penis! More startling had been the realization that she was simply staring at that part of him, unable to take her eyes off it, even though she could feel her face burning bright red.

She couldn't possibly do this. Especially not now, not after she had peeked in that awful sex room. She could still feel that queasy, unwanted longing burning deep in her belly. And now she was looking at Wayne naked!

A strange excitement was building within her, like an electric charge. She could feel her body reacting to her unwanted arousal and fresh fear sprang from within her. She *especially* couldn't take her clothes off *now!*

"We *have* to be naked?" Olivia asked.

"Even if you didn't," Wayne explained, "you'd be miserable walking around in soggy clothes."

That, Olivia supposed, was true. Perhaps naked was the best way to make any trip like this one. What were clothes, anyway, besides a tool for warmth and modesty? Wet clothes would not keep them warm and perhaps modesty was a concept that simply did not exist to the kind of people who were capable of constructing a place such as this.

Wayne turned and stepped into the water. Andrea heard him hiss at the icy touch of it on his bare skin.

"Wait!" called Olivia. In one quick motion, she stripped off her shirt. "I'm coming."

Wayne turned and looked at her. Andrea expected some amount of interest in his expression. Olivia was a gorgeous girl and she was stripping naked right in front of him, but there was no eagerness, no lustful leer, not even bashful admiration. All she saw on his face was a sort of deep sadness, as though someone had just strapped an enormous burden onto his back.

Andrea did not want to disrobe. She did not want Wayne to see her breasts, much less that other part of her. Especially now, especially while the sight of the sex room's horrible statues were still so fresh in her mind and her body was doing embarrassing things.

And yet the mysterious voice in the woods had told her to follow Wayne and Olivia. She was instructed specifically to go wherever they went, that she was important to them, that they would *need* her. She could not simply abandon them and run away. Besides, the last thing she wanted was to be alone down here. She was afraid of these tunnels. She was afraid of getting lost. She was afraid of losing her light or running into a nest of rats. And more than anything else, she did not want to go back into the sex room again.

Why hadn't she listened to Wayne in the first place? He was right. It hadn't mattered that she was not the sort of person who wanted to throw herself at every handsome man she met. The sex room still affected her. She understood now how Albert and Brandy could do the things they did in there. She could have been made to do that too. She was convinced that if she'd kept her eyes open for any longer, she might have done something unthinkable.

Even now, well after leaving that horrible room behind her, she wasn't sure she'd have the willpower to resist Wayne—or any almost man for that matter—if he should suddenly decide to turn around and try to take her. For the first time in her life, the thought of a man forcing himself on her actually made her feel excited!

What was happening to her?

Olivia stripped off her panties and bra and dropped them to the floor with the rest of her clothes. She was probably fifty or sixty pounds heavier than Andrea, but she was by no means fat. Her body was not flabby, but soft and curvy. She was *very* pretty, with a narrow, hourglass waist and breasts that were considerably larger than her own. Her body did not remotely compare. She felt like a skinny child standing next to her, with her bony hips and shoulders. She couldn't possibly do this.

But Olivia turned without hesitating and charged stark-naked into the water after Wayne, squealing at the water's icy touch, and Andrea was left staring after her, alone on the dry stone, unable to put it off any longer.

Strip down to her birthday suit or remain behind, alone in this awful darkness.

Whimpering under her breath, she began to take off her clothes.

Now she stood naked and trembling at the water's edge, her arms crossed over her private parts, blushing furiously and hoping desperately that no one could tell that her body was burning with unthinkable desires.

Bracing herself, she waded out into the cold water.

Chapter 13

The cold was almost overwhelming, but Wayne welcomed it. The cold drew his thoughts from the discomfort of the situation. Both girls followed him, remaining with him even past the part where they had to leave their clothes behind. They would not turn back for anything now. Like it or not, they were with him to the end.

And he had no idea what kind of danger he might be putting them both in. The absence of the man with no eyes at the water's edge was extremely bothersome. Why hadn't he shown up? Was the old man right? Did the Sentinel Queen refuse to help him? It certainly did not appear to be a move in his favor. Would they be able to reach the City of the Blind without his help? Or would the hounds be drawn to them as soon as they set foot in their territory?

He supposed he would find out soon enough. The first of those lower passages waited directly ahead. There was nothing he could do but press forward and hope for the best.

He glanced back as he stepped onto the dry stone to make sure they were both okay. Immediately, he wished he hadn't. Olivia was just a few steps behind him, hugging herself fiercely across her ample breasts. The bandage was still taped to her shoulder, protecting the bite, and her arm was still well wrapped, but the rest of her beautiful body was uncovered to his eyes.

A little farther back, Andrea was doing a better job of covering herself. She was very thin compared to Olivia, whose full and gorgeously curvy figure almost made the subtle shadows of the girl's ribs appear unhealthy. She was also very pale in comparison, her complexion much whiter. Without her clothes, all the jewelry she wore jumped out at him. Her pigtails now sagged, dripping over her shoulders, almost black in the combination of the wetness and the gloom, and he was struck by how childlike she looked. Covering herself that way and shivering, she looked like a girl barely touched by puberty.

He forced himself to turn away, embarrassed, but before he could face forward again, his eyes were captured by the spreading bruise on Olivia's thigh. He turned toward her now, looking only at the big purple blemish so that he did not see her eyes flash across his naked body and then flit away, embarrassed.

"Your leg…" he said, surprised that his voice could escape

the shivers that racked his chest. "Does it hurt?"

She looked at him again, directly into his face, and saw that her bruise had caught his eye. She might have laughed at his insistence on worrying about her injuries if that bruise hadn't been so close to that other place, where she now dropped a hand to shield herself from his eyes.

Wayne saw the motion, glimpsed for just an instant the soft, dark tuft of hair between her thighs, and then looked away from her altogether, ashamed that his eyes should wander like that for even a moment. "Sorry…" he stuttered.

"It's okay." And it was. How could she expect him not to see her? She'd removed her clothes of her own free will, despite the offer he'd given her of turning back and going home. She glanced down at her thigh. The bruise had grown some, as she'd known it would. "It's a little sore to touch," she said. "But it's fine. Really. It never even broke the skin."

"That's good." He glanced back at her, careful to look only into her face, and for a moment she held his eyes. "I was worried."

She smiled at him, her lips quivering with the cold. He was so kind to her. "Don't be. You've already rescued me." She looked down at herself now and saw that there were other bruises, too. Lots of them. Her back was probably covered with them from her fall through those trees into the Wood. She had always bruised easily.

He smiled at her. "Okay." He glanced at Andrea and saw that she had turned away from them and was rubbing her hands up and down her arms for warmth. He could see the gooseflesh that ran all the way up her naked back. "Come on," he said. "Let's keep moving. We'll stay warmer."

"Oh god I hope so!" Andrea sighed through teeth that Wayne could hear chattering even over the hammering of his own.

As Wayne turned away, Olivia put an arm around her. "Come on," she said, her own voice racked with shivers. "In a little while we'll probably be sweating."

"That would be nice," Andrea stuttered.

Chapter 14

Albert smeared the last of the yellow chalk onto the wall and then paused to give his tired hand a quick shake. It lasted longer than he expected it would. He'd done a good job of conserving it.

"No more yellow?" Brandy asked.

"No more yellow," he confirmed. "From now on, if we come to an intersection and see a yellow line, it'll mean we were there sometime before now."

"Do you think that'll help us?" Nicole asked.

Albert shrugged. "Who knows?" He unshouldered the backpack and removed the tube of sidewalk chalk. For a moment, he examined the remaining choices. There was blue, red, purple and green remaining. "I guess we'll go with green," he decided. "We'll just go in order of the rainbow. That way, we'll remember which trails are older."

"Roy G. Biv," Brandy said, nodding.

"Who?" asked Nicole.

"It's an acronym for the color spectrum," Brandy explained. "Roy G. Biv. Red, orange, yellow, green, blue, indigo and violet. We use that term at work when we merchandise clothes by color."

"Except we never had any orange or indigo chalk," Albert observed. "So we're already down to just four colors." He replaced the plastic tube and returned the backpack to his back. Then he pressed the new stick of chalk to the wall and started walking again.

For a moment there was silence among them, and then Nicole asked, "Do you guys think Wayne's okay?"

"Sure," Albert replied. "He's a big guy. He's strong. He's definitely smart enough. He can take care of himself."

"I just wish I knew how he was doing," Nicole said. "He's all alone out there. That's got to be scary. Even without all the other stuff we've seen, just being *alone* like that has to be really scary."

It did not cross her mind that Wayne might already be working his way back through the temple, already nearing the hate room, in fact, much less that he was no more alone than she was.

Brandy nodded. "And he's just one guy."

"Come on," Albert urged. "We can't let ourselves think that way. We'll see Wayne again later. The Sentinel Queen seemed to have faith in him."

Nicole said no more. That was true. (Assuming the Sentinel Queen could be trusted.) How far had he gotten, she wondered? Had he reached the Wood yet? Was the journey hard on him? A part of her wished that she could have gone with him, but that would have meant separating from Albert and Brandy and she did not want that.

Ahead of them, the road forked into two tunnels, each of which held the promise of new choices for them to make. Somewhere, hidden deep within this collection of lefts, rights and straight-aheads was a formula that would take them exactly where they needed to be. (More than one, if the Keeper was telling the truth.) But finding it, finding *any* correct path, was like blindly navigating the stars. The odds that they were going in the right direction in such a place were too slim to even consider.

They fell into silence and Albert led them on through the labyrinth, choosing directions at random, hoping to find what they were looking for merely by blind chance, since they had no other way to navigate.

Chapter 15

Wayne led the way through the hate room without incident. It was easier than he could have hoped, in fact. As soon as he set foot in the angry man's mouth, he saw the light from Beverly's flashlight illuminating the square opening on the other side. All he had to do was turn off his own light and dodge the statues.

It was a stroke of luck, as was navigating the decision room with its scarred floors for the second time tonight without encountering any hounds, regardless of the blind man's failure to help them. But he hated that *this* small bit of fortune originated from such a grim tragedy. He would have gladly given up this advantage to have caught her when she fell. It seemed wrong to reap any sort of luck from someone's untimely death.

But even navigating by Beverly's flashlight alone, he was unable to ignore all the features of the statues. Things still crept through the shadows. Never before tonight had he ever wished for poorer eyesight, but right now he envied Brandy's more profound nearsightedness.

Surrounded by shadowy human shapes, he found himself reminded of childhood bullies and some old friends he'd grown to strongly dislike. He was brought to the brink of something that was probably grumpiness, but thankfully never felt anything he would consider *hate*.

Olivia clung to his hand, her eyes pressed tightly closed. She gnawed nervously at her lower lip as she waited for him to tell her she could open her eyes again. It was torture not being able to look around. She was half-convinced that there were monsters waiting to seize her with every blind step that she took.

She had no idea how she was ever going to sleep again.

Andrea, on the other hand, had no problem keeping her eyes closed this time. The sex room had sufficiently frightened her. She wanted nothing to do with this awful-sounding "hate room." She was more than happy to live the rest of her life without knowing what *these* statues looked like.

"I can't believe I'm actually naked down here," Andrea said, breaking the unnerving silence that had settled around them. She hated the silence. The silence let in too many frightening thoughts. It was why she kept talking. She couldn't bear to let herself think too much about what she'd gotten herself into. "I've never done anything like this before."

"I know," agreed Olivia. "Me either. It's strange."

"It's *so* strange."

"I just want to hide."

"I know."

"At least you're a skinny little thing. I feel like a cow."

"Oh, please. I'd love to have your body. I feel like a boy standing next to you."

Olivia gave a huff of a laugh. "Believe me; you don't look like a boy."

"Well I'd still rather look like you. You're *so* pretty."

"No I'm not," replied Olivia, embarrassed.

"Yes you are."

"*You're* prettier than I am."

"No way. I have, like, no butt or boobs."

Olivia laughed. "If I could, I'd give you my boobs. All these things're good for is dropping the IQ of every guy in the room."

"Huh," said Wayne suddenly. "Is that why I keep forgetting where I'm going?"

Olivia smiled, her face flushing red in the darkness.

Andrea giggled.

"I didn't mean you," Olivia apologized. "*You've* been a perfect gentleman."

Wayne laughed. "Yeah. Especially the part where I drag you both into the sewers and make you get naked. That was real classy of me."

“You didn't make us get naked. We made our own decision.”

“That's right,” Andrea agreed. “*You* told us to go home.”

“I did, didn't I?”

Olivia gave his hand a squeeze and had to resist the urge to open her eyes to look at him. He was such a nice guy. He was nothing at all like Andy...

But she didn’t want to think about Andy right now.

She forced herself to concentrate on keeping her eyes closed.

As soon as he was in the doorway between the hate room and the spiked pit beyond, Wayne returned his glasses to his face and prepared himself to look upon Beverly’s body once again.

She was right where he’d left her, impaled on the stone spikes, staring up at the ceiling with lifeless eyes. When last he looked upon this scene, her life’s blood was still flowing from her motionless body, onto the stone floor beneath her, and her eyes had grown glazed and distant, void of that brilliant glow that was too often underappreciated in the living until death scrubbed it away.

Now her body had grown ashen, her life’s color washed from her in a great pool of tacky blood.

So much blood.

The air was heavy with the smell of it.

"Brace yourselves," he cautioned. "It's ugly." He could not take his eyes off the stone spikes that protruded cruelly from her skin.

"Oh *god!*" gasped Olivia. Wayne warned them both of the gruesome sight that awaited them before they entered the hate room. She had prepared herself for the worst, but it was still a tremendous shock. "That's *her...*" she said, her voice quivering. "She's the one who sent us into Gilbert House."

Andrea stared at the body and the pool of congealed blood below it. This was the woman who had written the notes and collected the newspaper clippings inside the envelope that had appeared at her window. Beverly Bridger. She turned away, unable to look any longer. The only other dead body she had ever seen had been her grandfather's, and he'd been embalmed and resting serenely in his casket. He had looked wrong to her, she recalled, not quite like she remembered, but he had at least looked peaceful. This was different. There was no peace here, no illusion of sleep, only death, cold and harsh and raw and violent.

Suddenly, this thing felt a lot more real to her.

Olivia, on the other hand, could not seem to pull her eyes away. That woman had nearly gotten her killed. She had sent Andy, Nick and Trish to their violent deaths. She hated that woman, despised her...but she never would have wished this upon her.

"She was insane," Wayne said, also unable to remove his

eyes from her body. "Completely nuts. I was so mad at her. I hurt her. I sprained her wrist, maybe broke it, I don't know. And then…" He shook his head. "I tried to catch her. I really did."

Olivia finally was able to look away. She turned her face to him and then took his hand and squeezed it. "I know," she soothed.

"It was Gilbert House," he said. "That place drove her crazy."

"Can we keep going?" Andrea asked. She did not want to look upon this woman's body any more. It upset her. It made her feel sick.

"Yes." Wayne tugged softly at Olivia's hand and the three of them made their way carefully along the ledge to the next passage.

As Olivia followed Wayne out of the room, she found herself looking back at Beverly's body one last time. The stained spikes and congealing blood beneath her reminded her too much of the blood she'd seen oozing down the wall in Gilbert House.

Nick's blood.

She wondered if there would ever be a night she would not have some sort of nightmare about watching him die.

Chapter 16

"What do you think it is?" Nicole asked. "The Caggo, I mean."

"Could be anything," replied Albert. "After the Sentinel Queen and the Keeper and that thing in Gilbert House, I couldn't even begin to guess. Probably something really nasty. Or, for all we know, 'Caggo' could just be another name for a bear. That wouldn't be much worse, really."

"Hopefully we'll never find out," Brandy said.

The three of them had not seen any sign of the reservoir system or the hounds' passages since leaving the chasm behind them half an hour ago. Instead, they had encountered several more hills, some climbing, others descending, a few rising and falling like the backs of mythical sea creatures, until they no longer had any idea how high or how deep they might be.

They walked on for a few minutes without speaking and soon the silence began to feel uneasy to Nicole. She wanted to jump at every little noise they made, thinking that the Caggo was right behind them or waiting just beyond the next turn. "Do you have any ideas about where we'll end up if we solve this thing?" she asked, hoping to take her mind off the monster.

"I assume it'll take us to wherever the Sentinel Queen wants us to go. To whatever place those fourteen pregnant women were coming from when they passed through the City of the Blind. To 'where all humanity began,' wherever that is."

"What does that mean, exactly?" Brandy asked. "Where *did* humanity begin?"

"In some primordial ooze just like everything else," Albert replied. "No one really knows. Africa, I thought, but apparently it was a tunnel in the Midwest of what would eventually become the United States of America."

"That's a little odd, since the earliest civilizations were on the other side of the world," Nicole added.

"That's true," Albert admitted.

"Is history wrong?"

"History before records is just speculation and scientific guesses," Albert explained. "I think the margin of error has always been there and if you throw in something like the City of the Blind, then I think that margin of error grows quite a bit."

"Maybe it doesn't have anything to do with history and

science," Brandy suggested. "Maybe this is about the Garden of Eden."

Albert shrugged. "Just as likely, I suppose." Although he'd never really believed in an actual, physical Garden of Eden. He always thought it was a metaphor. But was it any less believable than the Temple of the Blind? Thinking about it now, he realized it wouldn't surprise him at all if that was exactly what awaited them at the end of this journey.

"Wherever it is we're going," Nicole said, "they spared no expense in keeping people away from it."

"This place is unreal" Albert agreed. "Without help, I can't imagine anyone ever even finding their way in, much less back out."

"Why even have all that if no one can get through it?" Nicole asked.

Albert again shook his head. He did not know. No one knew. If they were lucky, they'd live to be the first to find out.

He walked on for a while in silence, watching his flashlight beam as it slowly gave up its struggle against the darkness. "That's it for my batteries," he said as he stopped and removed his backpack.

"I'm so glad we have more than one of these," Nicole observed. "Can you imagine being down here by yourself and having to change the batteries in your flashlight?" She shuddered at the idea of having to sit down here in the dark for even a moment.

Brandy compared hers to Nicole's. "I think mine's going, too," she worried.

"We've still got plenty of batteries," Albert assured her. "We'll get as much use as we can out of each one and hopefully they'll last long enough for us to find our way out of here."

"And if they don't?" Brandy asked.

His light shining at full strength again, he slipped his arms back into the backpack and resumed walking. "We'll worry about it when we get there, I guess."

They followed the current passage as it curved to the left and chose left when it ended in an adjoining tunnel. In just a short amount of time, the path dead-ended and they had to back up and make a right instead. This tunnel curved to the right and led them to a fork at which they chose right. About fifty paces later, they found themselves exiting from the left side of the fork, having gone only in a small circle. They were going nowhere at all.

Brandy closed her eyes as Albert led them back the way they'd come, squeezing his elbow and trying hard not to be discouraged. She was beginning to feel as though she were in a dream. It seemed so long ago that she woke in her own bed, fearful of a ringing phone. It felt like days ago, perhaps weeks or even months, yet it had been only a matter of hours. Back then, she had never heard of Wendell Gilbert or Gilbert House. She had never dreamed of a City of the Blind or a Sentinel Queen. Yet here she was now, lost in an ancient labyrinth, trying to find some mysterious doorway she knew nothing about. It was impossible. There was no way this nightmare could be real, yet it was because of this place, because of the Temple of the Blind, that she had Albert in her life. If not for the sex room and the hate room and the fear room and all those other chambers they explored the last time they were inside this underground hell, she would not have him in her life. So if the dream was real, why shouldn't the nightmare also be real?

They backtracked out of the area where all the passages dead-ended and then turned left where they'd previously made a right.

Soon they found themselves at another intersection and the beams of their flashlights fell on a crooked yellow line.

"Shit," Brandy spat.

"It's okay," Albert said. "At least we know we've been here."

"What do we do?" Nicole asked.

Albert considered their options, trying to remember how far back the last untaken tunnel was. "Let's go forward," he decided. "We'll take the next unmarked passage."

They pushed on, drawing a green line over the yellow, indicating that they had traveled this way twice. The two colors would also help them distinguish the approximate time that they traveled these paths. The yellow lines always came before the green ones. Soon they reached an intersection where they had previously taken a right and turned left. Within five minutes, this newest tunnel abruptly ended.

"This is impossible," Brandy groaned. "There's got to be a better way." She opened up her dying flashlight and traded the dead batteries for fresh ones from Albert's backpack.

"Just relax," Albert said, although relaxed was one thing he was not. The longer he was in these tunnels, the more anxious he became. "We can't let ourselves get discouraged. We sure as hell can't panic. We just have to stay calm. That's our best bet."

Brandy dropped the dead batteries into the backpack and zipped it back up. Hopefully it would be a long time before they needed any more.

Chapter 17

Wayne had grown silent as he descended the long, spiraling staircase. The fear room lay ahead, and he grew more anxious with each step he took. It was not merely the thought of all those intolerable statues he would soon have to endure, but *all* the things that still stood between him and the friends he sought. He was so tired already.

After leaving the room that had claimed Beverly Bridger's life and body, the three of them passed through the mysterious empty chamber that apparently hadn't been empty at all to Beverly, and then followed the next passageway to the stone bridge. There, Wayne had heard the strange and ominous noise of the hounds lurking below him, but it was not nearly as loud as it had been when he first crossed it with Albert, Brandy and Nicole. A fear had begun to grow inside him that too many of the hounds might have begun to roam beyond that maze. Was it possible that they had grown wise to the blind man's underwear trick? At the very least, they had probably grown bored with such stubbornly elusive prey. If so, they could be anywhere, and before they reached the City of the Blind, they were going to have to travel through their territory again, territory he was sure was rich with Albert's and Brandy's and Nicole's scents as well as with his own.

He hadn't voiced his concerns. He didn't see that it was necessary to alarm the girls. He had already told them about the hounds. They knew the risk. That the odds might be stacked a little more out of their favor didn't make a lot of difference in the end. Such knowledge would only make a difficult trip even harder.

He led them into the next passage, just as he had led the others on his first trip. And just like his first visit, he nearly managed to get his big ass stuck. This time he had at least wedged himself within reach of the opening so that he could simply grasp the edge of the passage and pull himself to freedom.

Now the top of the spiraling staircase had risen well into darkness above them and below them the bottom would be coming into view any minute. Behind him, Andrea was saying again how weird it felt to be walking around naked and he wished she'd stop bringing attention to it. It was the forgetting that he was naked that made the lack of modesty bearable.

But Andrea could scarcely stop talking at all.

Though Wayne had only known her for a few short hours, he was rapidly learning a lot about her.

She was eighteen years old and a senior in high school. She intended to attend Briar Hills University next year, though she still hadn't decided if she wanted to major in nursing or forensics or veterinary medicine or education or maybe something else. Her best friend's name was Rachel Penning, and they were supposed to be roommates when they started college but Rachel was apparently acting like a bitch lately, so maybe she wasn't really her best friend anymore. And she had an uncle who used to tell her stories about the tunnels under the city and she always wanted to explore them but she always thought she'd be too scared. She knew a girl who claimed to have sneaked into some of the tunnels and saw a ghost, but she never really believed her. And she had never been naked in front of anyone until tonight and it was really weird being naked. But maybe not as weird as she thought it would be. And she still couldn't believe she was doing this.

Anywhere else and Wayne might have been extremely annoyed. But somehow he found the sound of her voice unexpectedly relaxing. It was nice to have a distraction from all the strangeness of this unearthly temple.

But he did wish she'd stop bringing up being naked.

Olivia, on the other hand, was still mostly quiet. She could not believe that she was here in this place. For two days she'd sat perched atop the seat of a dry toilet in a restroom stall without even the slightest glimmer of light to ease her troubled mind. Her legs cramped, her mouth and throat parched from thirst, her stomach aching with hunger, she had never in her life been so miserable. She still had very little strength, *far* too little to be here in these dangerous corridors, in fact, but she simply could not remain behind. It was the obligation she felt toward this man who had saved her life, her moral inability to let him go on alone into whatever mortal peril awaited him, but it was also more than that. What happened to her was no freak accident. It was not just some lunatic serial killer who murdered those people in Gilbert House. They had been attacked by something that, as far as she knew, should not have existed, something much deadlier than anything her formerly narrow view of reality would have allowed her to imagine. There was something else out there, something far greater than the world she knew. If she was ever going to learn to live with what happened to her, she needed to know that all these terrors were not going to come crashing through her bedroom window while she slept. It might not be possible to find closure, but at the very least, she could find some way to explain it all.

The long hours she spent inside that restroom stall were nightmarish. She sometimes dozed, sometimes rocked herself comfortingly, but always listened, expecting the door to open and that thing to come rushing in, ready to finish the job it began with Nick's skull.

Several times she'd had to pee and had been forced to use the toilet on which she sat, even though there was no water in the pipes, and the whole time she was terrified that the monster would either hear the sound of her urine striking the porcelain or smell it on the air and hunt her down the way it had hunted down Andy and Trish.

The memory gave her a hard shiver.

"Are you okay?" asked Andrea, derailing from her ramblings.

"I'm okay," Olivia assured her. "Just… You know. Memories."

"You went through a lot, didn't you?"

That seemed like the mother of all understatements.

"You want to talk about it?"

"No," she replied bluntly. "I don't."

"Okay."

"But thank you. You're sweet. I just… I don't want to talk about it. Not now. Not down here."

"Okay. But whenever you *do* want to talk… I know I don't sound like I shut up much, but I'm actually surprisingly good at listening."

Olivia smiled up at her. "I'll remember that." Andrea was such a sweet girl. She was glad she came along. She was a breath of freshness in this otherwise stale dungeon of a place. But she couldn't put words to all the things that weighed on her mind. Not here, not with a woman's corpse lying in a pit of spikes behind them and the dreaded fear room looming ahead of them. She could not possibly speak the words aloud.

Andrea went on talking, telling them about how this place reminded her of a friend of hers named Helen who used to dare her to do all sorts of scary stuff when they were kids. And as she talked, Olivia found that she could not stop thinking about all the things that had happened to her.

Particularly, she could not stop thinking about Andy and his friends, all of them dead and lost inside that awful dormitory.

It was all so pointless.

The whole damn thing had been pointless. She never should have even been there. She never should have become involved with Andy in the first place.

Dating Andy Lanott was the worst decision she'd ever made. She still couldn't believe that she fell for his ridiculous charms. He said he was fascinated by her, that she intrigued him, that she was the most beautiful creature he'd ever seen, and somehow she actually believed him. But what he'd really meant, of course, was that he just wanted to fuck her. The only thing that *really* fascinated him was her bust size.

She met him in the hallway while waiting for her Biology class to start. He simply appeared next to her while she was sitting on a bench, reading one of her textbooks. He was cute. And he seemed so smart and charming. He said all the right things. She was delighted that he wanted to meet her for a drink that evening.

It took only about three days to figure out that he didn't care anything about her beyond getting into her pants. And to that end, he turned out to be tireless. He made every effort to get her alone. He sweet-talked her. He flirted with her. His hands were constantly wandering. But he took absolutely no interest in her life. He didn't want to talk about her. He didn't want to meet any of her friends. He couldn't even be bothered to walk her to class.

She was only with him for a week. She could hardly say that she even knew him. (Although she knew him considerably better than he knew her, because if he absolutely *had* to talk about one of them, it was damn well going to be about *him*.)

It was her own fault that she was still with him on that awful evening. She knew it would never work. He never *intended* for it to work. She should have been through with him the moment she realized this, but for some reason she was lazy about it. She put off telling him it was over, half expecting him to tire of her pushing his hands away and dodging his come-ons and end it for her.

By Wednesday she had decided to tell him not to meet her anymore, that he simply wasn't the one she was looking for. She couldn't say exactly why, but she decided to let him walk her home from the cafeteria one last time before ending it. (He liked walking her *home*, of course; *home* was where her bed was.)

But they hadn't gone home after dinner. Earlier that afternoon, someone left a curious letter beside his books in the library, a letter that offered to pay him one thousand dollars to poke around someplace called Gilbert House.

She tried to talk some sense into him. It didn't add up. Why would anyone just give away a thousand dollars like that? He had no idea what kind of mess he might be getting himself into.

But he wouldn't listen to a word of it. He had his sights set on that money. He assured her it would be fine, that he'd invited Nick along, just to be sure. As if that were any kind of improvement.

Andy at least pretended to be charming. His best friend, Nick Shrewd, was arguably the most annoying person she had ever met. He was rude, vulgar, immature and obnoxious. He thought he was funny, and a lot of the people he surrounded himself with seemed to think so, too, but Olivia found nothing that came out of his mouth the least bit amusing.

She had no business going with them into Gilbert House. She knew it was a bad idea. She knew that something bad would probably happen. She should have simply walked home and left them to their little adventure. Even better, she should have broken off their relationship (if you could call it a relationship) and *then* walked home. But she followed them anyway. She was a little curious about Andy's mysterious letter, after all. And her sister had told her once that doing crazy, stupid stuff was just a part of being in college. But she supposed the real reason she went along was Trish.

Trish was Nick's girlfriend, although she couldn't fathom what it was she saw in him. Olivia only met her twice, but she seemed like a very sweet girl. She liked her much better than any of the other people Andy introduced her to. She seemed genuinely interested in getting to know her. The only attention she ever received from anyone else was when his fraternity pals were blatantly ogling her chest.

Trish was uncertain about the offer in Andy's letter. She was scared. Olivia saw it in her pretty blue eyes. And she wondered at the time whether Nick had given her any choice in the matter. It was the idea of those two idiots blindly following the directions in that letter and dragging poor Trish into it against her will that made her hesitate when she was ready to walk away. It just didn't seem right to leave her alone with them.

It was stupid. She should have left anyway. It was none of her concern. They weren't her real friends. She wasn't responsible for them. And for all she knew, maybe Trish would have refused to go through with it if Olivia hadn't tagged along to lend her courage. Perhaps she even would have convinced Nick to leave, too. And then maybe none of them would have gone into Gilbert House.

On the other hand, maybe there was no stopping Andy and Nick from going down that cellar door to their deaths. Maybe what she should have done was take Trish by the hand and walk away with her. At least then she could have saved *one* of them.

There were so many things she could have done differently. She wondered if any of them would have changed what happened…or if cruel fate had always had it in for Andy, Nick and Trish.

She remembered the woman who was waiting for them in the clearing outside Gilbert House. Wayne said her name was Beverly Bridger. Olivia had not liked her from the start. She seemed half crazy. She kept looking up at the empty space above the windowless walls and telling them that all they had to do was go inside, just go inside and look around. Look at *everything*. She kept stressing that they had to look at *everything*, yet she would not say what it was that she was looking for or why she could not go in herself. She wouldn't even tell them her name.

Even then, she hadn't been smart enough to run away.

But she never could have dreamed that there was an actual monster waiting for them inside.

She couldn't forget the silence that greeted her when she first sealed herself in that flimsy bathroom stall, trying to calm herself enough to hear over her breathless sobs and the pounding of her terrified heart. It had gone on for so long.

Hours and hours, it seemed, though it must have only been one or two. Then the silence was filled with the bloodcurdling sounds of poor Trish's screams. Olivia had clasped her hands over her ears, but still she heard them. They went on and on, screams so horrible that she was sure to hear them in her nightmares for years and years.

If she survived that long.

She remembered rocking herself atop the toilet seat, her hands pressed over her ears, sobbing as she waited and waited for it to end. She could not imagine what that thing must have done to her to make her scream like that for so long. And she never wanted to know. Only Albert had seen her body and she desperately hoped that he never told her what he saw. She never wanted to know what happened in that third floor room of Gilbert House.

When the screaming finally stopped, there were other noises in the darkness. Thumps. Bangs. Thuds. They would stop for several hours at a time and then start back up again. And her imagination made the noises more disturbing each time she heard them, until she was nearly convinced that the noises were coming from the bodies themselves, that Andy and Trish and Nick were stumbling around the dark corridors, searching for her.

For a long, long time, Olivia did little more than weep silently, forcing herself to hold back the desperate sobs that wanted so badly to burst upward from her throat. But even then, that little voice was there in her head, telling her to just hold on, to be strong and patient because someone was coming for her. It was an irrational thought, since no one on earth knew where she was. No one except that insane woman outside. And she had probably fled when she first heard the screaming.

But that irrational voice in her head had somehow been correct. Wayne had come for her. He rescued her, even though he ultimately had to face the Wood to do it.

And now, after all that, she had followed him into *this* strange little corner of hell.

Perhaps she had lost her mind in that bathroom stall after all.

Below them, the bottom of the stairs finally came into view. Wayne was breathing heavily, his bare body slick with sweat. He needed to rest, but when she suggested it, he refused. He was determined to catch up with his friends and nothing was going to hold him back.

"How far is it now?" Andrea asked.

"The fear room's just ahead," Wayne replied.

"The fear room's the hardest, isn't it?"

"Yes."

"Can we make it?"

"I made it through before with my friends," Wayne said. "But it wasn't easy then, and I don't think practice makes it any better." *Besides*, he thought but did not say, *last time I had Albert with me. I only had to do* half *of it.*

"We're going to be okay, right?" Andrea asked.

Wayne assured her that they would, but he felt like a liar. Who was he to say that they were going to make it? He didn't know.

Olivia watched Wayne as he made his way down the last of the spiraling steps. This man, this wonderful, incredible man, had risked his life for her, had walked alone in the dark for what might have been miles to find her, suffered painful injuries and had worn the soles of his feet bloody in places. And even now he continued to push on, determined to catch up to the friends he'd left behind.

She hoped she could be half as brave for him.

Chapter 18

Brandy groaned as she finally reached the top of the incline.

"I know," said Nicole between labored breaths. The hill that was now behind them was the steepest they had encountered and must have taken them up at least four stories. "If there's a dead-end up here I swear I'm going to scream."

"Please don't do that," Albert gasped. He was out of breath, too, his body aching. "We don't need to draw anything's attention."

Nicole nodded. "Right," she panted. "Maybe just some choice words then."

"That should be fine," Albert agreed.

Nicole turned and leaned against the wall, pressing her back to it. The coldness that had settled into her from their frigid swim had finally passed and she had even begun to perspire a little. With her eyes closed, she stood there, trying to catch her breath, and Albert found himself distracted for a moment by her lean, muscular build and the rhythmic heaving of her full breasts.

He turned his eyes away from her and gazed down into the darkness behind them. He didn't want to see Nicole that way. He didn't want to think about her like that. But her beauty was distracting. It was difficult. Ever since he and Brandy returned from the temple after their first adventure, the experience they shared in the sex room had lingered in him. It did something to his libido, permanently increasing his sex drive so that it took very little to make him aroused. Though he had never before been all that preoccupied with sex, he now found himself frequently distracted by it. *Everything* seemed to turn him on. Fortunately, it was the same for Brandy and together they could release their sexual tension as often as they needed.

But down here he had no such luxury. Down here there was no time for sexual games. They had to stay focused. They had to stay aware, alert for the many dangers that awaited them throughout the labyrinth. And even if the urge became too distracting to ignore, it wasn't as if they were alone together.

He had to keep his mind on the task at hand.

It wasn't even as if he had any interest in Nicole. He was in love with Brandy. He adored her. He was happy being with her. He wanted no one else *but* her. He didn't lust after his girlfriend's best friend. He didn't have fantasies about her.

Well… Maybe one or two about his girlfriend *and* her best friend… But he was pretty sure that was normal male thinking… He was even pretty sure that was normal *female* thinking, too. They just refused to admit it.

Besides, it wasn't as if Brandy was any less distracting. If anything, the sight of her naked body was even harder to ignore. She was, after all, his lover. If they were alone (and not lost in a terrifying labyrinth with a deadly monster), there would be nothing to stop him from walking over to her and running his hands over her supple body.

He had thought that as he grew wearier, he would become less distracted, that by now he would simply be too tired to even notice the two gorgeous bodies that were constantly passing before his tormented eyes. But it was exactly the opposite. Apparently, the more exhausted he became, the more difficult it was to muscle his thoughts *away* from them.

Searching for something to focus on besides beautiful, naked women, he considered the urges themselves. He contemplated how the sex room had changed him and Brandy, enhancing their sexual appetites so that they lusted after each other like they never lusted for anyone before that night. He supposed it could be argued that it had nothing to do with the sex room besides thrusting them together in the first place. He was, after all, a virgin before he entered that chamber. Some would say that he simply didn't know what he was missing, that when the statues worked their unusual power on them, it showed him how pleasurable sex could be and how much he enjoyed it. Even Brandy, who had been with two other boyfriends before him, might simply not have had as strong a connection with them. Perhaps they hadn't been good at it. They were both merely teenage boys, after all. Or perhaps there was something about the way Albert made love that was much more alluring to her. Perhaps Albert was simply much better at it than both of them. (There was an appealing thought.) It could be that the sex room merely drove them into each other's arms and they discovered quite by accident that they very much enjoyed making love to each other. *Very* much enjoyed it.

But Albert wasn't sure that was true. It didn't feel like just something they enjoyed doing. It was practically an obsession. Sometimes the two of them would come home after a long day apart and be so madly horny for each other that they never made it to the bedroom. They frequently made furious love on the couch, the chair, the floor, the table, in the kitchen, the bathroom, the dining room. More than once they did it in the hallway on their way to the bedroom. Almost every morning and night they made love in their bed. Rarely did either of them finish a shower without sharing a soapy quickie. They even occasionally left the table in the middle of a meal.

More than that, Albert wasn't sure that other men were capable of having sex as often as he did. He could usually be ready to go again within five or ten minutes. Sometimes considerably sooner.

"I don't know how much more of this I can take," Brandy groaned.

"I know," agreed Nicole. "I'm dying for a cigarette."

"Me too."

"I'd settle for some Taco Bell, though. I'm starving."

"I think I'm too tired to eat. I just want my bed."

"Lucky. I'm never too tired to eat."

Brandy rolled her eyes.

Albert turned and faced them both. Nicole was bent forward, resting her hands on her knees, her magnificent breasts pulled gently toward the floor and swaying voluptuously as she lifted her face and gazed forward into the darkness ahead. Brandy had stood up straight and was stretching, her lean arms crossed over her head, her pert breasts lifted sensuously, her belly flattened, her legs lengthened as she lifted herself onto her toes. The small tuft of fair, blonde hair where her thighs met was softly illuminated by the beam of his flashlight so that it glowed almost golden in the darkness.

He wondered for a moment if they might both be doing this to him on purpose.

Without speaking, he walked past them and led the way forward. He liked being in the lead. The darkness that lingered ahead was unnerving, but at least there were no gorgeous, naked women to distract him.

If he kept getting distracted, he would eventually lose his focus. And he desperately wanted to avoid the embarrassment of an ill-timed erection. He was fairly sure that Nicole would not let him forget it. She was so fond of trying to make him blush.

The tunnel that stretched out in front of them leveled off and then converged with three more in an eight-way intersection.

"Any suggestions?" asked Albert.

"Like we know any better than you do," Brandy said, a little too grumpily. "We'll never find our way through this."

"Just pick one," Nicole agreed. "It doesn't really matter, does it?"

"I guess not," Albert replied. He picked the path to the right of the one straight ahead and soon they found themselves walking downhill again. At the bottom of this hill, the path converged with another and they continued forward. Soon, this passage made a sharp left turn and Albert spied a large room looming at the end of the passage ahead of them. He swelled with hope that they had somehow lucked into finding the end of the labyrinth, but he knew better. What awaited them ahead was most likely one of any number of large chambers scattered throughout the temple. Perhaps they had circled back to the reservoir or maybe to that disturbingly enormous chasm.

Instead, they walked out into an open darkness.

They stood there for a moment, gazing out at the enormous

chamber. The floor continued forward into the room, but everything else receded into the darkness, far beyond the reach of their flashlights, so that nothing but a flat, stone walkway could be seen.

Again, Albert cursed himself for not thinking to pack flares. Here was yet another place he could have dropped one to get an idea of what might be below them.

Brandy seized his elbow and squeezed nervously. She wasn't exactly afraid of heights, but neither was she terribly fond of them. She was usually fine, but she disliked climbing on ladders and standing on precarious ledges. The walkway before them was plenty wide enough to safely cross, even side-by-side, if they wanted, but there were no rails of any kind and it was disorienting in the darkness. Not being able to see anything beneath them was especially unnerving.

"I don't like this," she whimpered, pressing herself closer to Albert.

"This place is stupid," Nicole growled, but there was more apprehension in her voice than anger. "Everything about this place is just fucked up."

"It could be worse," Albert offered.

"Oh, I'm sure it will be."

Brandy stared out at the walkway, her stomach sinking. She didn't want to do this. The very sight of it made her feel queasy. She couldn't even see what was holding it up.

"We might as well get it over with," said Albert, and with Brandy still clinging to his elbow, he started forward. Almost immediately, the wall behind them dissolved into the shadows and left them walking through the darkness with nothing to be seen but the small strip of floor beneath their feet.

"Seriously," grumbled Nicole, "whoever designed this place was not right in the head."

Albert didn't disagree. There was something definitely twisted about the temple. He wished he could see what was around them. It made him nervous not knowing what might be out there.

He couldn't help but wonder if the Caggo was here, watching them, stalking them.

In a sort of optical illusion, the floor seemed much smaller than it had in the confines of the labyrinth's many passageways, making him feel as if he might teeter off balance at any moment. And with the bottom of the chamber hidden beyond their vision below them, it was easy to magnify that feeling by imagining that they were suspended over a bottomless abyss.

But this chamber was definitely not bottomless.

From somewhere directly below them, the furious clamor of a hound suddenly burst from the silence and Brandy and Nicole screamed.

Chapter 19

Albert, Brandy and Nicole each stood motionless, their hearts pounding in their chests, as the strange and threatening roar of the hound rose up from beneath them, filling the chamber and echoing off the walls so that it took on a terrible, warbling tone that was indescribably menacing. Then other hounds joined in. Dozens of them, it seemed, though it was probably only four or five, and it felt as if there were a thousand monsters roaring at them with their awful, clattering voices.

Brandy held Albert's arm in a death grip. And the instant the noise began, Nicole pressed herself against him as well, so that they stood in an intimate huddle, terrified.

Had they wandered into a den of some kind? There was a very subtle reek to the air that he hadn't noticed at first, a stale and musty animal stench.

Brandy shouted something at him, but it was impossible to hear her over the imposing roar of the creatures. What the hell was that sound they made? He just couldn't grasp how they were doing it. It didn't sound like any kind of animal call that he had ever heard. It didn't even sound organic. As if they were not beasts at all, but unthinkable, murderous machines.

The creatures were directly beneath them, perhaps only twenty or thirty feet down. This walkway obviously passed right over a large chamber in their territory. But they should be safe up here out of reach. There was no evidence that the hounds had any means of climbing up to them. The two parts of the labyrinth had been kept separate so far and Albert was fairly certain that they would remain that way.

Knowing this, however, did not make it any less challenging to move forward. With the very real and very deadly threat of the hounds to frighten them, and with the creatures' enraged racket assaulting their ears from every direction, the walkway seemed to become even narrower, threatening to spill all of them off the side and into the snarling jaws of something unthinkable.

It was almost dizzying.

Step by step, Albert crept forward, his eyes fixed on the platform at his feet, reminding himself over and over again that there was plenty of room, that he was in no danger of falling to his death.

Brandy continued to cling to his elbow, digging her nails

into the flesh of his arm. He welcomed the pain as a distraction from the disorienting roar that practically shook the chamber around them.

Nicole, too, remained attached to him. Her hand on his shoulder, she pressed her body against his bare back whenever he paused. Suddenly, he was no longer aware that she was naked. His only awareness was of the floor beneath his feet and the hellish din of the hounds.

But as they clung to him, afraid of the monsters that filled the chamber around them with their terrible noise, they threatened to throw him off balance. Albert had to pause and focus himself to keep from staggering.

Was it only his imagination, or could he also hear the underlying sound of menacing snarls? There was no doubt in his mind that if they should stumble and fall from this platform, they would immediately be set upon and slaughtered by whatever those things were, and yet he remained fascinated by their mystery. What were they? What did they look like? How did they make that unusual noise?

Eventually, they reached the other side of the chamber and hurried into the passage that awaited them on the other side, breathing a sigh of relief as the noise of that chamber began to fade into the shadows behind them.

"Okay, that was terrifying," squealed Nicole when it was quiet enough to again be heard.

“I think we stirred them up a little,” said Brandy.

“You think?” retorted Nicole.

Brandy ignored her. “You don’t think all that noise they’re making will lure the Caggo, do you?”

“It could,” he admitted.

“Oh god,” sighed Nicole. “I don’t know if I can take much more of this.”

An intersection appeared ahead of them and they turned left. At the next intersection they turned right. Then right again. Albert barely thought about it now. It made no difference. It seemed that the quickest way through this labyrinth now was to cover as much ground as possible. At some point they would have to stumble across the exit.

He turned left and then stopped as another dead end emerged from the darkness ahead of him.

“You know,” he said as he turned to retrace his steps. “For a maze this size, there haven’t been as many dead ends as you would think.”

“That’s true, I guess,” agreed Brandy.

“Most passages go somewhere, even if it’s just to another passage,” Albert continued.

“So, what?” Nicole asked. “Instead of getting hopelessly lost and running into one dead end after another, we’ll get hopelessly lost and just go in circles?”

“Pretty much,” Albert replied. “Except that we have the

advantage of our chalk line. Because we know where we've already been, we should be able to find our way through. It's just a very long process of elimination."

"*Too* long," decided Brandy. "We're supposed to stay lost in here until the Caggo can hunt us down and kill us."

"I think so," Albert admitted. It was a grim thought, but perfectly accurate, he was sure.

From somewhere ahead of them, they heard the distant droning of hounds again.

"Are we circling back to that same room?" Nicole asked.

"It's possible," Albert replied. "Or somewhere near it."

The noise grew louder, and when they reached the end of the passageway they found another dropped tunnel crossing theirs. Twice as wide as the ones to which they had been confined, it looked like another major thoroughfare for the hounds. The stench was much stronger here. It reminded him of the zoo, where some the habitats always inevitably smelled foul no matter how well the animal keepers cared for them. It was the very nature of wild animals. They stank. And the hounds were likely no exception.

The noise was coming from somewhere to the right. Albert felt certain that if they were to follow the sound, they would probably find that it sloped into a ramp that led down to the unseen chamber beneath the precarious walkway.

But that was no place they wanted to be.

"Let's just go back," Brandy suggested.

But Albert was already looking at the passage across from them. "I don't like to backtrack unless I absolutely have to."

"The hounds are right over there," Nicole argued. "We don't know how far away they are or how fast they can get here."

"We can make it."

"I don't care if we can or not," snapped Nicole. "It's a chance we don't have to take."

"I don't think we'll get out of here alive if we avoid taking chances," Albert said as he turned and fixed his eyes on hers.

"You don't know that," she said, but it was hard to meet his gaze.

"Maybe I don't. But it feels right to me. The more time we spend going back through passages we've already taken, the longer we're stuck down here and the more likely we are to attract the Caggo."

Without waiting for more arguments, Albert dropped down into the passage and hurried across to the other side.

Brandy and Nicole followed quickly, unhappy, but unwilling to risk being separated from him should a hound come racing toward them. And in a mere few seconds they were all standing on the other side, safely out of reach.

"I'm going to bet that we'll stir those things up again," Albert said as he shined his light down the passage in the direction of the noise. "And we won't be able to cross these intersections if they get too riled up. That's reason enough to explore as widely as possible now."

"I guess," said Brandy.

"I just want to *see* one," Albert said. "I want to know what they look like."

"I'm sure you'll get your chance," Nicole assured him. "Now come on. I'm not hanging around here to wait for one to come begging for a treat."

Albert nodded, but he lingered another moment, hoping for a fleeting glance at something extraordinary.

The mysterious roar of the hounds faded away behind them and they resumed their blind trek through the labyrinth. Albert turned left at the next intersection, and then left again. Then straight ahead. Then right. Before long, he'd lost track of which direction he was traveling. Not that he had known which way was which in this insane temple since he first stepped foot in it.

A few times, they encountered intersections where the buzzing of the hounds could be heard from somewhere deep inside one of the passageways. They chose to avoid them and continue their search in the silent corridors. None of them wanted to risk having to cross another of those treacherous bridges any time soon. The next one might not be nearly as wide as the last. Or as sturdy.

Eventually, they made their way to the end of a long passageway, where they found themselves looking out at another large chamber.

But this one was different.

It *felt* different.

"What is it?" Brandy asked, although she was sure she already knew. The chamber was wrong somehow. It was ominous. *Sinister.*

Albert stared into the enormous emptiness for a moment, contemplating it. Then, at last, he spoke it aloud: "It's the meadow."

Chapter 20

"Do you guys think I'm talking too much?"

Wayne almost laughed. It came bubbling up from inside him like a geyser, filling his throat and mouth. It took a significant amount of effort to hold it back. "Why would you say that?" he asked, marveling at the evenness of his voice.

The three of them had entered the fear room and had already managed to navigate the first two rooms, but Wayne was already feeling the weariness that plagued him on his first visit to this awful place.

"I just do that sometimes," Andrea replied, her eyes still tightly closed. "It bugs my dad. He makes fun of me."

Wayne could scarcely imagine why. "You're definitely chatty," he told her. "But I don't mind." This was the truth, actually. In this chamber, any distraction from the statues around him was more than welcome.

"I think it's nice," Olivia agreed. "Takes my mind off things a little." The darkness, she discovered, was a little easier to bear when it was filled with the girl's sweet chatter.

"That's good," Andrea said, squeezing Olivia's hand. "Because when I get nervous I sometimes talk more than when I'm not and right now I'm pretty nervous."

Olivia squeezed her hand in return. "That's okay."

"Yeah," Wayne said. "You can keep us entertained so we don't freak out in here."

"You guys are really nice," Andrea said. "Thanks for letting me come along."

"I didn't think I had a choice," Wayne said, easing around a statue that made him want for some reason to look at the floor and watch for little slimy things. He had no idea what these things might be, but he was suddenly very certain that he never wanted to step on one of them.

"I guess you didn't," Andrea replied.

"I just can't believe you both wanted to come," Wayne said. "It just floors me."

"We're complicated girls," Olivia said.

Andrea giggled.

"I guess," said Wayne.

"We can help," Andrea told him. "We have useful qualities."

"Like what?" he asked, amused.

"You just said I'm keeping you distracted, didn't you?"

"That's right," Wayne admitted. "You are doing that." Although he could have used a little *more* distraction. He was beginning to feel jumpy, his nerves already a little frayed. How many rooms did this place have again? He couldn't quite remember.

"And Olivia knows what her qualities are."

"Yeah," said Olivia. "Sitting on a toilet seat for two days. I'm really good at that."

Wayne laughed. "I can't imagine it. You're a tough chick."

"I guess I am."

"I wouldn't have made it," Andrea decided. "I would've gone completely nuts."

"There were times I thought I might," Olivia remembered.

Andrea shuddered at the thought.

Wayne kept his eyes half-open, trying to block out the things he saw lurking in his peripheral vision. This was harder than the last time he did it. His eyes had been inferior for as long as he could remember, forcing him to wear glasses for years when he was a boy, but now they were failing him because they were not inferior *enough.*

He was beginning to wonder if he was capable of making it past all of this without going utterly mad.

A large shape loomed before Wayne, blocking the path

forward. It was difficult to see the way past it without glimpsing details that fixed themselves firmly into his mind and filled him with uneasiness. It seemed to be reaching out for him with many arms. And he could not help but think that there was something disturbing about the mass of shadows at its center, as if the thing's belly were bloated and bulging, filled with something unspeakably vile.

No. That wasn't possible. He couldn't possibly know such a thing. He couldn't see that well. It was only shadows and shades of gray.

And yet he found himself thinking for some reason of an old dirt road and thick smoke hanging in the air.

Wayne stopped and closed his eyes. He wanted nothing more than to catch up with Albert, Brandy and Nicole as quickly as possible, but he had to make time in here. He couldn't do this himself unless he rested. He had to let the horrible thoughts fade in his mind or they would accumulate and overwhelm him. Albert made that mistake and he experienced a gruesome death-hallucination that scared the hell out of everyone.

He didn't care to experience that for himself.

"Wayne?" called Olivia, concerned.

"It's okay," he assured her. "I'm just taking a second. The statues in here put some weird things in your head. If you push yourself for too long it can really get to you."

"What's it like?" Andrea asked suddenly.

"You don't want to know," Wayne assured her.

"I do. I want to know what you're going through. I want to know what you're doing for us."

Wayne considered it for a moment. He didn't really want to focus on it, but talking seemed like a good idea somehow. It would help him to ignore that strange, cold breath that was currently falling across his bare shoulder.

"The statues are…*unthinkable*," he began. "Most of them are monsters, of some sort. Things you can't even imagine. Big ones. Small ones. All shapes and sizes. It doesn't just make you feel scared. It makes you feel like these things are real, that they've *always* been real. You just *know* they're real. Every one of them seems to have a story and it's *terrifying*. Sometimes I can hear it growl at me. Sometimes I feel it touching me. Sometimes I just feel absolutely certain there's something there, right beside me, ready to strike. You know it's too terrifying to look at, but you feel like you *have* to look, like something bad is going to happen if you don't. But if you do… That's when it gets you."

Olivia shuddered at the thought. Her time in Gilbert House had left her with a keen impression of what her imagination was capable of producing. She could scarcely imagine the added terror of being surrounded by things that actually added their own horrors.

"It's all different sensations. Albert and Brandy said it's different than the sex room. There, the images just kind of…get to you somehow. Like it's all subliminal. It just makes you feel like you can't control yourself."

Andrea considered telling him that she'd peeked in the sex room, that she knew a little bit about how that felt, but she bit back the words, still too embarrassed to admit what she'd done. She remained silent and anxiously chewed her lower lip.

"But here," Wayne continued, "you walk away absolutely certain that everything in here is *real.* And you don't leave it behind when you go. You keep it. Maybe forever."

"My god…" sighed Olivia.

"Wow," agreed Andrea.

"I know. It's like being in a nightmare, the way they feel so real while you're stuck in them. It doesn't matter how irrational the situation is or whether you know none of it can possibly be real or even if you *know* it's a nightmare. While you're asleep, it's as real as anything you could wake up to."

He opened his eyes and fixed his gaze on the floor directly ahead of him. The fears were still there. He could still see that smoky dirt road. It still felt as if things were watching him. But at least that disturbingly cold breath was no longer falling across his neck.

"Sounds awful," Olivia said.

"It is," Wayne assured her. "It's worse than you can imagine because it's worse than I can ever describe it. It feels… *indescribably* bad in here."

Olivia gave his hand a gentle squeeze. "We're right here if you need us for anything."

Wayne turned his head a little, as if to look over his shoulder at her, but he closed his eyes as he did it, not daring to risk glimpsing any more of these demented statues than was absolutely necessary. "Thanks."

"We're all in this together."

"That's right!" exclaimed Andrea. "We're a team. Like it or not."

Wayne smiled. Like it or not. That was definitely true. He liked having them here. They really were helping him. He didn't know what he'd do if he didn't have them to distract him from these stone nightmares. But he felt nearly sick at the thought that he might be leading them into something neither of them could handle.

God, he hoped he was strong enough to keep them both safe.

Chapter 21

Albert stood there, staring into the large chamber. Near his feet, the smooth floor of the passage gave way to coarse, black soil. Farther away, at the very edge of their flashlights' reach, he could see the gently rippling surface of a small pond and what appeared to be the naked branches of a shadowy tree stretched out over it.

The meadow.

It was not difficult to understand why the Keeper warned them to stay away from this place. There was something wrong with this chamber. He could feel it, like a faint vibration in his very thoughts. A queer energy radiated from within. It was a bad place. And yet there was something about it that called to him, that made him want to go inside, to see what secrets were hidden there.

"The Keeper said we can't go in there," Nicole said, as if everyone needed reminding.

"I know," said Albert. "It's a dangerous place."

"It's bad," Brandy agreed.

And yet…

"It doesn't look like a meadow," Brandy observed. "I thought meadows were grassy."

"What kind of grass did you think would be growing down here in the dark?" challenged Nicole.

"I don't know," defended Brandy. "I just pictured a grassy meadow. That's what a meadow is. Grass."

"Maybe 'meadow' has a different meaning to whoever built this place," suggested Albert. "Maybe it has another definition. Like a lagoon. On a tropical island, a lagoon is a great place for a romantic walk. Where my grandparents live, it's the nasty green hole where things go when you flush them down the toilet."

"Gross," said Nicole.

Albert stepped a little closer, willing his flashlight to reach deeper into the shadows and show him something more.

"What are you doing?" Nicole asked.

"Just looking."

"What's there to look at?" Nicole didn't like this place. Not at all. Even without the psychic abilities the Sentinel Queen claimed Albert and Brandy possessed, she could feel that there was something wrong here. "The Keeper said to stay away from this place. I don't know how much we can trust that…*thing*…but this is a subject I definitely think I agree with him on."

Brandy nodded. "I think you're right. It feels…*bad*…in there." She turned and looked at Nicole and her eyes looked strangely distracted. "I can't explain it."

"Did you see that?" Albert asked.

"What?" said Nicole and Brandy simultaneously.

"There's something in there."

"Where?" asked Brandy.

Nicole stepped up beside him and looked out at where he was aiming his flashlight. "I don't see anything," she told him.

"I thought I saw something moving," Albert explained. It was just a shadow, but it was definitely there. Something small and dark, moving quickly across the ground.

"I still don't see anything," Nicole said after watching for a moment. "Come on. Let's get the fuck out of here. This place is creeping me out."

She was right. There was something wrong with this place. But there *was* something moving out there. A small shape. He started to take one more step forward. He just wanted a quick glimpse at whatever that was.

Nicole seized his arm and halted him, digging her nails painfully into his flesh. "*What the fuck are you doing?*" she demanded.

"Ouch," he said flatly, finally pulling his eyes from that

room and looking at her. "What's wrong with you?"

"What's wrong with *you?*"

"I was just trying to see what's in there."

"You were trying to *go* in there!" she corrected him, gesturing at his feet.

When Albert looked down, he saw that his raised foot was hovering just above the black soil.

He pulled his foot back, startled, and backed away.

"What are you thinking?" Nicole asked.

Albert shook his head. "I don't know," he confessed. "I just really wanted to see…" His eyes had drifted back into the meadow as he spoke. Now his voice died away as he stared past Nicole at the chamber the Keeper warned them about.

Curious, Nicole turned to see what had caught his attention.

"Do you see them too?" he asked.

Nicole nodded. "Uh-huh."

"What are they?" Brandy asked.

Out in the meadow, lots of things were moving now. The ground churned with dark, scuttling shapes. As they watched, the coarse soil heaved upward and then sank again. Black, shadowy shapes slithered just into view and then out again. Something the size of a small cat emerged from the ground and scurried out of sight.

"I don't know…" breathed Albert.

"Can we go now?" Nicole asked.

"Please?" added Brandy.

Albert nodded. No longer did he find the chamber compelling in any way. All he felt when he looked in there now was a rapidly rising panic. The Keeper had been right. This was a place to be avoided. A bad place. A place of pain and misery and death.

Nicole took him by the arm, more gently this time, and urged him to move away. "You're starting to scare me," she whispered.

These words were enough to draw his attention from the meadow. He looked at her, gazed into her eyes. "I'm sorry…"

"Just come on," she begged. "Let's just go. Please?"

Albert nodded. His eyes became more alert at once. "I'm sorry," he said again, more firmly this time. "You're right. I don't know what's wrong with me."

She let go of his arm and placed her hands on his cheeks. She leaned close to him, her nose nearly touching his, as if about to tell him something very intimate. "You're a dickhead," she told him. "That's what's wrong with you. And if you go all hypnotized on me like that again while we're down here, I'm going to put my knee in your balls. Is that clear?"

Albert's mouth twitched into an amused grin. "Crystal."

"Good."

She smiled at him and then turned and looked at Brandy who was standing next to them, watching them. "The same goes for you, too."

"As everyone can plainly see," she replied, spreading her hands in front of her naked hips, "I don't *have* any balls."

"I'll think of something," Nicole promised. "Now let's please get the hell out of here."

Chapter 22

Wayne's whole body trembled as he approached the doorway between the final chamber of the fear room and the second spike room. His teeth clenched, his knuckles white upon the handle of his flashlight, he fought the urge to vomit. He'd made this second trip through the fear room in much less time than the first, but with no less mental exertion. In fact, he could almost feel himself teetering at the very edge of consciousness. Waves of vertigo washed over him. He could feel things crawling on him. They slithered up his legs, scuttled through his hair and wriggled into his ears. There were even things moving around *inside* him, burrowing beneath his skin, swimming through his veins, squirming through his guts. But none of it was real. Not anymore. Not to him.

But somewhere out there…a very long time ago…

The worst part was the way the room made it all seem so vividly *real.* He could not help but believe that these things had actually happened out there somewhere, in some long lost time. And if these horrendous things *ever* existed…what was keeping them from returning?

He forced himself to focus on the doorway, on avoiding the wicked spikes that jutted up at various angles from the floor on either side of the opening, threatening to gouge out his eyes if he was not careful.

As before, he'd run into one of those damned spikes while trying to feel his way around the monstrous statues, this time taking it in his right arm instead of his belly, and in his state of weariness, he again felt as though he were bleeding to death.

Fortunately, he'd somehow managed to keep from suffering the same, horrifying illusion of being slain that had temporarily crippled Albert when he was last in there. But there were several times when panic nearly overwhelmed him. Many times, he'd had to stop and close his eyes and force himself to calm down. Once, he actually had to bite back a scream as he made himself accept that there was not actually something cold and bony crawling up his back.

He hadn't realized until tonight just how much willpower he could muster. He might have been proud of himself if he didn't feel like such an exhausted wimp.

"Are we through?" asked Andrea as she felt her way

cautiously toward the door behind Olivia. Three times, something had scraped her as she walked, once on her left arm and twice on her right hip. She had also bumped her head on something and a small red mark was already growing into a bump on her forehead just above her left eyebrow.

"Almost. I'm in the doorway now. There are spikes everywhere, so be careful." He stepped out of the fear room and leaned against the wall beside the doorway, his eyes closed. He had to calm his nerves. They still had far to go and he would need his wits if he was ever going to catch up to the others.

Olivia, too, had suffered a few little scrapes and bruises as she passed through the winding chambers, but anyone would be hard-pressed to identify them among all the others she had collected during the night. She opened her eyes and peered out at the thousands of stone spines that filled the next chamber, horrified once more at the deadliness of the Temple of the Blind. "Oh my God," she sighed.

"I know, right? It's not as bad as it looks though." He could already feel his heart gradually slowing to its normal pace, but that weariness was not yet letting up. And it still felt as if a swarm of insects was crawling up his legs. "There're places to step. It's for tripping up anyone who beat the fear room by doing it blind."

Olivia nodded. That made sense. She could understand how the two rooms might work together like that. It took a combination of blindness and sight. "Are you okay?"

"I'm fine. I just have to rest a minute. That room drains you."

She stepped away from the doorway and stared into the spiked room. "I can't believe this place." She turned and looked at Wayne, her eyes suddenly widening. "You're bleeding!"

"It's okay," Wayne promised. He was still holding his glasses in his hand. The blurry images of the next room were strangely relaxing. "It's just a little poke."

"No, it's not!"

Wayne returned his glasses to his face and looked down at his arm. There was a gash just above his elbow and a steady trickle of blood was running freely down his arm and dripping onto the floor at his feet. "Oh," he said, surprised. For a moment he stared at himself, watching the blood pool in the palm of his open hand, and then he chuckled at the irony.

Andrea had been feeling her way slowly through the opening, careful to make sure she was well clear of the fear room and all its horrors before opening her eyes. "What happened?"

"I ran into one of those spikes. The same thing happened the first time I was in there, except I took it in the belly." He chuckled again, feeling a little delirious. Last time he'd been sure that he was badly injured and yet the wound had turned out to be nothing but a harmless scratch. This time, he had erroneously assumed that the injury was just as superficial as the last one, when in fact he was bleeding considerably.

"We need a bandage," Olivia said. She was quickly approaching a panic and Wayne could hardly blame her. There were no first aid stations down here. No hospitals. No help. They were entirely on their own and at the mercy of the temple.

This was part of the reason he was feeling weak, he was sure. How long had he been bleeding like this? How much had he lost?

Olivia forced herself to calm down. She closed her eyes and took a slow breath. She wasn't useful to anyone if she couldn't think straight.

When her head had cleared a little, she remembered the cut on her arm. The monster that snatched her from Gilbert House dropped her into the trees and one of the limbs gouged her as she fell. She'd stopped the initial bleeding with her torn shirt, but after she and Wayne were safely out of Gilbert House, Wayne had cleaned it for her and wrapped it properly with gauze. He went overboard, using far more than the injury required. And she was still wearing all that gauze.

She reached up and untied it. As she expected, she was able to unwind several feet that she had not bled through, more than enough to fix Wayne up for the time being.

"I don't have anything to disinfect it with," she told him as she tied it around his arm.

"It'll stop me from bleeding to death," he told her. "We can worry about infection later."

Olivia stepped back and looked him over. Now he had bandages on each arm, one below the elbow, the other above, as well as on both feet. "I'd feel better if we could take you to a hospital though."

"No deal. You wouldn't let me take *you*."

She smiled at him. "I hate doctors."

"*I* hate needles."

Olivia laughed. For a moment they stood there, looking at each other.

She was beautiful. Her eyes were so deep and dark, yet brilliantly bright, as though a warm glow were breaking through from somewhere within. Even with her face smudged and her makeup smeared and her hair dirty and damp and tangled, she was probably the most beautiful woman Wayne had ever seen. He could hardly believe that he was the reason she was still alive.

And yet, he couldn't help but wonder if he might merely be the reason she almost wasn't. He still wondered how things might have been different if he'd followed the instructions in Beverly's letter and shown up when he was supposed to, the same night Olivia and her friends arrived. Could he have prevented all that carnage? Could his absence that night have been the only reason those people were dead?

"How are you feeling?" asked Olivia.

"Better," Wayne replied. And it was true. He could already

feel the weight of the fear room lifting.

"Good."

Wayne stood up, ignoring the pain in his arm. It wasn't hard. He'd been ignoring the pain from his other arm and his feet since escaping Gilbert House for the second time. Compared to being bitten by a zombie, this was nothing.

The three of them moved on, making their way past the menacing spikes and ever deeper into the temple. They were closer now. Not much stood in their way. Soon they'd be in the City of the Blind.

And Wayne had some questions for the local sovereign.

Chapter 23

For more than an hour, Nicole had been leading the way through the tunnels of the labyrinth for no reason other than that she had wound up in front when they turned away from the meadow. Behind her, Albert dragged the chalk along the wall, carefully laying the trail that he hoped would prevent them from walking in circles, thereby helping them find their way more quickly to the exit.

Or at the very least back to the entrance.

She didn't know where she was going. The choices she made were entirely random, and even with Albert's blue chalk line leading the way back (the green ran out about a hundred yards back) she felt terribly uncertain about these walls, unable to shake the feeling that with every turn they were becoming more and more lost.

She chose left and then right, and then went straight through two more intersections. The passage then began to curve to the right and they soon found themselves staring in at the meadow again.

"Shit," she spat. "Another circle."

"No," Albert corrected her. "A circle would be if we were right back where we were the first time. We're in a different place, looking in from a different angle. We've gone around it a little."

From here, they could see neither the small pond nor the tree. There was nothing beyond the end of the passage but coarse, black soil.

"So we've gone, what, fifty feet? A hundred?" Brandy asked.

"Maybe. But in a maze, fifty feet could be as good as fifty miles."

"Or as good as fifty miles *backward*," Nicole argued.

"Don't think that way. Come on. At least we know we've made some progress. At least we haven't seen the Keeper again."

Nicole and Brandy said no more. That was true. The worst-case scenario would be if they exited a tunnel and found themselves right back at the entrance to the labyrinth, looking out at those two rows of sentinels.

Well, the *worst*-case would be turning the corner and finding the Caggo or a pack of hounds or some other voracious beast.

Albert turned and led them away from the meadow, not willing to remain too close to it for too long. He did not know what was in there, but it sure as hell wasn't kittens. Something was wrong with that room, and he didn't intend for it to take hold of him again like it did the last time he stood this close to it. More than that, he had no idea if the things that scurried and slithered through the dirt were specifically bound to that room or if they could be drawn out into the labyrinth.

"What do you think it is?" Brandy asked. "A trap?"

"I think so," replied Albert. "That's what it feels like."

"I still don't understand why all this is needed," Nicole said. "It's impossible. No one could find their way through this place alone."

Albert considered this. Maybe she was right. Maybe that was precisely the point. Maybe this place was not supposed to be found. Maybe only someone hand-picked by the Sentinel Queen would have enough of an advantage to pass through all of these obstacles.

But if so, then why choose *them*? Of all the people on the planet, why Albert Cross, Brandy Rudman and Nicole Smart? Why were *they* so special?

When they had returned to the previous intersection, Albert turned left and then made his way through each one that followed, forcing himself to think as little about each decision he made as possible. It did no good to over-think his decisions. It was a labyrinth. He was supposed to get lost. Analyzing each decision would only waste time and probably drive him crazy.

About ten minutes later, they found themselves looking in at the meadow for a third time.

Nicole and Brandy both swore.

"I don't like that we keep coming back here," Nicole groaned. The place gave her the creeps the first time she saw it. Now it almost seemed as if it were intentionally luring them back to it.

Albert peered into the enormous chamber. A large, leafless tree branch was visible on the left side, its naked branches spread out over the black soil. "What kind of tree can survive down here?" he wondered.

"Maybe it's dead," Brandy suggested.

"For how long?" Albert countered. "It should rot away if it's been dead for any amount of time."

"Frankly," said Nicole. "I don't give a shit. Let's go."

Albert did not dare to linger any longer. Risking the chance of being lured into that nightmare chamber was bad enough. But Nicole's tone warned him that she did not intend to tolerate his annoying curiosity for another moment.

They retreated back down their blue line.

Again, Nicole found herself in the lead. She still had no idea where they were going or how they were going to get out of this insane labyrinth, so she continued to choose her paths without thought. It didn't seem to matter anyway. They were hopelessly lost down here.

Albert had begun to wonder how much longer they could possibly avoid the Caggo. They'd been in here for so long now that he could scarcely comprehend why it hadn't already caught their scent and tracked them down. He was reluctant to believe that it was mere luck.

Maybe the Sentinel Queen had something to do with it. She sent the man with no eyes to take their underwear, after all, so that he could distract the hounds and make it safer for them to travel in the first chambers of the temple. Maybe the blind man was doing something similar to distract the Caggo. That would be a comforting thought.

But even so, how long could they possibly hope to keep avoiding it?

Ahead of them, the passage opened once more into a large chamber and Nicole nearly cursed her luck again. But it was not the meadow that was waiting for them at the end of this stretch of tunnel. Instead, they found themselves back inside the temple's vast reservoir system.

A narrow channel of water lay before them and ran beyond their sight both right and left. A bridge spanned the water from the mouth of the passage to the walkway that ran along the other side.

"Which way?" Nicole asked, as if she expected anyone to

have an answer.

Albert peered down into the water as he crossed the bridge and glimpsed something swimming past in the gloom way down where his flashlight's beam faded. "What was that?"

The three of them paused and peered down into the water.

"I don't see anything," reported Brandy.

"Gone now," Albert explained.

"What did it look like?" asked Nicole.

"It was too quick. I couldn't tell."

"A fish?" suggested Nicole.

But Albert wasn't sure. There was no reason why there *wouldn't* be ordinary fish down here. There could be an entire ecosystem in these waterways. Or, for all he knew, one of these chambers could be connected to a lake or river somewhere and the creatures that lived down here could simply wander in and out as they pleased.

But no answers presented themselves in the depths below, so they turned and continued on their way.

Since nobody had an opinion about which way to go, Nicole turned right at the other end of the bridge and followed the channel past two more passageways and into a large chamber very much like the first one they came across. In fact, Nicole had to wonder if it might *be* the same chamber. It had the same layout: a wide ledge along the wall, multiple openings leading back out into the labyrinth, and a large, deep pool of water stretching out as far as her light would reach. If she could somehow illuminate this entire room, would she be able to see their yellow chalk line from here?

They turned left and ventured deeper into the reservoir.

Albert continued to shine his light down into the water, curious about what else might inhabit these mysterious waterways.

Something splashed a short distance ahead of them and sent waves racing past them. Albert probed the gloomy depths with his flashlight, trying to get a glimpse of the mystery creature as it swam away, but there was nothing to be seen.

Brandy, however, was less interested in what might be beneath the water than in what might be hiding in the darkness that shrouded the chamber all around them. For all they knew, the Caggo could be somewhere in this very room, watching them from the darkness, preparing to pounce.

She walked a few steps ahead of Albert and Nicole, carving at the darkness with her flashlight, and another heavy splash arose from the water's edge in front of her.

This time, Albert *did* see something beneath the racing ripples. "Did you see that?" he asked.

Nicole did. But there was little to be made of it. It was nothing more than a dark shape deep down in the gloom, visible for only a second and distorted by the waves.

Brandy did not even glance back at them. "Come on you

guys. Let's go."

Albert knew she was right. Lingering here would not help them. He was sure that catching a glimpse of the mysterious jumpers in the reservoir would do nothing to help them escape. But after all this time, it was frustrating how the creatures down here continued to elude his sight. At the very least, knowing what they looked like would put to rest all the things that his imagination insisted on suggesting. More often than not, the monsters in movies and books became a lot less frightening once they stepped out of the shadows and revealed themselves.

Brandy shined her light out over the surface of the water, but there was nothing to be seen out there. When she aimed it at the floor in front of her again, however, she caught a glimpse of something small and black darting across the floor.

She stopped, frozen in mid-step. Her heart was suddenly racing. It was only there for a second, but she didn't dare dismiss it as her imagination.

"Guys?" she called, but she didn't dare look away from where she thought she saw the thing to see if her hushed voice reached anyone. Could it have been a mouse? Or a rat? It wasn't the most pleasant thing she could imagine running into, but she could deal with that much more easily than something unknown. In her sudden fear, however, she couldn't help but remember the small, black shapes they'd seen scurrying across the grimy soil of the meadow.

Albert must have heard her because he was suddenly at her side. "What is it?" he asked.

"I saw something."

"What kind of something?"

"I don't know. It was…just *something*. Small. And dark."

"Be careful," Nicole whispered. She was standing a few steps behind them, adding her light to theirs.

Albert crept forward, pushing farther into the darkness, trying to see what was there.

Brandy seized his arm and clung to him, moving forward with him, not daring to let him out of her reach.

"The floor's wet over here," he observed. Something from the water had recently crawled up onto the walkway.

"Something's here," Brandy breathed.

Albert was about to point out that the water on the floor proved only that something had *been* here, that there was no proof it was still with them, but at that instant something splashed into the water nearby and all three of them swung their lights toward the sound, startled.

"You guys…" Nicole whispered.

"It's okay," Albert assured her. "Nothing to worry about." Although he knew no such thing. Not really. He turned back to the wet floor he'd been examining before his attention was redirected and his light fell across something strange. It looked like a lumpy piece of pale, rubber tubing with black, bristly hair growing all over it. As he watched, it slithered back into the shadows.

Brandy took another step forward, thrusting her light ahead of her, trying to see what the darkness was hiding, and several more of these meaty, hairy coils spilled across the floor into view and immediately wriggled from sight again. At the same moment, there was a wet, gurgling noise and a stream of brown fluid squirted from the shadows where the creature had disappeared, striking the ground next to Albert's bare foot.

Before either of them could react, two more jets shot at them. The first struck Brandy on her right thigh, splashing up onto her belly and down her right leg. It was cold and vile. The second, only an instant behind the first, struck her in the face just as she opened her mouth to scream.

For a couple of frantic heartbeats, Brandy convulsed. Her eyes bulged. The flashlight dropped from her hand.

Albert grabbed her and pulled her back, away from the creature, terrified. What just happened? What did that thing do to her? He heard it as it slid away, a great mass of soggy, hairy coils, splashing heavily into the water, but he paid it no attention. It didn't matter. Nothing mattered at that moment except Brandy. If anything happened to her…

Brandy made a horrible sound, deep in her throat, as if she were choking to death, and then she doubled forward and retched violently and repeatedly.

Nicole, too, was by her side in an instant, her heart pounding with fright. What had those things done to her? What was that horrible stuff they shot at her? Was it toxic? Corrosive? Something else unthinkable?

Brandy retched again, this time harder than ever, her body trembling from the force of it. Then she spat a mouthful of foul bile onto the floor and gasped for air.

"What's wrong?" Albert asked, his voice trembling. "What's going on? Talk to me."

Brandy tried to catch her breath and then gagged again, her whole body clenching with the force of it. Her every muscle strained against her naked skin. It seemed to go on and on, relentlessly, violently. But finally she relaxed again and gasped for air as she began clawing at her face, trying to pull away the disgusting goo that was smeared across her mouth and chin. It was somehow sticky and slippery at the same time, and she couldn't seem to peel it off.

"Does it hurt?" Nicole asked.

Again, Brandy retched. She couldn't stop herself. Her eyes bulged horribly with the force of her heaving.

"Albert, help her!"

"Take it easy, Baby," Albert urged, not sure what else to do. He was mentally inventorying the contents of the first aid kit in his backpack, trying to think of what might help, but he still didn't even know what this stuff was doing to her.

Brandy gasped for air and managed a labored, "I'm okay!" before another violent retch overcame her, this one dropping her to the floor on her hands and knees.

"Does it hurt?" Nicole asked again.

Brandy shook her head. "Just…" Her chest heaved again and she gasped for air. She was sure that if not for the fact that she hadn't eaten anything since before they set out for Gilbert House hours and hours ago, she would have been vomiting all over the stone floor. "Oh god!" she cried. "So nasty!"

The taste in her mouth was unspeakably disgusting. It was far beyond vile, like a festering concoction of everything nasty and putrid, mixed with a strange, sickly sweet flavor that reminded her somehow of tomatoes and citrus. It clung mercilessly to her tongue, refusing to let her go no matter how hard she spat.

Albert wiped at the fluid that clung to her chin and examined it. It had a slick and slightly gooey, mucus-like texture and was a sickly brown color. It had a powerful, pungent stench and he had little trouble understanding why Brandy had become so violently sick.

Brandy coughed and then retched again, her back arching with the force of the heave. Then she collapsed onto the floor, gasping for breath.

"Is she going to be okay?" Nicole asked. The sight of her best friend in such a state scared the hell out of her.

"I think so," Albert replied. He was kneeling over Brandy, his hand on her bare back, trying his best to sooth her. The brown fluid he'd wiped from her chin was still between his fingers. It wasn't burning him. It wasn't numbing his skin. It wasn't making him feel sick—except for the way his stomach flopped over when he sniffed it. It didn't seem to be poisonous, at least not to the touch. And somehow he didn't expect it to be. Something this vile was likely created specifically to be vile. If it was toxic, it wouldn't matter what it tasted like. The toxin would do its work regardless of the flavor. Brandy's violent reaction to the mere taste of the stuff was more than adequate to ensure that they kept their distance from these things from now on.

This was likely something similar to the spray of a skunk; harmless, but overpowering. Perhaps it was how these things protected themselves from the hounds and whatever other predators might be hiding down here.

Of course, he could be wrong. He knew nothing about the creatures that lived in the temple. For all he knew, the people of the City of the Blind had spent millennia breeding these horrors so that they were as nasty as possible.

But Brandy didn't seem to be in mortal danger.

"Oh god, that was so gross!" she gasped, rolling onto her back. There was still a smear of brown bile on her chin and cheek. A strand of it ran to the floor where she'd pressed her face to the stone a moment ago. A rope of spittle clung to her lower lip. Tears streamed from both bloodshot eyes. "That was the most disgusting—" She gagged again, as if on the very words, and had to force herself to relax.

Albert wiped tenderly at her face with his hand. "Even worse than my Salisbury steaks?" he asked.

Brandy laughed. Her body shuddered with the force of it as she was still trying to catch her breath. Albert's Salisbury steaks was one of their private jokes. It was a dish he'd attempted to cook for them the first week they moved into their apartment. It was an utter disaster. Completely inedible. They'd been forced to order pizza instead. To this day, they still had no idea what he did wrong, but it was as funny now as it was that evening. "Nearly," she told him when she caught her breath.

Albert laughed.

Brandy wiped her eyes dry and sat up.

Nicole slapped her gently on the arm. "You scared the shit out of me!"

Brandy slapped her right back. "I'm ever so fucking *sorry*. Next time *you* take the monster spunk in the mouth."

"Just be more careful. Both of you."

"Yes, ma'am," Albert replied.

Brandy spread her knees apart and looked down at her body, groaning. The cold, brown goo was splattered across her lower belly and right leg and had oozed down between her thighs.

"Let's get going," Nicole pleaded. "I don't like it in here."

"We *should* keep moving," Albert agreed. He didn't like remaining anywhere too long. He stood up and helped Brandy to her feet. "Are you okay?"

"I think so."

"Can you go on?"

Brandy nodded. She wiped at the mass of brown goo on her belly and attempted to fling it from her fingers, but it was stubbornly reluctant to let go. She groaned and fought back another retch. "Just go," she said as fresh tears sprang to her eyes. "I'm coming."

Nicole started walking. She turned down the next passage that led away from the reservoir, happy to put those nasty creatures behind them once again.

Chapter 24

Wayne found Wendell Gilbert without any trouble. The old man was right where he and the others had left him. Unlike Beverly's body, Wendell's filled him with no emotions whatsoever. It could have been a discarded mannequin for all that it mattered to him. For one thing, he had never met the man. He'd been dead for decades. Secondly, it was this man's insane obsession that had ultimately destroyed Beverly. If he had never built that hellish dormitory, perhaps she would not have ended up entombed in that bleak pit.

They moved on, past the body and into the empty room that lay beyond. Wayne thought nothing of this chamber. He was far more concerned with the area beyond it. There were hounds there. They'd even heard one when he and the others came through here earlier that night. He didn't know what he'd do if they arrived at the drop-off and discovered one of the creatures waiting for them. This was, after all, the only path to the City of the Blind that he knew. He doubted they would get very far if they strayed from it.

As he stepped into the mouth of the next tunnel, Wayne suddenly realized that he was alone. Pulled from his thoughts, he stopped and turned around.

Olivia was standing just inside the chamber across from him, staring up at the dark ceiling above her, an expression of fearful puzzlement on her face.

Andrea was standing next to her, her flashlight scanning the stone above them, trying to find whatever it was that had captured her attention.

"What's wrong?" Wayne asked.

Olivia shook her head. "I don't know. I thought I heard something up there."

"Something like what?"

Olivia stared up into the darkness for a moment, listening, but whatever she thought she heard had fallen silent. "Like chains," she replied at last. She lowered her eyes and looked at him, her expression uneasy. "It was like chains rattling."

"That's really creepy," Andrea said.

"Come on," Wayne told them. Suddenly this room frightened him. In his mind's eye, he saw Wendell Gilbert's corpse lying in the tunnel with no visible wounds. The Sentinel

Queen said that he was killed by the same sort of thing that killed Beverly, some kind of horrific creature that could only be seen by those with strong, psychic minds. He still remembered the look of utter and maddening terror in her eyes as she staggered backward to her death.

Andrea saw the concern on Wayne's face. "What is it?"

"Just come on."

Olivia and Andrea crossed the room without incident and the three of them entered the next passage together.

"You're like Albert and Brandy," Wayne said.

"What?" Olivia had no idea what he was talking about.

"You're psychic. Not a lot. Not like Beverly was, or Wendell Gilbert, but a little."

"No I'm not," Olivia said.

"I think you are," he insisted. "Albert felt something in there when he passed through it, too. He stopped and looked up at the ceiling, just exactly like you did just now. He said it felt creepy."

"I don't believe in psychics," Olivia said. "It's all a con, like magic."

"So it's easier to believe in parallel universes full of zombies and groping trees?"

Olivia opened her mouth, but then closed it again. She had never thought of herself as psychic. Not in the least, but what did she know about the universe? If something like Gilbert

House could exist, why couldn't she have a faint sixth sense?

"Come on," Wayne said. "When we get to the city, we'll talk to the Sentinel Queen. Maybe she'll have some answers for you." *She sure as hell better have some for me*, he thought, remembering the accusations of the old man.

Farther down this tunnel was the small drop-off that Albert had compared to a cattle guard earlier that evening. It was walls like these, he remembered, that kept the hounds from roaming the entire temple. Wayne hopped down into the lower part and listened. When nothing greeted his ears but silence, he helped Olivia and Andrea down and the three of them hurried on.

Wayne remembered the bridge that crossed over the maze where his underwear had been hung and that the noises from below were much quieter than the first time he crossed it. That meant only one thing to him: that there were not as many hounds in the maze as there had been before. If that was the case, then where, exactly, had they gone? He had no doubt that this area was connected to that chamber somehow, and he, Albert, Brandy and Nicole had all tracked their scent through this tunnel mere hours ago.

But no hounds awaited them as they stepped out onto the bridge and over the dark chasm.

"Unbelievable!" Andrea sighed. "How big is this place?"

Olivia gazed down into the infinite darkness below. It was like nothing she had ever seen before, a veritable abyss.

"Enormous," said Wayne. He had not stopped walking. He had seen it all before. And he didn't care to dwell on the insurmountable size of the task before him.

But Andrea and Olivia lingered for a moment, transfixed by the awesome sight. How could this place be so big? It didn't seem possible.

Finally, they pulled their eyes away and followed Wayne into the next stretch of empty tunnel. Ahead of them were the four passageways and the sentinel statue that invited them to choose a path.

Wayne paused. For a moment, panic welled up inside him as he realized that he couldn't quite remember which one Albert had chosen before.

"Wayne?" Olivia watched him, concerned, as he shined his light into one passage and then another.

"I'm okay." He remembered the knife. That was what they were looking for. He searched the floor, but it wasn't there. He moved on to the next passage and still could not find it.

"Wayne, what's wrong?"

"It's nothing. I'm just…" He moved to the next passageway, sweeping the floor with his light. "I'm not seeing it…"

"Not seeing what? What's wrong?"

"Are we lost?" asked Andrea. The dread in her voice was unmistakable.

Desperate to find it before something caught their scent, he almost turned away and missed it, but then he saw it there, lying on the floor, almost too far away for his light to reach. "This way," he sighed. "Hurry."

He took several steps and then abruptly stopped and cocked his head, listening.

"What is it?" Andrea asked.

Wayne shook his head. "Thought I heard something."

"What kind of something?" asked Olivia, her voice tense.

Wayne did not answer. He stood there, holding his breath, listening. Again, he thought he heard it, a soft clicking noise. It was coming from somewhere behind them.

He motioned Olivia and Andrea to go ahead of him and then took a few steps back the way he'd come, still listening. After a few seconds, it came again. He was sure he heard it this time, a sound like something hard tapping against the stone.

The sound made the hair on the back of his neck stand up.

Then there was only silence.

"What is it?" Andrea asked. Wayne could hear the fear in her voice and did not blame her for that.

It was time to go.

He turned and gestured at Olivia and Andrea to keep going, not daring to raise his voice for fear that the man with no eyes might have been lying when he said the hounds were deaf. When they turned and started forward, he shined his light back the way they came and listened for a moment longer.

There was another soft click from somewhere nearby, barely audible over the loud pounding of his heart, and then a sudden explosion of violent noise erupted from one of the other passageways, as loud and terrifying as a chainsaw. It was a ferocious sound, a noise with which he was perfectly familiar by now, but still utterly incapable of describing.

It was a hound.

And it was startlingly close.

Wayne turned and dashed toward the girls, screaming at them to run. Shrieking with terror, they sprinted ahead of him, rushing toward the end of the tunnel and the wall that would allow them to climb out of harm's way.

How far did this passage go? He couldn't quite remember.

Behind him, he could hear the thing tearing after them, the terrible noise rapidly growing louder and louder.

The girls were faster than him. The distance between them slowly grew as they all ran for their lives toward the safety of the next passage. Darkness parted before Andrea's darting flashlight beam and revealed only more darkness, as if they were going nowhere at all.

The hound drew closer and closer, its hellish roar growing louder with each desperate second that passed. It was a dreadful feeling, knowing that it was back there and rushing toward him. He did not even know what it was, and yet it was only moments from rending his flesh with its teeth or claws or whatever it might use to slaughter its prey.

At the very least, he supposed the girls would likely be able to escape. By now, they should be able to find their way to the City of the Blind. They might still be able to catch up to Albert and warn him about the things the old man told him.

But he wasn't ready to stop running and turn to face whatever was there. Perhaps if he had known what it was that chased him he could have more bravely faced his fate, but not knowing what horror was bearing down on him was intolerable. He pumped his legs as hard as he could and tried not to scream at the sound of the loudly approaching doom behind him.

When Andrea finally reached the wall at the end of the passage, she grabbed the ledge and swung herself neatly up and out of peril. Even in spite of his fear, Wayne was impressed with her litheness. Olivia, on the other hand, was not nearly as graceful. In her rush, she did not try to swing herself over the ledge but instead attempted to pull herself straight up. Perhaps it was the weariness she must have been feeling, the lack of both food and sleep for the past two days, but she was only able to lift herself a couple of feet off the floor, her bare toes sliding across the smooth stone of the wall as she desperately tried to push herself upward.

She cried out, her voice overtaken by sheer horror, and Andrea turned and seized her arms. But Andrea was not strong enough to lift her into the upper passage with her. She screamed for her to climb and Olivia begged her to pull her up, to get her out before it was too late. She could hear the hound racing toward them and the thought of not being able to climb to safety in time filled her with icy panic. She did not want to die like this. Not after all she'd been through.

At last, as the furious sound of the hound grew deafening, Wayne caught up to Olivia and tossed his flashlight up into the next tunnel. Both hands free, he grabbed Olivia, gripping each of her legs just above her knees and heaving her upward with all his strength.

She squealed as she was lifted, surprised by his ungentle touch, but desperately grateful to be shoved from death's outstretched hand.

Behind him, the roar of the hound was thunderous. The thing was damn fast. It was right behind him.

He grabbed the ledge and swung his leg up into the higher tunnel. Had he been there thirteen months ago when Albert and Brandy had their first encounter with a hound, he might have laughed at the similarities between the events of then and now. Albert had also investigated something odd in the tunnels, had also drawn the attention of a hound and yelled for his companion to run. He had even paused before climbing to safety to give Brandy an urgent and ungentle hand.

But one thing was terribly different: Wayne was much less

lucky than Albert.

As he swung up over the ledge, his right foot first, something very large slammed into his left leg and sent a jolt of excruciating pain straight to his brain. He screamed as much in surprise as in agony and would have let go of the ledge completely if Olivia and Andrea had not been there to grab him and pull him up.

"*Oh God!*" Andrea cried.

His leg was bloody and chewed, the flesh torn and ragged, as though the thing had actually had time to gnaw on him.

Below them, the hound beat frantically against the wall, trying to find the prey that had somehow eluded it.

"We've got to get out of here!" Andrea screamed over the violent noise.

"My leg!" Wayne cried.

"*We've got to go!*"

But Wayne shook his head. "We're safe up here. They can't jump. Tell me how bad it is."

Olivia did not want to take her eyes off the ledge behind them. The hound was right there, just beneath her sight, still making that horrible noise. She could not trust that the thing was actually trapped there.

But if Wayne said they were safe, then they must be safe. He was her hero. He wouldn't let anything happen to her. Reluctantly, she bent over his leg and examined him.

It wasn't as bad as she thought. Not really. The thing had nearly taken the skin off more than half of his shin and left several deep gashes in the side of his calf, but his leg was neither broken nor severed. The wound looked bad, but it was mostly gnarled and twisted flesh. He was bleeding more than she liked, and must have been in a hell of a lot of pain, but overall he was in better shape than she would have expected. "I think you're going to be okay," she told him.

"Hurts like hell."

"I know. It *looks* painful. But it's not too bad. I think you're going to have a nasty scar."

Wayne uttered a prayer of thanks under his breath. He had actually feared that his leg had been torn off. The pain was excruciating. Being bitten by that zombie thing did not even compare.

"Come on," Olivia said. "Let's get you away from here."

"Not yet." Wayne sat up and looked around. "My flashlight…"

It had slid a good fifteen feet into the passage when he tossed it. Andrea stood up and retrieved it for him.

As soon as it was in his hand, he turned and began crawling toward the ledge where the hound was still making its horrible noise.

"What are you doing?" Andrea shouted.

"Fucking *freak!*" Wayne screamed at the creature. "*Bastard!*"

To Andrea he said, “I want to see it. I want to know what got me.”

“Wayne, *no!*” The terror in Olivia’s voice was unmistakable. That thing was dangerous. They needed to get away from it, not stay and look at it.

“Wayne, please!” Andrea begged.

Wayne leaned over the edge and shined his light down onto the hound. Immediately, his rage melted away. “Jesus Christ…”

Olivia and Andrea crept up beside him, their curiosity overwhelming their fear.

The sound that the creature made was not really a shuffling or a rattling. It was a clashing, like the sound of blades beating and grinding together. When the man with no eyes first warned them to beware of the hounds, Wayne had immediately pictured some demonic version of a dog, a canine terror like Cerberus, the three-headed guardian of the entrance to Hades, or the sleek, mechanical killers who were the firemen’s pets in Ray Bradbury’s *Fahrenheit 451*. But this creature was not canine at all. In fact, it was like nothing he’d ever seen. It was like nothing he’d ever even imagined.

It was low to the ground, standing less than three feet in height, but its breadth was enormous, filling more than half the width of the passage. It was a deep, reddish-brown color with curious patterns of darker and lighter shades. It had two short tails that were frantically whipping around, slashing at the air in a ferocious rage. And looking down at the shape of the beast, Wayne thought that they were extensions of two separate spines that ran along its wide, flattened back and converged at the base of its skull. It had no neck that he could distinguish. It had powerful, but very short legs, perhaps part of the reason why it could not jump, and no eyes or ears that he could see. It did have jaws, however, and they were currently snapping viciously at the stone wall that stood between it and its prey. Its snout was not long and sleek like most canine's, but wide and short, with small but wicked-looking teeth. It had no hair on its body that he could see and its skin was covered in rigid scales that resembled square razor blades standing on end. Each of these blades were in motion, gnashing back and forth against one another like jigsaw blades, causing the creature's flesh to ripple rhythmically and creating the loud, metallic clashing sound that had been the only proof of their existence until now.

Wayne stared down at this creature, amazed that such a deadly beast could even exist. It was like something from a horror movie, essentially a chainsaw with jaws on legs. If this thing had caught him before he reached the wall, he would have been shredded as easily as if he were cast into a giant blender.

No wonder it had done so much damage to his leg in such a short amount of time.

"What is it?" Andrea asked, her hands pressed to her ears.

Wayne did not know. "A hound," he said. "Something that

doesn't exist above ground."

"Why won't it stop making that noise?" Olivia asked. She had to scream to be heard over it.

"We should go," Wayne said. "Before more show up."

"You're leg," Olivia said. He was not gushing blood, but still he was bleeding pretty badly. If he kept this up, he wasn't going to have any left by the time they found the others.

"We'll wrap it when we get farther ahead," he promised. "Now help me. Please."

Olivia and Andrea helped him to his feet and he limped away between them, leaving the enraged hound to batter pointlessly at the walls of its stone prison.

They were well on their way now. Ahead of them lay the lake of mud they would have to cross. Beyond that lay the entrance to the City of the Blind.

Wayne wanted to catch up to Albert and Brandy and Nicole, wanted to already be by their side, but he also needed to stop in the city. He needed to speak with the Sentinel Queen. Perhaps there was nothing more to be said, but he felt that he needed to face her. Perhaps she had intended him to go to his death, but she had also helped him. If she had really wanted him to die, then why had she warned him of the dangers of that terrible tunnel? It would have been much easier for her to say nothing and let him perish.

But that was too much to consider right now. For the time

being, the only thing he could think clearly about was the screaming pain in his leg.

Chapter 25

"I can still taste it," Brandy groaned.

"Could have been worse," Nicole reminded her.

"I know."

"Some kind of cephalopod," Albert reasoned.

"Some kind of what?" asked Nicole.

"Octopus. Squid. That sort of thing. I didn't see much of it, but it looked like a mass of tentacles."

"Looked more like a spider or something to me," Brandy said. "It was *hairy*."

"It was," agreed Albert. "But it wasn't rigid like a spider's legs. It was…*fleshy*."

Brandy threw her hands up and half-gagged, shaking away the image.

"That stuff it squirted was probably a specialized ink. But

instead of blinding predators and covering their escape, it's engineered to put a bad taste in their mouths."

"Well, maybe it'll work out for the best," suggested Nicole. "Maybe the hounds won't want to eat you now that you taste like nasty-hairy-squid juice."

"Great," groaned Brandy. "I'm *so* lucky."

"So you think all these monsters down here are bred intentionally?" Nicole asked, glancing back at Albert.

"I don't know about that," Albert replied. "I mean, I suppose they've had all the time in the world for a science project or two, but I'm guessing these things might've already been around when they built the place. It seems like it was designed right from the start with the hounds already in mind."

"So then where'd they come from?"

"Wherever all this leads us, I guess. Wherever those fourteen pregnant women supposedly came from."

"Another world?"

"Maybe. Or maybe just another time. Who knows?"

They reached the end of the passage and found themselves in the chasm once again.

"We're here again?" Brandy asked.

"I wonder how far we've gone now," said Nicole.

Brandy stared down into the darkness below them. It was unsettling, the way she could see neither the ceiling nor the floor. It was as though the labyrinth went on and on into eternity. "I don't know," she replied. "I just want to be out of here. I'm sick of this game."

"Me too," agreed Nicole.

Albert stared up at the four bridges that crossed above them and wondered if one of them had his yellow line scrawled across one side. It never crossed his mind that just a few minutes ago, three others might have crossed this same chasm somewhere else in the temple, their lights illuminating a tiny portion of the endless darkness.

He kept walking. He didn't like it here. He didn't like how small it made him feel.

It was as they stepped into the opening on the other side of the chasm that they first heard the paralyzing shriek of the Caggo. It echoed down from somewhere high above, too distant to pinpoint, but far too close for comfort, seeming to rattle the very walls around them.

"*Oh my god!*"

"What the fuck was that?" Brandy asked, though she already knew the answer.

"The Caggo," Albert replied. There was not a doubt in his mind that this was true. The sound had filled him with unspeakable dread. There was something unsettling about the scream, something almost evil.

He turned and peered out into the chasm again. It was out there somewhere, probably on one of the other bridges. Had it caught their scent? Or perhaps it heard them talking or saw their light. Just because the man with no eyes told them the hounds were deaf and blind didn't mean the Caggo was. Would it be hunting them now? Was it tracking their scent? How long might they have before it caught up to them?

"What do we do?" Brandy asked.

"We just keep going," Albert replied.

More terrified than ever, the three of them continued onward, desperately hoping that the exit was waiting for them somewhere nearby.

Chapter 26

"You've got to be joking," Andrea exclaimed as she looked out over the vile, black sea of mud.

"I wish I was," Wayne replied. "I really do." He stared into the sludge-filled chamber, mentally cringing at the task before him. He had not yet forgotten the stench from his first visit here. This time, he was considerably more tired and he had no idea how this stuff would affect his injuries. What if it burned like iodine when introduced to a fresh cut?

But if that were so, he likely would have noticed it on his first trip. He'd collected a number of cuts and scrapes in his first visit to the fear room and none of those had caused him any trouble. But his recent run-in with the hound had left his lower leg half-skinned. He'd had to recycle the bandages he'd been wearing to cushion his raw feet in order to sufficiently stop the bleeding. It still hurt like hell, and he had no doubt that dragging his leg through this stuff was going to be excruciating.

But there was no sense in putting it off. They sure as hell couldn't turn back, not with that hound prowling the area behind them. He stepped out into the mud, his bare foot sinking beneath the cold, grimy surface.

"This place is twisted," Andrea said, as if she'd just decided this. She could not believe that anyone would willingly wade into something so foul.

Olivia stepped out after Wayne, but hesitated as she felt the cold mud ooze between her toes. "Oh god!" she squealed. "It's so gross!"

Wayne did not stop. "Sorry. I did warn you about this."

"You did," Olivia admitted. "*Oh!*" She threw her hands up and fanned the air around her face. "It *reeks!*"

Wayne hissed as he pressed the tender flesh of his shin against the thick mud. Even with the gauze padding the wound, it was like using his freshly torn skin to push a heavy weight across the floor.

Andrea had hesitated as long as she could. Slowly, her companions were making their way out into the vile darkness, leaving her alone on the shore of this disgusting lake of horrors. Bracing herself for the worst, she bit her lip and rushed forward before she could lose her courage. Immediately, the cold, grimy muck squished between her naked toes and an awful stench rose around her.

"*Ew-ew-ew-ew-ew!*"

Olivia clasped one hand over her nose and mouth. The other she held out to her side, trying to maintain her balance as the deepening mud threatened to trip her and spill her into it.

"I can't believe I'm doing this!" whined Andrea.

Relentlessly, the cold, foul-smelling mire rose around their naked bodies, climbing their exposed flesh, oozing between their thighs and churning up the nauseating stench of soggy decay. The effort it took to stay upright quickly overwhelmed Olivia and Andrea's desire to complain and so they fell silent and restricted their expressions of disgust and discomfort to their pretty faces.

For Wayne, the nauseating stench and the awful feel of the slimy and grimy mud between his toes and thighs was the least of his discomfort. The journey was agony. He could feel the gritty sludge oozing up under the gauze and into his wounds. It burned and it grated in the raw, bloody flesh as he dragged his leg through it step after step. He could almost feel the germs taking root, threatening to infect him, rotting away the meat and poisoning his blood.

He could not believe the amount of hell he'd been through tonight. It never seemed to end. If he survived all of this without contracting gangrene in any one of his bloodied limbs, he'd consider himself blessed.

"Maybe you should stop and rest," Olivia suggested, glimpsing the hard, white knuckles of his fist as he struggled against the pain.

But Wayne shook his head. They hadn't even reached the deepest part yet. They still had far to go and the journey was only going to get harder. "I'll be fine. I just have to keep moving."

"These people are really important to you, aren't they," she said, her voice beginning to waver. She was shivering against the numbing cold that came with the awful, reeking touch of the mud against her skin. "Even though you just met them today?"

Wayne was silent for a moment as he pushed himself through the torturous sludge. Then he said, "It's complicated."

"Complicated how?"

"They're good people. I'm… Well, I'm not."

"Yes you are," Olivia argued through chattering teeth. "You're a wonderful person. How can you even say that after all you've done? You *rescued* me. *Twice*."

"I stumbled across you," he corrected her. "I just happened to run into that bathroom where you were hiding, scared to death and cursing my dumb luck."

"So? You still rescued me. You came all the way into that forest to find me."

Wayne didn't know what to say. He promised her he wouldn't let anything happen to her. Then he lost her. He thought she was dead and it was all his fault. He should have kept his promise. When the Sentinel Queen told him she was still alive, he had no choice. He couldn't leave her there to die. No part of that made him any kind of hero. If he'd done it right the first time, he wouldn't have had to go out there to rescue her. And they wouldn't have nearly been eaten by those zombie things.

"It doesn't make me a good person," he said at last. "Believe me. I'm not."

"Why?" Olivia pressed. It was good to talk. Talking took her mind off that disgusting stench and all the horrible things her imagination kept suggesting might be its source. "What have you done that's so bad?"

For a moment, Wayne was silent and she didn't think he was going to answer her, but then he did. For the first time in his life he said the words aloud: "I cheated on my girlfriend. For starters."

"Oh." Olivia was lost for words for a moment, caught off guard by this sudden and brutally honest confession.

"Yeah."

"That *is* pretty bad," Andrea agreed, speaking through her hands as she covered her jittering mouth and nose from the nauseating mud.

"Yeah."

"But it's not the *worst* thing in the world," said Olivia.

"It's right up there, I think," replied Wayne. "I never

forgave myself for it."

"How long ago did it happen?" asked Andrea.

"Few years ago. Between high school and college."

"Did she leave you?"

Wayne didn't care for all these questions. They were almost as uncomfortable as the mud that grated his torn flesh. "*I* left. Didn't seem fair to stay."

"Did you tell her?"

"No. I didn't want her to know. She deserved better."

Andrea was quiet for a moment as she considered this, then she said through chattering teeth, "That seems kind of selfish."

Wayne stopped and looked back at her. "What?"

"You just left her to think *she* did something wrong."

For a moment, Wayne just stared at her, considering. "Huh," he said at last and then turned and pushed his way forward again, gritting his teeth against the pain. "I never thought of it that way." He'd only wanted to protect her from the truth. Leaving the way he did…it was kinder than letting her think she wasn't good enough for him to be faithful to her. Wasn't it?

"It still doesn't make you a bad person," Olivia insisted, and she found that she believed it. Although she had always felt that cheating was the worst kind of betrayal, she found it difficult to condemn Wayne for it. She wondered if it was because he had saved her, because he was her hero, that he could do no wrong, or if it was the remorseful way that he spoke of it, the way he said that he never forgave himself for it, that made her believe that he meant it. Perhaps it was a great many things, but she found it impossible to despise him the way she'd instantly despised other men who cheated.

But Wayne did not reply. He was thinking about what Andrea said. Did Gail really think she did something to make him leave her? It wasn't her fault. He never meant for her to think that.

"*I* don't think you're a bad person," Olivia assured him.

"Neither do I," added Andrea, catching the disapproving look that Olivia gave her.

"Thanks," Wayne said. But he knew better. They didn't see the way he made Gail cry that night. They didn't see how he walked away from all the friends who cared about him. They didn't even see how he treated Beverly when she caught up with them in the entrance to the sex room. He was so rough with her, so cruel. He was so *angry*.

"*I* think," continued Olivia, determined to make her point, "that if you still feel like such a bad person after all this time, then you can't possibly be as bad a person as you think. It seems to me like it hurt you just as much as you hurt her."

Wayne said nothing. He could explain the situation if he wanted. He could tell them exactly what happened that day, explain how he and Claire just sort of…did it…how he never intended it, how it never even crossed his mind until he'd already done it. But he did not want them to understand. Understanding meant compassion and he did not deserve that compassion.

He was not done punishing himself yet.

Andrea cried out as her feet became bogged in the dense mud and she fell forward, submerging her body and half her face in the sludge. "*Oh gross!*" she cried through chattering teeth. "*Oh yuck! Oh gross!*"

Olivia turned and offered her hand. "Come on."

"*It's so gross!*" Andrea whined as she regained her feet and tried to fling the mud from her small fingers.

"I know."

Andrea took several small and awkward steps and took Olivia's offered hand, squishing the black goo into her palm. "I don't like it down here," she groaned, her voice distorted by her shivering.

"You'll be fine," Olivia promised, ignoring her dirty hand. It was nothing compared to the grossness she felt between her thighs. "We'll go together."

Andrea nodded. But with her very next step, she stumbled again and this time they both went down into the awful mud with identical squeals.

Chapter 27

Brandy looked at her watch and was startled to see that it was already well past six o'clock. "Shit, you guys." She looked up at Albert, who had noticed her looking at her watch and was now checking his own. She could see that he was as surprised by the time as she was. "I'm supposed to work tonight."

Albert looked back the way they'd come. How long would it take to find their way back to Briar Hills, he wondered. It was right around sunset that they entered the steam tunnel. That was nearly twelve hours ago. It didn't seem possible. He tried to remember how those hours had been spent, but couldn't quite manage it. The gray monotony of the tunnels had absorbed his sense of time, blurring the chain of events in his memory until he could no longer remember which set of walls he'd seen when or for how long.

"You do too, don't you?"

He nodded. He was scheduled to go in at one o'clock, but at this rate he wasn't going to make it. Even if he did, he wouldn't be in any condition to work. His feet were killing him and he hadn't slept a wink since the previous night, when those bizarre telephone messages kept waking him up. If he attempted to go to work, he was sure it would be the longest shift of his life.

"Will you get fired if you don't show up?" asked Nicole.

Brandy shrugged. "I don't know. Paula will probably throw a tantrum." Paula was the store manager at Old Navy and an insufferable bitch. Albert was surprised that Brandy hadn't walked out already. She wasn't the kind of person to put up with someone like that. But she had her reasons for staying, he knew. She genuinely liked most of the other people she worked with. And she was comfortable there. It probably had more to do with not wanting to find a new job and start all over as a trainee again than anything else.

"Oh well," Albert said. "Let them fire you."

Brandy didn't reply. She supposed he was right. So what if they fired her? She could get a job somewhere else. Besides, their loan money paid the rent and they had some savings to live off of for a while, too. And it wasn't like it was already time to clock in. They could still make it home in plenty of time to call in properly.

If they made it home at all…

She could still hear the awful cry of the Caggo ringing in her head. If that thing had its way, they'd never see the light of day again.

Ahead of them, the tunnel branched off to the right and Albert chose the new passage without a thought. He doubted he needed to worry about losing his job. He had a good work record. He could think up an excuse. Things came up, after all. People had emergencies. People confused their schedules. Half the people he worked with called in all the time for one reason or another, and half of those reasons were usually stupid, in his opinion. He couldn't see them firing him for missing just one shift.

Brandy turned to Nicole and said, "Did I tell you Emily Walshen quit?"

"No. When?"

"Week before last, I think."

Emily had gone to school with Brandy and Nicole. She was a likeable girl, but not very outgoing.

"She wasn't there very long, was she?"

"A few weeks."

"Because of Paula?"

Brandy nodded. "Paula had her in tears one day, it got so bad. The next day she called in and then she just never came back."

"She's such a bitch."

"I know."

The tunnel around them was curving again, spiraling to the right. It would either dead end or spiral back out again. They'd only know when they got to the center.

In the end, Albert supposed he didn't care about making it to his job. It wasn't worth minimum wage to miss out on something like this. So far, what had lain beyond the fear room was more spectacular than he had ever imagined and he was not willing to give up on this adventure just to keep a job that already took up time he could be using to study or spending with his lover.

Except for the Caggo.

That shriek had been terrifying.

It hadn't made another sound since they left the chasm, but that didn't mean it was gone. He was sure that it was only a matter of time before it found them. And he still had no idea what they were going to do when it did.

"Does Molly still work there?" asked Nicole as she shined her light behind them again, unable to shake the thought that something horrible might come rushing out of the darkness back there at any moment.

"Yeah. But not for long, I don't think. Seems like Paula's trying to make her quit."

"Why?"

Brandy shrugged. "She's a malicious bitch."

Nicole shook her head. That wasn't right. Molly was a nice girl. She'd known her for years. She hated people like Paula. She couldn't express how thankful she was not to have to work for someone like that.

She did not have a job to worry about. She was still living with her parents and they were perfectly content with paying her credit card bill (within reason, of course) as long as she continued attending college. And since both of them were well-respected instructors at the same university she attended (and held very high expectations for her), she'd chosen to avoid the added stress of trying to hold down a job while going to school.

At the center of the spiral, they found four passages. Theirs turned out to be the innermost. Albert chose the farthest of the other three and exited the spiral along the outer passage. After several widening circles, the path straightened out and then converged with two other tunnels. They turned left and soon found themselves climbing another hill.

"God, I wish we were out of here," Brandy groaned. "I don't know how much more of this I can take."

"I'm really starting to hate this place," Nicole agreed, glancing back again.

Albert said nothing. He was beginning to feel trapped down here. How long would it take to get back to the entrance from here? And if they tried, would they find their path blocked by the

Caggo? If it had caught their scent, it might very well be tracking them through these many passageways, following the very chalk lines that were meant to lead them safely home.

How long did they have before it caught up to them?

Chapter 28

The City of the Blind towered over them. Enormous columns of stone rose into the unyielding darkness like skyscrapers in a silent, black metropolis, the countless windows dark and empty. Alternately, inverted towers plunged into the black void beneath the floor, rows upon rows of unlit windows circling the walls of each abyss. To Olivia and Andrea, the enormity of this chamber was a marvel unmatched by any before it. Small and infinitely insignificant, they both became acutely aware of the cold darkness that pressed in on them from every angle. It was ominous. The weight of their journey suddenly grew burdensome upon their shoulders and they both began to wonder what the hell they were doing here.

But Wayne refused to feel small here. He led them between the towers of stone and around the wide, round pits, limping with every step he took. His feet were filthy and raw from the many miles he'd walked without shoes and he could feel the gritty mud that had invaded his bandages, grinding like glass into the bloody wounds the hound had carved into his leg, burning and stinging his flesh.

He'd finally made it back. After all that he'd been through, he was once again walking the streets of the Sentinel Queen's city. It felt like days since he was last here, since that freakish woman placed her disturbingly long hand upon his bare shoulder and pulled him away from Albert and Brandy and Nicole, since she locked him inside that nightmarish tunnel and set him loose into the darkest night he'd ever known. But it had only been mere hours.

The words of the old man came back to him as he walked. They rang in his head, dominating his thoughts. He had some questions for the so-called Sentinel Queen and he intended to ask them.

Olivia and Andrea followed close behind him. Both of them were caked with mud. All but the upper half of Olivia's face was black, even her mouth having been submerged in the nasty sludge while crossing it. But Andrea was even worse. After stumbling forward several times, the only part of her body not black was a small spot high up on one of her blonde pigtails. But they were not bitter from the experience. To their credit, the two of them had giggled at the sight of each other when they finally reached the far side.

Wayne had been taken by surprise. He'd thought that chamber would be the last straw, the final insult, that they would hate the Temple of the Blind and finally despise him for allowing them to suffer all these indignities.

But they *laughed.*

There simply wasn't any reason not to. There was nothing to be said. The stuff in that room was vile. It was foul. It smelled of death and decay. It was as cold as ice against their skin and as awful as the caress of a corpse. But it was the only way forward and there was no way backward but into the jaws of a ravenous hound. Besides, they'd already made up their minds to stay with Wayne, no matter what the temple threw at them. And when Olivia turned and saw Andrea's big, blue eyes staring back at her from that disgusting black mask, all she could do was giggle like a little girl. And all Andrea found that she could do was giggle back.

Ahead of them, the fountain in which Wayne first met the Sentinel Queen emerged from the gloom.

"Is that where we're going?" Andrea asked. It was the only structure they had seen besides the windowed towers and their inside-out counterparts.

"That's right."

"I feel like Dorothy in the Wizard of Oz," she said, and to this Wayne actually chuckled.

"It does sort of have that feel, doesn't it?"

The Sentinel Queen wasn't in the fountain. Wayne stared into the empty pool for a moment and then gazed up into the darkness that surrounded them. First, the man with no eyes had failed to appear and take their underwear into the labyrinth. And now the Sentinel Queen was missing. Were they avoiding him? Did this mean the old man was right about them?

If she wasn't here, then how would he ever find her? She could be in any one of those thousands of windows, and on any of the countless levels that might exist above or below them. Or she might not even be within the city walls. For all he knew, she might have left the temple entirely by now. If she did not want to be found by him, then she simply would not be found.

"What now?" Andrea asked.

Wayne lifted his head and startled them by screaming into the darkness, *"Where are you?"*

Nothing but his own voice returned to him, bouncing off the distant walls of the city.

"Come out and talk to me!"

But again there was no answer but his own echoing voice.

"Maybe she doesn't want to talk to you," Andrea suggested. "You said she tried to kill you."

Wayne nodded. It made sense. She was apparently very psychic. She would have known he was coming. She would have had plenty of time to hide from him. But that seemed wrong somehow. The Sentinel Queen hadn't seemed like a coward. She had seemed like someone who would stand up for her actions, perhaps even to the death.

"*Damn* it!"

"Wait." Olivia was moving away from them now, toward one of the stone towers they had passed on their way to the fountain.

"What is it?" Wayne asked.

"I don't know. I think I…heard something…" She turned her head to the side, listening. "Or something." It was very faint. And it didn't seem to touch her ears, exactly, as if it wasn't a sound at all. Yet she was certain it wasn't her imagination. "I'm not sure."

Wayne recalled the empty room beyond Wendell Gilbert's mummified corpse, where she claimed to hear a sound like rattling chains. If she was psychic—and he was almost certain she was—then perhaps she had not *heard* something so much as *sensed* it. And the last time they were here, it was Albert and Brandy who had first "heard" the Sentinel Queen's strangely alluring song.

Olivia felt drawn toward the tower. She began to walk, her eyes fixed on one of the window-like openings at the bottom. There was something in there, she realized, a pale figure, just visible in the darkness.

Wayne and Andrea followed her closely, illuminating the

way for her. Immediately, a faint voice touched their ears and quickly began to grow clearer. Within seconds, their heads were filled with lovely singing.

But this was not exactly the same singing Wayne heard the first time he came here. This song was different. It was quieter. And it was much softer, much *sadder.*

The Sentinel Queen was there, kneeling with her back to them just inside the square opening. *I see you made it back*, she said, her voice soft and lovely inside their heads. Before her lay the blind man, as still as the air around him. *I've been waiting for you.*

Olivia and Andrea stared at these two, afraid of them, yet fascinated. Wayne had described them both, and although they thought that they had believed him, they realized now that they really had not. How could they have? They could see the woman's impossibly long fingers as she caressed the blind man's head, and the shallow impressions where the man's eyes should have been. And the voice inside their heads was almost overwhelmingly surreal.

You're in a lot of pain, the Sentinel Queen said. It was not a question.

"Yeah," Wayne said. His voice was cold, controlled. "I am."

Her face had been lowered, as though she were staring at the blind man, although he knew that was impossible, for she had no eyes. Now, she lifted her face and "stared" at the wall across from her. *You're very strong. Despite your injuries, you succeeded in your task.*

"Did I?"

Again she lowered her head. She seemed to sigh, though she made no sound.

Rising onto her knees, she crawled backward and out of the little room. It was an awkward sort of motion, but she managed it with surprising grace. Wayne, Olivia and Andrea stepped back to give her room and she stood up, revealing her full height as she turned to face them.

Olivia and Andrea gasped a little at the sight of her and Wayne felt a strange sensation rush through him. He remembered the way she had seduced him in the first chamber of that nightmare tunnel and was infuriated to realize that he felt the beginnings of an unwanted erection.

Despite what you were told, Wayne, I did not send you into that tunnel to die.

"Then why did you send me in there without any way to survive the Wood?"

Because I didn't need to. Why would I be concerned with your well-being in the Wood when someone else has reason to keep you safe?

"You mean the old man." The old man had told him as much. He said that the Sentinel Queen might have anticipated his involvement.

Older than you know, Wayne. You would be wise to remain cautious of him.

"Who is he?"

For a moment it seemed that she wouldn't respond, but then she did, and her words struck him like a punch in the gut: *He is the devil.*

"The *devil?*" asked Andrea, surprised.

The Sentinel Queen turned her eyeless face to her and she felt a strange sort of arousal rising through her virgin body, one that made her very uncomfortable. Was that another result of what she saw in the sex room, she wondered. *Yes. The Devil. Throughout your people's history he has been perceived many times as the very demon of which so many religions warn. A personification of pure evil. The ultimate deceiver.* She turned back to Wayne and added, *The father of lies.*

"That sounds a little hard to swallow," said Wayne.

As hard to swallow as zombies and hounds?

Wayne had no response to this.

The old man lied to you, Wayne. He arranged all the things that happened at Gilbert House. You were merely his contingency plan, in case I interfered, which I of course did.

Wayne was as confused as ever. He did not know who to trust. One of them was lying to him. Perhaps they both were.

The others must reach their destination, Wayne. If they do not, your world is dead. There will never be another chance to make this happen. You must not interfere.

"I'm going to help them."

I cannot stop you. If you feel you must go to them, then you must. They've left a trail that you can follow. You'll even find that they've left you shortcuts to help you catch up. But remember, the future of your world depends on reaching that doorway.

Wayne didn't know what she meant by a trail he could follow or shortcuts, but he supposed he'd figure that out when he reached the labyrinth.

"This is too weird," Andrea exclaimed.

Yes, replied the Sentinel Queen. She stared at Andrea with her eyeless face. *It is. And you, Andrea, are another mystery. Even to me.*

"What do you mean?"

The "old man" of which Wayne speaks sent someone to steal that envelope from Beverly Bridger and deliver it to Albert Cross, to lure him and Brandy into Gilbert House. He used the same person I used to deliver the box and the key to them more than a year ago, but somehow it got sent to you instead. I do not know how it found you or why.

"I'm just lucky, I guess," replied Andrea timidly. She did not know what else to say. She did not like the way the Sentinel Queen was "looking" at her. It made her nervous.

"She said a voice told her to follow us," Olivia said thoughtfully.

"Yeah," remembered Andrea. "That voice I heard in the woods. It said they'd need me."

I'm sorry. I cannot tell you where that voice came from or to whom it belonged. It is another mystery.

"*Everything's* a mystery," Wayne challenged. "You aren't even telling us anything! What is this doorway you claim is so important? Where does it lead? What is it for?"

I cannot tell you.

"Of course you can't. But you expect me to believe that it's going to save the world, when that old man says it'll destroy it."

He expected her to tell him that this was merely the way it was supposed to be, that she could tell him nothing more, but she surprised him by saying, *The truth, Wayne, is that I don't know what lies on the other side of that doorway. No one does.*

"Then how the hell do you know its going to save the world or whatever?"

I just do.

"How?"

Faith.

"Of course. Well excuse me if my faith is a little thin right now. I've been through hell tonight, in case you haven't been following along. That tunnel of yours was a real treat, by the way. I've been mauled by a hound. Olivia and I were both bitten by those…*zombies…*"

Don't be concerned with those injuries, Assured the Sentinel Queen. *You are not infected with anything from the corpses of the Wood. Even bacteria cannot survive there.*

Wayne felt a wave of relief flow through him in spite of his anger. Even if there was no such thing as the zombie virus from those old horror movies, he had not known what sorts of diseases such creatures might carry.

The same is true of the hounds. They are clean. They carry no diseases and their bites are not toxic.

"So they've had all their shots, then," Wayne remarked. "That's good to know. Makes having my leg nearly chewed off so much better."

I understand your anger, Wayne.

"Of course you do. You're obviously so great with people." He couldn't help himself. After all that he had been through, he deserved more than this. She wasn't even apologizing for what she put him through.

The end of the world is not waiting on the other side of that doorway, Wayne.

"But what if you're wrong?"

I'm not. The doorway is the salvation of the world. Leaving it closed *is what would destroy it.*

"How can a doorway decide the fate of the world?" Andrea asked. "I don't understand."

"Well," suggested Wayne, "if that doorway happens to stand between our world and a horde of flesh-eating zombies, opening it would be apocalyptically *bad*, wouldn't it? Isn't that how you described Gilbert House earlier? Destroy Gilbert House, throw open the door, destroy the world?"

The Sentinel Queen seemed somehow to smile. *That is true. But Gilbert House was built by an obsessed genius who was tampering with things he had no hope of controlling.*

"Yeah? And who built this place, exactly?"

The sentinels.

Wayne had to stop for a moment. "Wait. The *sentinels*? You mean those statues we've been seeing all over the place? The ones that look like—"

Me?

"Those things are *real*?" Andrea asked.

I'm *real, am I not? The world has not always been so small.*

Wayne rubbed tiredly at his temples. What did that even mean?

"So *you're* a sentinel?" Andrea asked.

My father was a sentinel, she replied.

Wayne remembered her telling them when he came here with Albert, Brandy and Nicole that one of the fourteen women who passed through the Temple of the Blind remained in this city and gave birth to her. He had assumed that woman was human. This would certainly explain why she had such a strong resemblance to those statues.

But he still found it difficult to believe that those statues could be real beings. They had no faces. He could buy that they were probably psychic, like the Sentinel Queen, communicating telepathically, with no need for eyes or ears or voices, but how did they eat? How did they breathe? "So then what were the sentinels?" he asked. "Gods? Angels? Demons? Aliens? What?"

They were the sentinels. Nothing less.

"So no straight answer then," Wayne deduced.

The Sentinel Queen stood before him, her empty face staring down at him, and said no more.

"Do the sentinels still exist?" Olivia asked.

Not that I know of. But then, I don't have eyes in all the worlds. It is possible that they still exist. Somewhere.

"All the worlds?" Andrea inquired. "How many are there."

No one knows for sure.

"That's what the old man said," Wayne recalled. He lowered his eyes from her featureless face and gazed at the eyeless man lying on the bare floor within the tiny room.

You are concerned about my son.

Wayne stared at the blind man. It surprised him to think of this ancient-looking man as her son. "Yeah," he told her. "I am."

He's not dead. Not yet. But he will be soon. Like all my children, his time here with me has come to an end.

"How old was he?" Wayne asked.

Four hundred thirteen years.

Olivia and Andrea exchanged a look of surprise. Could anyone really live so long?

He lived much longer than many of my children, she explained, *perhaps only by his will to not leave me alone, but my children all lived long lives. They did not know disease. And their sentinel blood gave them longevity.*

"I'm sorry," Wayne said.

Of course you are. Aren't we all when life is at its end? Suddenly, she turned her face toward Olivia. *Come here.*

Olivia hesitated for a moment. She glanced at Wayne, unsure, and then cautiously took a step toward the Sentinel Queen, fearful, but curious.

Olivia Shadey. She reached out with her long, bony fingers and tenderly caressed Olivia's cheek.

"You know me?"

Of course I do. We've already met.

"We have?" She stared at the woman's outstretched hand. She moved so gracefully and yet she looked so awkward with those unnaturally long limbs.

Yes. Inside the second-floor restroom of Gilbert House. I was with you the whole time.

"You were?"

Though this woman had no features upon her face to do so, she seemed to smile at her. *Don't you remember me? I whispered to you. I eased your fear. I said, 'You'll be all right. Someone's coming for you. Just hold on a little longer.' I kept you company the whole time you were in there. I kept you safe.* She dragged the tips of her long fingers down Olivia's cheek and beneath her chin. Then, in the same, fluid motion, she ran her bony knuckles affectionately up the other side of her face, sending a shiver down her spine. *I was even with you in the Wood, telling you not to be afraid, that help was still coming.*

Olivia stared up at her, astonished. The only thing that kept her sane throughout the past few days was that voice she'd thought was her own, deep inside her head, whispering to her to not be afraid, to just hold on a little longer. "That was you?"

I was with you both out there. I showed you the light in Gilbert House. I urged you in the right direction. I distracted the monster that chased you and made it go the wrong way.

Wayne remembered the way the towering monster crashed to the ground without any obvious reason. And later, inside Gilbert House, it had suddenly changed course again, crashing into the ceiling instead of following them down to the basement and out of the building.

All psychic things are susceptible to suggestion. By suggestion, I made Olivia control her fear and in the same manner I confused the beast and made it stumble.

This was not new information. The first time he met the Sentinel Queen, she told them that she could manipulate psychic minds. It was how she made Albert and Brandy leave their cars unlocked so she could deliver the box and its key. It was no stretch to think that she could use this same power to help Olivia retain her sanity for two days in an abandoned bathroom stall. And the old man had told him that she had used this ability to trip up the monster in Gilbert House.

Olivia stared at the Sentinel Queen as she ran her long hand over her dirty hair. "Are you saying that I'm psychic? Like Wayne said?"

Of course you are, the Sentinel Queen replied. *I only wish that your friends had also been. I might have saved them as well. Unfortunately, their fear overwhelmed my ability to calm them and get them out.*

Olivia lowered her eyes to the floor. This was all so strange. She was psychic. Was that the only reason she was still alive?

"Am *I* psychic?" Andrea asked.

No, replied the Sentinel Queen.

"Oh," said Andrea. She sounded disappointed.

Wayne was even more confused now. That was her voice in Olivia's head? Why would she be protecting Olivia if she was trying to kill him? "That old man said that you sent me into Gilbert House on purpose. To kill me."

I did *guide you to Gilbert House. I did it so that you would watch over Albert, Brandy and Nicole.*

"Let me guess. It was the old man who sent *them* there to die, right?"

Not to die, the Sentinel Queen insisted. *He knew I wouldn't let that happen, just as I knew he wouldn't let anything happen to you.*

"Then what was the point?"

I believe Olivia *was the point.*

Wayne and Olivia looked at each other, confused.

He told you that those other two envelopes were random, but it was always his intention to lure Olivia into Gilbert House.

"What?" asked Olivia. "Why?" It was startling to think that someone could have sent her into that awful hell intentionally. What kind of monster would do something like that?

To manipulate Wayne, replied the Sentinel Queen.

"Me?" Wayne asked.

He knew that she was psychic and that I would be able to protect her from the beast inside. He also knew that I was aware of his plot to lure Albert and Brandy there. He knew I'd send you to keep them safe and that I would make sure Olivia was found.

"So she was a part of this all along?" Wayne asked.

Of course.

"Why?" Wayne demanded. "What's the point of all that?"

To send you back to Albert and Brandy, replied the Sentinel Queen. *To make them doubt their purpose and leave the doorway closed.*

"Why not just go to them himself? Why not tell them what he told me? Or for that matter, why not just kill them?"

"Because she wouldn't let him," Olivia said, answering for the Sentinel Queen.

Wayne turned and stared at her for a moment. "Yeah," he decided. "I guess she wouldn't."

It's all very complicated, explained the Sentinel Queen.

Wayne nodded. "Yeah. No shit."

According to the Sentinel Queen, the old man lied about her trying to kill him. He also lied about Olivia's boyfriend receiving his letter from Beverly by chance. And he was sent to Gilbert House not to die, but to protect Albert, Brandy and Nicole.

One of them was clearly lying, but which one.

Olivia felt violated. She couldn't believe someone would deliberately put her through all that psychological torment. It was bad enough when it had all been a random accident, but that someone might have actually orchestrated it all… She thought of Trish, and that horrible screaming that went on and on in the darkness. How could anyone consciously let that happen?

"He also said that my going to rescue Olivia was to put distance between me and the others," Wayne added. "Did you arrange to have her taken into the Wood? Did you call the monster that took her?"

Olivia looked at Wayne, startled. Was *all* of her suffering deliberate?

The Sentinel Queen lifted her hands to her blank face in a gesture of weariness. *I did not*, she replied, her voice fading a little from their minds. *That was another of his lies.*

"Are you okay?" asked Andrea.

For now, she assured her. But she seemed to be growing dimmer somehow.

"Are they all right?" asked Wayne. "Albert and Brandy? Nicole?"

Yes. For now they are.

"How far ahead are they?"

She did not answer for a moment. She stood as she was, with her long hands pressed to the empty plane of her face. When she did speak, her voice was dimmer still, as if she were speaking to them from a great distance. *I'm sorry, Wayne. I'm growing weary. Just know that if you continue forward, you all will be a part of something much greater than you can imagine, something that began long before I was brought into this world and will continue long after I am gone. The doorway is the future. Don't let the man you met on your way to the Wood let you destroy that.*

"I don't know what to do," Wayne said. "I don't trust you."

You don't have to. Just trust yourself.

"I don't even know what that means."

I'm very tired, said the Sentinel Queen. *My son is dying, and I will be dead soon after him.*

Wayne wanted to say more, wanted to ask more, but she seemed to be fading like a candle at the end of its wax.

I'm very tired, she said again. *I need to rest…but before you go, I owe you an apology, Wayne.*

"An apology?"

Yes. When I took you into the first chamber of the road to the Wood, I told you I had something for you. In reality, I took *something from you. It was selfish of me. It was wrong.*

Wayne said nothing. He did not know what to say. She had essentially raped him. He'd awakened feeling dirty and violated.

An apology seemed rather insignificant, in all honesty.

I seduced you, Wayne. I fornicated with you and it was not your fault. I am the Mother, the giver of life inside these walls. I can make you give yourself to me if I wish. When I took you in my hand, you did not have enough will to say no to me, even if I had not clouded your mind with your own desires.

Wayne remembered thinking about such women as Laura Swiff, Nicole Smart and even Olivia. He had spiraled into a sort of fantasy dream and lost consciousness. She had done all that to him?

It is why you feel such arousal when you look at me. All of you. I give off psychic urges. To be perfectly blunt, you could say that I am in heat. She lowered her long, bony hands to her belly. *I apologize, Wayne. I did what I did to put myself with child. I intended to birth a new breed of children, a new race of keepers for the Temple of the Blind, with you as their father.*

Wayne did not know what to say. He was stunned. He stared at the Sentinel Queen's belly. Was she saying…?

I succeeded in becoming pregnant, but still I failed. I can feel my deathwatch ticking. I will be dead within hours, alongside my last son, and with me will die your child. I've begun a life I cannot complete and I am deeply ashamed.

Wayne wanted to say something, but no words would come. He felt as though a storm of emotions were raging in his own head, beyond his control. That she seduced him was bad enough, but she took from him a *child*?

"Can we do anything?" Andrea asked. The thought of the child in this woman's belly not having a chance to even be born made her sad. It was dreadfully unfair.

I had only one purpose in my long life. I was the keeper of this city, the guardian of the gate that leads back to the place from which we all came. Please don't let my life, and the lives of all my children have been for nothing. Albert and Brandy must *reach that door.*

"What door? How do I even get there?"

Please go… Her voice had faded to a faint whisper. She was growing desperately weak.

Wayne hesitated a moment longer and then turned and walked away. He felt a wide range of emotions inside him, too many to even count. He felt violated, sad, angry. He felt both relieved and disappointed. He felt lost. They went on and on. He could practically feel them swirling around in his chest, whirling like a tornado.

Olivia and Andrea joined him as the Sentinel Queen disappeared back into the little stone room where her last son lay dying.

Wayne had so many more questions to ask, so many more things he wanted to know. He did not know whether to trust her or the old man and so he trusted neither of them. He needed to find Albert and Brandy and Nicole. Together, perhaps the six of them could find the truth among all the lies.

Behind them, the Sentinel Queen began to sing. Her sad song drifted after them, dragging their hearts into a deep sorrow as they walked toward the north gate and the mysteries that lay beyond it.

Chapter 29

As a little girl, Brandy wanted to be a movie star. Now she was studying history. As they walked the endless corridors of the labyrinth, she found herself remembering those old dreams and wondering whatever happened to that little girl. She supposed that as she grew more mature, so did her dreams. She no longer wanted fame, but just a pleasant future somewhere. She did not need to be rich, but merely comfortable. She wanted to someday take that vacation to Paris that she always wanted and live in a nice house and have two or three gorgeous children. More than that, she wanted to do it with Albert Cross. Looking at the blank walls around her, she was beginning to wonder if, just as those childhood dreams of riches and fame were lost in her transformation from girl to woman, these new dreams of simple bliss might soon be lost in a spray of warm blood and terrible screams.

Brandy shivered, her whole body actually jolting with the reality of where they were and how much danger they were in.

"You okay?" Albert asked her.

"I'm fine. I'm just ready to be out of here, that's all."

"I know," he said. "We'll get there eventually. Just don't give up on me, okay?"

Again she nodded. It was hard. She had arrived at the point where she was ready to leave this awful place and just go home.

But she was stronger than this. After all they'd been through tonight, she wasn't about to give up on Albert and Nicole. Hearing the shriek of the Caggo had rattled her courage. It was a chilling reminder that getting lost and starving to death were the very least of their worries.

What was the Caggo? The Keeper made it sound as if it were more than merely a vicious beast. It said that slaughtering intrudes was its only joy, as if it were a sadistic killer that took perverse pleasure in disemboweling its victims. It sounded more like a sociopath than a monster. They weren't dealing with any kind of animal. This was certain to be more like the thing that attacked them inside Gilbert House. Except that she was sure the Caggo would be considerably worse somehow.

Lost in thought, she almost ran into Albert when he abruptly stopped in the middle of the next intersection. For a moment, she did not understand what he was doing, but then she saw what he was looking at. A single yellow line ran down the wall of the intersecting passage. They'd circled back to their own trail again. And an old one, at that.

For a moment, no one spoke. The discouragement of the labyrinth's size and difficulty was beginning to take its toll on them. They were tired. Their feet hurt. They were afraid and thirsty and hungry. They'd had only a small supper. Had they known that such hardships awaited them, would they still have come here?

They probably would have. Albert had no doubt in his mind that *he* would have. He would have come alone if need be.

"What now?" Brandy asked. The only choices were left or right, which would have them retracing steps they'd taken earlier in the night, or else back the way they just came.

"We keep going," replied Albert. "Take the next unmarked path we find."

"Do you think we've had time to get completely lost yet?" Nicole asked. The question was more a whine than an inquiry.

"Probably," Albert said. "But give me another fifteen or twenty minutes and I think we can be sure."

"Fabulous," Nicole replied.

"We're still okay, though." Brandy's tone as she said this was less than reassuring.

"Yes," Albert replied optimistically. "At least we know when we're retracing our steps. If we hadn't been leaving that line behind us we might be walking around in circles and never even know it."

"I'm still scared," said Nicole.

"Me too," seconded Brandy.

"Yeah," Albert told them. "I think that's going around just lately."

As they started walking again, Albert's blue line neatly drawn just above the yellow one, Brandy began to think about her first trip to the temple and the sex room. It wasn't the most romantic of circumstances for the memory of the first time they had sex. But it had been unavoidable. And perhaps if they hadn't come down here they wouldn't be together now. Therefore, she refused to regret the events of that night. Instead, she remembered it fondly. And it was an incredible thing, really. A wonderful thing. Not like how she lost her virginity. That she *did* regret.

It was not that she hadn't wanted to do it. It was more the fact that she gave in to Ben Anshen before she realized that she simply did not and would not ever really love him. It was because when it was all said and done it was not making love. It was just having sex. It was just being a slut.

She was fifteen at the time, so young. It had seemed like such a good thing when they started. They were friends first. Then they became more than that. She made out with him because it seemed okay and she had sex with him because she thought she wanted to. She was curious. But as soon as it was over she found that she was not satisfied. It had hurt, for one thing, and she found that, rather than feeling something special, she had merely resented both him and herself for it. She knew as soon as it was over that someday she would be holding the man she really loved and she would hate herself for doing that.

But she didn't really hate herself. She didn't even hate Ben, as easy as that would have been. She accepted it. And later, when she was a senior in high school, she also gave herself far too soon to Kevin Lefreys. She told herself at the time that she thought she loved him, but really, she only let it happen because she'd already given herself to Ben. If she and Ben had never happened, she probably would have waited longer before giving into Kevin. After all, it wasn't as if her virginity was at stake.

She and Kevin remained together for a few short months and they made love half a dozen times during those months. But it was never real. It was never satisfying. And he always seemed to want more than she was willing to give.

She didn't love him any more than she'd loved Ben. She loved him less, in fact, because at least Ben had been her friend before he was her lover. She walked away from that relationship wondering if there was something wrong with her, if she was incapable of distinguishing petty lust for real love.

But the sex room had shown her that lust could be every bit as overpowering as hatred and fear. The experience had been horrifying. It had been humiliating. Right after it happened, she felt briefly as if her world had fallen apart. The only comfort she could find was that she was not a virgin. That awful room, for all the things it made her do, hadn't taken that away from her.

But that was precisely what it took from Albert. He had gone inside perfectly innocent, and while the room was raping her of her dignity and self-respect, it was tearing from him all the wonder and beauty that might have been his first time. It was making her do to him what she let Ben do to her.

But it wasn't really like that at all.

She didn't realize it until after that night was over, but there was something different about doing those things with Albert, something besides the obvious perversity of those statues. There was something there, something that was missing that day with Ben and each time she was with Kevin.

She remembered lying on the cold stone floor in front of the sex room door while Albert lay atop her, kissing her as if he meant to devour her lips and thrusting himself violently and painfully into her as the sentinels watched on with their massive erections. It was the second time they passed through the sex room, the second time it made them do these things. And like the first time, there was nothing romantic about it. It was pure, animal lust. But this time Albert had managed to get them through the statues and out of the chamber before losing control, and as the intensity of the sex room's desires began to fade, so did the fierceness of their sex, until Albert's kisses became tender and sweet, and the motion of his hips slowed to a gentle rhythm.

That was the first time she'd ever felt satisfied being with a man. Though she hadn't realized it yet, that was the first time she truly made love.

Ahead of them, another intersection came into view. The yellow line went straight ahead into the darkness. The passages that led left and right remained unmarked and unexplored.

Albert turned right without speaking and Brandy and Nicole followed him, their flashlights prodding the passages they left behind, half expecting to see a pair of sinister, glowing eyes peering back at them.

In the eerie silence, Brandy continued to think about the sex room and whether or not she would have Albert in her life today if they had not been driven together by its insatiable urges.

Chapter 30

"What's that smell?" Nicole groaned, her face scrunching into a sour expression of revulsion.

The air in this passage had grown rank. A deep, pungent odor was permeating the air in the narrow space through which they walked.

"The hounds," Albert said. "Or if not them then *some* sort of animal. Smells like the zoo down here." Although he never remembered the zoo smelling *this* bad. Not even at its worst. Down here, there likely weren't any animal keepers to clean up the exhibits.

"It's disgusting!" Nicole complained.

"One of the hounds' tunnels must be just ahead," Albert surmised. But as he walked forward, he found that the passage went on much farther than he expected, and likewise, the stench grew much stronger. By the time they reached the next intersection—which was, indeed, a crossing of one of those lowered passageways—the air was so pervaded with the pungent, ammonia-stench of animal waste that it brought tears to their eyes and threatened to strangle them.

The floor of this reeking passage bore the same scratches as those in all the other areas where the hounds were allowed access, but it was considerably more damaged than any they had encountered so far. The center was worn nearly to sand. Something about these creatures was obviously hard on the stone. Albert assumed that they must walk on incredibly formidable claws to do such damage. After hundreds of years, or thousands, or even tens of thousands, it wasn't unthinkable that the floor would eventually wear beneath the feet of such creatures, whereas the rest of the temple likely suffered very little traffic and therefore remained pristine. And this passage, for some reason, endured significantly more traffic than others.

"What *is* this place?" Brandy coughed.

"A lot of animals always do their business in the same place every time they go," Albert explained.

"So this is a giant litter box?" Nicole asked. Her hand was pressed over her mouth and nose, muffling her voice.

"Something like that." Albert shined his flashlight left and right. Once again, no hounds were in sight. But this was obviously a place they frequented. If the smell was any indication, somewhere very near this spot was a passage or chamber that was the equivalent of a sewer.

Directly across from them, the passage they were traveling continued forward.

"Come on," he said. "Let's go quick, before one of them comes back."

Brandy and Nicole didn't like the idea of crossing another of these passages, but they already knew that Albert wouldn't backtrack as long as there was an alternative. He was probably saving them hours of walking in the long run, but it still seemed like an unnecessarily dangerous risk. None of them knew how fast the hounds could run. If one caught their scent, there was no guarantee that it wouldn't be on them before they could climb back up to higher ground.

Quickly, the three of them dropped down and rushed to the other side. Albert gave Brandy and Nicole each a gentle boost and then heaved himself up and over the ledge, once again managing to avoid being mauled.

Coughing on the noxious stench, Albert did not even bother to glance back in hopes of glimpsing a hound. He pressed the chalk to the wall and hurried on, hoping the air would soon clear.

A few minutes later, the left wall of the passage opened up, revealing another lower passageway running alongside them. The same, foul stench filled the air and the same, telltale scratches covered the floor.

The Sentinel Queen told them that her children acted as caretakers for the Temple of the Blind. Albert had assumed that part of their job was keeping the place tidy, explaining the immaculate cleanliness of the corridors. There had not even been any dust to dirty their bare feet. He had also assumed, then, that their work must extend to cleaning up after the hounds, but this area suggested the hounds to be very clean animals that likely required little effort on the part of the Sentinel Queen's blind brood. Given that he had not detected any foul odors in other areas where the floor was scarred, it seemed likely that the hounds preferred to keep most of their territory clean.

Perhaps that meant that this was a fairly safe place for them to be. Clean animals usually didn't like their food too near their waste. If a hound should appear in that lower passage while they were passing through, it might not even be interested in them.

On the other hand, just because it was picky about where it evacuated didn't necessarily mean it was particular about where it came by its food. And the things might be violently territorial, in which case hunger wouldn't have anything to do with it. They would kill anything that wandered into their labyrinth on pure instinct.

However, he had to keep reminding himself that he knew nothing of these things. They could have been engineered specifically to break all the rules of nature. Someone, somewhere, designed the fear room, after all. There was no guessing what kinds of monsters someone like that might be capable of breeding.

They moved on, each of them keeping near the wall as they walked, their flashlights repeatedly drifting down into the shadows of the lower passage, their eyes watering from the pungent stench that pervaded the air.

The two passages parted again less than a hundred feet from where they met and the stench finally began to dissipate a little as they moved away. About forty yards ahead, they turned left at an intersection and immediately crossed another section of the hounds' labyrinth (this one mildly less rank than the last) and again there were no hounds to be seen.

Albert was beginning to think that there was something unnatural about their luck. Once again, he wondered if the Sentinel Queen had done something to distract the hounds beyond hanging up their undergarments, since they had surely grown wise to that trick by now.

They came upon another intersection and Albert turned right. Several yards beyond, Albert heard the curious noise of a hound drifting toward them from somewhere up ahead.

"I don't like it here," Brandy said. "There's way too many hounds."

Nicole agreed. "I keep thinking we're going to find ourselves trapped between two of those passages and they won't let us leave."

Albert had to admit, that was not a pleasant thought. But so far there had not been any two junctions between the two labyrinths with nothing between them. He would not, however, rule out that there might be such places somewhere down here. In fact, something like that would be just the thing to trip up someone like him, who was choosing to cross those junctions rather than spend extra time backtracking through the labyrinth. It made sense, even, when he considered the twisted logic of the temple. It seemed that for every advantage they found, there was an equal disadvantage. Entering the hate room blind protected one from the overwhelming emotions. But *exiting* the room blind could mean sharing Beverly's gruesome fate.

The Temple of the Blind had a way of punishing those who learned its tricks.

At the end of the passage, as expected, was another sunken tunnel. The noise of the hound was still droning on, but the creature itself was not within sight. It seemed to be lingering somewhere to the left, concealed in shadows.

"Tell me you're not planning to cross this one too," said Nicole as she gazed nervously toward the noise. As the chilling sound went on and on, it sounded deceptively like purring to her, as if the hound might be nothing more than a happy, napping cat, if a terrifyingly large one.

Albert glanced at the opening across from them. It was so

close, and yet so incredibly far. "No," he replied. "Not this time."

The hound was right there. It was making its noise, which might mean that it was agitated or at least that it was awake and probably alert. It would be only a matter of time before it caught their scent. It didn't take much time to drop down and climb back up, but when danger was so close, and so obvious, the risk became too great to justify. Perhaps if it was only him down here he might have considered taking the risk, but there was no way he would so blatantly risk Brandy's or Nicole's life just to save a little backtracking.

"So we go back to that last intersection," said Brandy, relieved that she didn't have to talk him out of risking it.

"Yeah." But Albert did not turn back. He lingered there, his light aimed toward the droning racket of the hound. It was becoming more than he could bear. He wanted to see one, wanted to know what to expect in case they had to deal with these things later. But it remained stubbornly out of sight.

"So let's go," Brandy urged.

Albert nodded, but still he lingered for a moment, waiting, watching. He wanted only a glimpse, just a fleeting flash of the creature. He began to walk only when Nicole started back ahead of him and Brandy took his hand and pulled him away.

Chapter 31

Rachel was never going to believe this. Not in a million years. There was simply no amount of swearing that could ever convince Andrea's best friend that there existed a place like the City of the Blind hidden deep inside a colossal *Temple* of the Blind that itself existed right beneath the very streets of Briar Hills. Rachel was also not going to believe that Gilbert House, those eerie, but otherwise boring walls practically in Andrea's own backyard, was actually an entire building that was somehow invisible and acted as a portal between their world and an endless, black forest populated with shambling, undead corpses. She was never going to believe there was any such thing as a hound or a Sentinel Queen or whatever that thing was that attacked everybody in Gilbert House. She was not even going to believe that always-modest Andrea took her clothes off in front of a guy.

Even Andrea wasn't sure she believed all of it. It was so much to take in. Even the things she'd seen with her own eyes seemed far too spectacular to possibly be real. As she gazed around her now at the walls of gray stone that stretched on and on into the relentless darkness before them, she could not help but marvel over all the things she'd discovered since that envelope first appeared on her window screen.

She couldn't stop wondering what she was doing here. What business did a girl like her have in a place like this? She was only eighteen, still just a kid. Had she really followed these two complete strangers into this terrifying underground labyrinth just because a mysterious voice in the forest told her to do it?

What business did any of them have down here, for that matter? From what Wayne and Olivia told her, they had never met each other or the three people they were trying to catch up with before tonight. They were all three of them strangers, yet here they were, alone in the darkness, far too deep within the earth for their screams to be heard by anyone, forced to trust in one another like family.

They were naked, even! They were walking around down here completely nude, their most private parts on display before the eyes of people they'd known for mere hours! Why? It was insane. She couldn't stop thinking about how utterly crazy this all was. She never would have believed herself capable of doing such a thing. Yet here she was.

And now that she was here, what was it she was supposed to do? The Sentinel Queen told her that she had no idea how the envelope found its way onto her window screen, or whose voice was in her head outside Gilbert House, instructing her to come here. She was an unexpected player in this game. Clearly someone intended for her to be here, but who? What was her role in it all? It was all so confusing.

What did she even have to give? She wasn't special. She was quirky, but otherwise just a perfectly normal teenage girl. She was not psychic like Olivia or Albert or Brandy. Certainly not like Beverly had been. She was not courageous like Wayne. She would not have been capable of walking through that horrible tunnel all alone and scared to death. She *certainly* would not have been able to take on all those zombies. She probably wouldn't even have been able to handle just one shuffling corpse without screaming herself into cardiac arrest. Neither did she have Olivia's courage. Even with the Sentinel Queen's gentle words in her head, assuring her that she would be okay, promising that someone was coming to find her, she would have been driven completely insane with terror after just an hour inside that dark restroom, much less after two long days. It did not make sense that she, just a gentle virgin in a harsh and emotionless world, would be chosen to come down here into this ancient, underground world, to strip off her modesty and walk naked through a nightmare labyrinth that, to her, had begun to feel a little like the valley of the shadow of death in that prayer her grandmother once taught her, the one that always made her shiver.

It was all so overwhelming. *All* of this was overwhelming. This whole place, the very reality of it all.

And even as she thought about all these things, her eyes kept drifting to Wayne. He was walking in front of her, his naked back and buttocks caked with stinking mud in the light of her flashlight. Until tonight, she had never seen a guy naked before. And until now, she had been too embarrassed to give him more than a fleeting glance. But she found that she was beginning to grow bolder as the night went on and now she found herself really looking at him, studying him, *memorizing* him.

He was a little soft around the middle, but he was still muscular. He had big arms and legs and broad shoulders. He also had a fairly attractive butt, she noticed. Maybe not the cutest she'd ever seen, but not bad…

It felt odd looking at him like this. It was sort of naughty. It gave her a nervous lump deep in her belly. And she was surprised to discover that she *liked* the way that naughty sensation made her feel. It made her body tingle a little. Even with the stench of the mud chamber still wafting from her body, she couldn't help but feel a little sexy as she watched him walk, his strong thighs flexing rhythmically with his ever-urgent stride.

Was this what the sex room had done to her? Was this her punishment for ignoring Wayne's warning and peeking at those insane statues? Was she now doomed to feel these urges all the time? Would she slowly lose herself to increasingly insatiable desires until there was nothing left of the girl she used to be? Or was this all perfectly natural? Maybe it was just her body's way of telling her that she'd grown comfortable with hers and Wayne's nudity. Perhaps this was nothing more than who she was and who she'd always been. She just needed the right circumstances to reveal it to herself.

Either way, it felt sort of good. And she found herself forgetting the Sentinel Queen and her unknown purpose as she studied Wayne's masculine shape, enamored with these fascinating new feelings.

No, Rachel was definitely never going to believe this.

Chapter 32

The now too-familiar roar of the hounds rose from the silence ahead of them and grew louder as they approached the source. The air no longer reeked, but there remained a mustiness to remind them that they were not alone down here.

Brandy and Nicole grew nervous, just as they did each time they heard the sound. By now there was little reason to doubt that they were safely separated from the hounds and not at all likely to enter their territory unknowingly. And yet, they found it difficult to trust that they were really safe from them. They knew so little about these beasts, so little about this whole place. Far *too* little when it concerned their lives.

Albert, on the other hand, couldn't help but swell with eagerness. It had been thirteen long months since he first heard the curiously hostile sound of a passing creature from a nearby corridor of the temple. He remembered how it filled him with terror that first time, freezing him in place. Ever since that moment, he'd wondered what these things were, what they looked like, how they made that amazingly dreadful noise.

On his way back out of the temple that night, one of them had very nearly run him down before he and Brandy could escape. At the time, he hadn't known that the walls were what kept them reigned in. He hadn't known he was safe and so he had kept running, straight through the frigid waters of the flooded passageway and across to the other side. He'd assumed that perhaps the creature couldn't swim, that the water had been the reason it called off its pursuit. And even then he hadn't lingered for fear that he was wrong and the creature might still be stalking them. Looking back now, he wished he'd been brave enough to peek over that ledge before fleeing. Then he would have known what he was up against. And he wouldn't have lain awake in his bed night after night, wondering what it was that so nearly snapped off his feet.

But then again, that was only one of many mysteries that had kept him up at night. If not for the hounds, he'd have obsessed over the man with no eyes or the purpose of the emotion rooms or how the box made its way into his car.

Now, he found himself hoping each time he heard one of the hounds that it would be waiting for him when he reached the end of the passage, that it would finally reveal itself to him so that he no longer had to wonder.

Nothing bothered him more than an unsolved mystery.

Fortunately for him, his wait was nearly over.

At the end of the passage was a large chamber. The entire room belonged to the hounds, so that they stood at the mouth of the passage, six feet above the badly scarred floor, gazing out into blackness far too deep for their lights to pierce. The strange, clattering roar of the beasts was nearly deafening.

Brandy squeezed Albert's hand and he read her thoughts as though she'd spoken them aloud: *How do we really know they can't jump out of there?*

The answer to that was simple: they weren't sure at all. For all they knew the damned things could have wings. But he didn't think so. If they could get up into this part of the labyrinth, then why hadn't they?

He could hear them moving around. They were here. Lots of them. Just beyond his vision. A jolt of childish excitement rushed through him. At any moment one of them might appear from the darkness and he would finally see them. After more than a year of knowing nothing more than that queer noise they made, he would finally know what they were.

And yet, they still remained frustratingly invisible. Seconds passed on. The noises moved around the chamber as they roamed, but none ventured into view. Next to him, Brandy and Nicole glanced at each other, anxious and ready to move on, afraid of allowing these things to get too near. He began to fear that the simple truth of what these things looked like would escape him yet again, and a deep disappointment welled up within him. He had a maddening urge to hurl his flashlight out into that darkness, for the simple satisfaction of glimpsing even a shadow of these elusive creatures.

But then he saw one. It emerged at the edge of their vision, dashing from right to left, visible for only a second, but utterly and shockingly real.

Large, low to the ground and dark-colored, it did not move like any kind of canine. Nor did it move like anything else that Albert had ever seen. It was exceptionally fast for something on such short legs.

Brandy and Nicole saw it too, and immediately Albert felt a change in them both. Though their apprehension grew at the brief sight of the creature, their curiosity seemed to nail them down so that they no longer inched away from the ledge. They stood fascinated, staring into the chamber, waiting for it to reappear.

Another hound darted in and out of view, dashing across the floor as if playing, with a second and noticeably smaller creature close behind it. Again, they remained too distant and too fast to get a good look. Albert still could not tell how they were making that noise, but he could see that they had short, blunt heads and very little neck.

Then one of them wandered into the light much closer to them. Its head was down to the ground, sniffing the floor. It wasn't making the noise that the others were, and Albert observed the many rows of upright scales that covered its body.

"I've never seen anything like it before," said Nicole. "Where did they come from?"

"Maybe they're some kind of extinct species," Albert suggested. "Or something from another world, like the place we saw through Gilbert House's windows."

Brandy gripped Albert's arm and pressed close to him. She didn't like these things at all.

The hound lifted its blunt snout from the floor and sniffed at the air around it. A moment later, its body shivered and that familiar noise began. Albert watched it, fascinated.

"What's it doing?" Brandy asked.

Its body rippled strangely, its skin seeming to vibrate with the sound that it made. Then it swung its snout toward them and rushed at them.

Brandy and Nicole both screamed and shrank away, but Albert did not budge. He stood and watched as the strange creature dashed across the scarred floor and threw itself into the wall beneath them.

"My god…" he sighed. These creatures were even more fascinating than he could have imagined. He knelt down in the mouth of the passage and shined his light down on top of the hound.

"What are you doing?" Brandy hissed.

But Albert paid her no attention. He studied the creature, taking it all in. He noted its two tails, its two separate spines. He could think of no other creature that was built like that. It had no hair, only the curious, blade-like scales, which stood upright in tight, crooked rows that ran the length of its body. They were in motion, slashing rapidly back and forth, many of them rubbing together in the process. It was the friction of these oscillating blades that made the noise that had for so long nagged at his curiosity. Different blades contacted differently. Some of them simply rubbed together, others slammed against each other. It was no wonder he couldn't place the noise. It wasn't a single sound, but rather hundreds of sounds at once, all of them blurring into a single, chaotic clamor with no two hounds sounding exactly the same.

"I'm pretty sure that tops the list of the scariest things I've ever seen," Nicole said as she stood beside Albert, staring down at the agitated creature.

The man with no eyes had been honest with them. The creature thrashed angrily against the wall, but uselessly. It didn't seem to be capable of jumping or climbing or even lifting itself onto its back legs to snarl up at them. It merely battered itself against the wall, its broad jaws snapping at the stone.

Another hound rushed out of the darkness and slammed

into the wall next to the first. This one was slightly larger, and after a moment of trying to bite the wall, it turned and threw itself into the first hound, knocking it onto its side and sending a spray of blood into the air where their armored bodies collided.

Albert caught a glimpse of the smaller creature's claws as it rolled over. Set into the padding of its paw were several long, pale protrusions that ran from the front of the foot all the way to the back, each one like the serrated blade of a knife. They were in neat rows, similar to the upright scales on its skin, but thicker and more durable-looking. Such curiously evolved claws were perfect for making all those scratches in the floor, especially over the course of thousands of years.

Other hounds appeared as they stood watching. Some rushed toward them, snapping and snarling at the stone, occasionally colliding with those that were already here and sending up sprays of blood wherever the slashing, blade-like scales bit into flesh. A couple more passed through the flashlight beams without taking notice of the commotion, perhaps having not yet caught the scent of the intruders. A much smaller one approached from the darkness, but lingered well beyond the reach of its larger pack mates, its blades slashing violently as it sniffed yearningly at the air.

Brandy and Nicole were standing with their hands pressed to their ears. The noise was deafening. It was amazing how loud these things were.

Albert did not move. He knelt there, above the creatures' reach, staring down at them, amazed. This was an entirely new creature. No one in the world had ever seen anything like this. It was so *alien.* The magnitude of seeing such a thing was overwhelming. He could scarcely believe he was really looking at it.

They were every bit as violent as they'd been led to believe. They were even dangerous to each other. Looking down on them, Albert realized that all of them were covered in scars. One was missing one of its tails. Another had only three legs.

Brandy nudged at his elbow again, urging him to move. She didn't like the way they were swarming.

Albert stood up. He knew Brandy was scared, knew that she wanted him to turn and leave, but he could not pull his eyes from them. They were terrifying, yet they were magnificent. Finally, after all this time, he was seeing them, and they were more than he could ever have imagined.

And yet, something wasn't right.

He stared down at the hounds, watching them. He knew what they were now. He knew how they made their noise. He even knew how they'd scratched up the floors in their territory. And yet, he still felt incomplete somehow.

Brandy tugged at his arm, more forcefully this time, and finally he relented. He turned and walked with her, back toward the previous intersection and away from the quarreling beasts.

But even as he walked away, he found that he still had a strong urge to see the hounds.

As the noise began to fade behind them, he paused and looked back the way they came.

"What's wrong?" Brandy asked.

Albert wasn't sure. He felt a strong compulsion to turn and run back toward that room. But it wasn't the same as what he'd felt as he stood looking into the meadow. This was different. This felt like…

"Feels like we were close back there," he realized.

"Close to what?" Brandy asked.

"To the end," Albert replied as he finally turned his eyes back to her. "I feel like we were close to the exit."

"Back *there*?" Nicole asked doubtfully, gazing back toward the hound-infested chamber. If that was the exit, they couldn't possibly reach it. Those monsters would skin them alive.

"No. Not there. Not exactly."

"Then what?" Brandy pushed.

"I'm not sure."

For a moment, the three of them stared back toward the hounds.

The answer was there somewhere. Albert was sure of it.

Chapter 33

In considerably less time than it had taken Albert, Brandy and Nicole, Wayne made his way from the City of the Blind's north gate to the second pool of water. Behind him, Olivia and Andrea struggled to keep up with his brisk pace. He was eager to catch up (if that was even possible) and share what he had learned from the Sentinel Queen and the old man. Together, perhaps they could sort the truth from all the lies and determine what it was they needed to do.

He did not even hesitate at the water's edge. As Albert had done, he simply hopped into the water, assuming it would be easier to jump in all at once and get it over with.

Just like Albert, he was wrong.

Instantly, all the breath was sucked from his lungs. It actually seemed to him that his heart stopped beating, and perhaps it *had* skipped a beat or two. Water this cold was like a bolt of electricity, with all the gentleness of a baseball bat to the gut.

Olivia did not wait for his reaction. She jumped in after him, her feet entering the water even as Wayne was struggling up to the surface. She came up with a breathless gasp. "*Oh my God!*" she cried.

"Is it cold?" Andrea asked.

"Course not," Wayne remarked, his lips quivering with the violence of his shivers as he turned and swam away from her. "Perfectly tepid."

Andrea hesitated. Again she stood alone on the edge of a psychological cliff, pushing herself to jump, though every fiber of her being begged her to turn back. Desperately, she wished she'd rushed in as Olivia did, without waiting to see how it would affect Wayne. She did not want to go forward, did not want to torture herself anymore, but there was nowhere else to go. She was sure she could not survive the journey home by herself. If the emotion rooms didn't kill her, the hounds likely would.

Wishing a little that she'd just stayed home, Andrea gripped her flashlight and jumped in. The cold was unbelievable. She could not help but wonder how deep the water must be to be so cold. At some point far below in the permanent darkness, was it completely frozen?

The swim to the other side of the chamber took less than a

minute, but it felt much longer, as would any form of torture. Soon, the three of them climbed shivering and dripping onto dry stone. Earlier that night, Albert, Brandy and Nicole paused here to warm up by sharing body heat, but Wayne pushed on, warming himself by exertion instead, almost dragging his weary companions along.

"We're going to get sick," moaned Andrea.

"Not if we don't let ourselves get sick," Wayne replied.

"I don't think we have much control over it," she retorted. In the biting cold and her growing weariness, she was beginning to feel considerably less perky.

"I know," he told her. "But being cold doesn't make us sick. It just weakens the immune system. It makes us more susceptible."

"Really?" Andrea asked.

"Yep."

"I didn't know that."

"I think I remember one of my high school teachers telling us that," Olivia recalled.

The cold made Wayne's arm and leg hurt. The cut he'd sustained from the spikes in the fear room did not bother him by comparison, nor did his feet, really, but the zombie bite and the injury he'd sustained from the hound were killing him. He did not think he could get much more miserable than this.

For a while they walked, the shivering and the chattering

slowly fading, their bodies gradually regaining their former semi-warmth. They crossed the room with the forty-two sentinels and entered the passage beyond without pausing to examine any of them.

As he approached the intersection ahead, he spied the yellow line that ran along the far wall to the right. He reached out and dragged his fingers across it, smearing it.

"What is it?" Olivia asked.

"Sidewalk chalk," Wayne replied. He remembered the Sentinel Queen telling them that the others had left a trail for him to follow and realized that this was what she meant. "Follow the yellow chalk line," he said, grinning a little. "We're going to see the wizard."

"Guys…" Andrea had turned and was looking back the way they'd come, her flashlight piercing the darkness that pushed in at their backs.

Wayne turned and added his beam to hers. There was nothing there. "What is it?"

Andrea shook her head. "I thought I saw something…"

"I don't see anything," said Olivia.

"I guess…" Andrea shook her head again. For a moment she would have sworn that there was something there, some dark form, short and hunched, darker than the rest of the darkness, but there was nothing there. "I guess not," she said at last.

"Come on," Wayne said. "Let's hurry. We've got their trail

now."

Andrea lingered for a moment, still not ready to dismiss what she had seen, and then she turned and followed Wayne into the labyrinth, their flashlights chasing the yellow line that would lead them to the others.

Behind them, in the thickening darkness at their backs, the Keeper watched with interest.

Chapter 34

Albert stopped at a merging of three passageways and listened to the eerie silence. There were five choices, discounting the way they came. From where he stood, he could choose to continue straight ahead or he could take either of the passages that branched forty-five degrees to the left and right. Alternatively, he could choose to go forty-five degrees backward, which in this labyrinth could actually be forward. It was impossible to tell which way they might be facing and equally impossible to guess where any path may ultimately take them. But at least he was finally beginning to develop a plan.

Albert listened to the silence. "Nothing," he breathed.

Brandy glanced up at him. "What?"

"I don't hear anything," he replied.

"What are you listening for?" Nicole asked.

"Hounds."

Brandy's flashlight beam dropped to the floor, where she searched the stone for any sign of scratches or dropped scales. "Here?"

"No. Just listening for them."

"Why?" asked Nicole.

"I want to see them."

"Maybe the air is getting a little thin down here, Sweetie," replied Brandy, "but you've already seen them. They're freaky, remember?"

The corner of Albert's lip twitched upward into a subtle grin. "I remember," he assured her. "But I still want to see them."

"Why?" pressed Nicole.

"I don't know. But I do. It was driving me nuts. I figured it's because they've *always* driven me nuts. I spent months wondering what they were, how they made that sound. And now I know. But I still want to see the hounds."

"That doesn't make any sense," Brandy told him.

"I know. I didn't get it at first. But the Sentinel Queen said I was psychic."

"We don't know if anything she said is true," Brandy warned.

"I know. But if she's right, then maybe it's not the hounds I want to see. Maybe it's the labyrinth's exit."

"I don't get it," Nicole said.

"It's not logical," Albert explained. "Curiosity makes sense. I wanted to see the hounds because I didn't know what they were. But now I know what they are and I still really want to see the hounds. That sounds more like something subconscious to me. If the Sentinel Queen is right, if I *am* psychic, then maybe I can feel this place somehow. Maybe it's what she meant when she said we have the ability to pick up the 'vibrations' of the temple, or whatever it was. Maybe I can sense the exit. This might be how my mind is relaying it to me." He shrugged. "On the other hand, maybe I'm not psychic at all, but that doesn't mean the Sentinel Queen isn't back in my head, like when she made us leave our cars unlocked last year. Either way, the result is the same. I want to see the hounds. I'm thinking wherever the exit is, there might be hounds. And we can *hear* the hounds."

Brandy and Nicole glanced at each other.

"Well it's not like we have anything else to go on," Nicole decided.

Brandy shrugged. "Fine. Let's find some more hounds, then."

Albert listened again to the silence, but there were no hounds to be heard here, so he selected a path at random and kept walking.

After about twenty yards, they found themselves back in the reservoir system.

"Those fucking squid things better not spray me again!" Brandy snapped.

As if reacting to her threat, something splashed into the water nearby.

"I hate those things."

"Come on," Albert urged. "You can walk behind me."

The three of them moved deeper into the chamber, Albert's chalk still pressed to the wall. Ahead of them, shrouded in the darkness, things slithered from their path and fled into the water.

Albert paused at the next opening in the wall and listened for the sound of agitated hounds, but the labyrinth was silent. Even if this new instinct could be trusted, he realized it could be hours before they came across another area where the hounds were active, and even then there was no guarantee that they would find the correct chamber. There must be miles of intersecting passages down here.

They moved on and Albert listened at the next opening and then the next. Still he heard nothing. Then, as they moved toward the fourth passage beyond where they entered the chamber, a sound did rise from the silence, but it was not the droning of the hounds. It was the splashing of the mysterious aquatic creatures. Several of them suddenly threw themselves into the water somewhere on the other side of the chamber.

He glanced back at Brandy and Nicole and saw that their eyes were wide with fright. Something had spooked the creatures over there. And they knew of only one thing down here besides the three of them…

"Maybe they're fighting with each other," Albert suggested.

But another splash touched their ears, followed quickly by a second and a moment later by a third. Something was moving over there, something that was spooking the squid things and causing them to hurl themselves into the water.

And it was moving toward them.

"Oh god…" whimpered Brandy.

"Come on," Albert urged. He turned and hurried to the next opening. As soon as the chamber was behind them, all three of them broke into a run.

Chapter 35

Wayne paused at an intersection and examined the yellow line. It disappeared down the left side of one passageway and then returned along the right. Apparently the others had found a dead end down there.

"Are we okay?" Andrea asked.

"Yeah," he assured them, although he honestly did not know. The line was on the left side of the tunnel previously. If Albert had kept the line on that side of the wall the whole time he was walking, then he could remain reasonably confident about which direction they were traveling. That meant that as long as Albert's yellow line was on his left, he was moving toward them, and if that line was on his right, he was moving away from them. But if Albert's left hand had grown tired, they very well could wind up going in the wrong direction and perhaps end up traveling in circles.

Olivia turned and looked back the way they'd come. She did not like it down here at all. She was getting a bad feeling from these walls. Something wasn't right down here. Perhaps it was the walls themselves, so close and threatening, like the cage of some man-eating beast.

They walked past the dead-end path and followed the single yellow line to a set of crossroads, and then into another passage.

Wayne had at last discovered how he could catch up with the others. They were in a giant maze. For hours they'd probably been going in circles. Ordinarily, it would have been impossible. They could wander for weeks and never necessarily cross paths. But here was the path they had traveled, and by marking both sides of the tunnels they'd backtracked, Albert, Brandy and Nicole had saved them the trouble of repeating their mistakes. They could see dead ends before they began. This would shorten the distance between them greatly.

But even so, how many hours had it been since Albert, Brandy and Nicole passed through this tunnel? How long since this yellow line was drawn? Even with these advantages, how long would they be chasing chalk lines in the dark?

It didn't matter, he supposed. He was determined to follow the line for as long as it took. He only hoped that they remained safe until he reached them.

Chapter 36

Whatever spooked the creatures back in the reservoir had either failed to keep up with them or had not bothered to follow them.

Or it chose not to reveal itself.

Albert turned randomly at each intersection without bothering to pause and listen for the roar of the hounds. He hoped that they could lose themselves back into the labyrinth, but if the thing behind them possessed any kind of advanced sense of smell, the effort would be pointless. Any mere dog could follow their scent trail. Unless they were running from a person, there was literally nowhere to hide. And all any human being would have to do was follow the blue chalk line.

Was it the Caggo they heard spooking the reservoir creatures? Or was it something else. It was unlikely that it was a hound, but not entirely impossible. For all they knew, the other side of that particular chamber could have been a part of their territory. They would have to have access to the water system somewhere. They were living creatures.

Could the blind man have been creeping around over there, perhaps checking in on them for his mother? Or perhaps it had been the Sentinel Queen herself. Or maybe it had been the Keeper.

Or it was always possible that there could be something else lurking around down here, something that they had no way of knowing about.

If it was the Caggo they heard back there, why didn't it come after them? Could it not swim? Was there no way across that room?

Or was it merely playing with them?

Albert turned down another path and ventured deeper into the labyrinth. All he could do was keep moving and hope they found the exit before something nasty found them.

Behind him, Brandy and Nicole remained as close as possible, their flashlights gliding across every surface and frequently darting into the blackness at their backs.

Chapter 37

Wayne lingered long enough to boost Olivia and Andrea up into the next section of the passage and then hurriedly lifted himself out of harm's way. To his nearly overwhelming dread, Albert's yellow line had crossed right over a passage with all the expected markings of the hounds. After his agonizing earlier encounter with one of the beasts, this was the last place he wanted to take unnecessary risks, but he couldn't afford to lose the trail. If he wandered off the path, there was no guarantee that he'd ever be able to find the chalk line again.

What was Albert thinking? Clearly, he still didn't know how nasty the hounds really were.

But then again, he supposed it could be possible that the only way to find the exit was to cross these areas, in which case, constantly turning back at the sight of sunken passageways would never yield a path to wherever it was they were trying to go.

Though he hadn't known him for long, this seemed to Wayne like something Albert would think of.

But he still wasn't happy about it.

What would he do if he came to an area where the others had crossed, the yellow chalk line leading off into the darkness on the other side, but with a voracious, blade-covered hound sniffing eagerly at the scent of trespassers? He would be unable to follow. He'd have to find another way around, which would mean leaving the path and probably getting lost for hours, if not forever.

He supposed there was nothing to do but worry about that if and when it happened. Until then, there was no point in concerning himself about such things. He would only succeed in making himself more nervous about being here.

But not thinking about the hounds was virtually impossible. The constant, screaming pain in his leg was a far too vivid and constant reminder.

Chapter 38

Nicole felt nearly sick at the thought of something horrible stalking them in these dark corridors. Hot acid churned in her empty stomach at the thought of a bloodthirsty monster leaping out at them and murdering them one by one. It was not even remotely an irrational fear. Something was in here with them, and she had no idea how they were supposed to protect themselves. They were unarmed, helpless and far too deep beneath the earth for their screams to ever be heard.

She searched desperately for something else to think about, something to distract herself from these awful thoughts.

What she found was Josh Larsh.

Josh had been her first boyfriend and her high school sweetheart up until the end of their senior year. There was no big drama, no cheating or lying or backstabbing. They merely grew up and began to drift apart. For almost four years they had dated, ever since the summer before her freshman year, and for most of those four years, she was absolutely certain that she was in love with him.

At first, breaking up with him had seemed like the right thing to do. They were both growing up. They had begun to go their own ways in life. They both had changed, as people so often did. The world did not end that day. Life went on. But Josh had been more than an impetuous relationship. He was four years of her life and her first of so many things. He was her first kiss. And two years later, he was the first man she gave herself to, the first to ever see her naked, the first to make her feel not just like a pretty girl, but like a beautiful woman. He was the first to whisper, “I love you,” in her ear. Her first valentine. Her first *love.* She loved him back then, so much, and still did.

But by the time she realized that she still wanted to spend her life with him, he had already moved on. And he left her behind. He left her all alone.

She did not hate him. She did not resent him for moving on without her. She still talked to him occasionally, in fact. He still lived in Briar Hills. He attended school right here, studying biology. He was also a manager at Blockbuster Video.

He was also married now.

It broke her heart each time she saw him.

And she was terrified of being hurt like that again. This was the real reason she chose the men in her life the way she did. She intentionally kept company with guys she knew she'd never want to marry. It held the crushing loneliness at bay while preventing her from falling into the kind of love that once shattered her poor heart while she waited for the next Josh to come along, knowing all the while that there might never be one.

And then Albert came along. Albert reminded her a lot of Josh, really. He had the same charming nature, even the same friendly grin. And she could see early on that he loved Brandy with all his heart. And Brandy looked at him the way she remembered looking at Josh.

But there was so much more to Albert than there had ever been to Josh. There was *this* place. When they sat her down that night and first told her the story of how they really got together, about Albert's box and Brandy's key and the incredible journey they shared, Nicole realized that Brandy had found much more than her prince charming. She found her whole fairy tale. She found the sort of thing Nicole had always fantasized about.

That was precisely the reason she was here tonight, to live the adventure of a lifetime, the way Brandy once did, for just a glimpse of a perfect romance story.

But it wasn't really very romantic. It was cold and terrifying and unforgiving. It wasn't at all like she'd imagined.

And there was no prince to sweep her off her feet.

All she had was Earl.

She had never loved Earl. She felt nothing for Earl but mild physical attraction. When she came to stay with Albert and Brandy two nights ago, the tears in her eyes were never for him. Those tears were for herself, for how low she had sunk. She was still mourning the happiness she'd lost when she and Josh went their separate ways.

The only reason she ever chose Earl was because she needed someone as impossible for her to fall in love with as Albert was perfect for Brandy.

And that was something she could never tell anyone.

Ahead of her, Albert and Brandy abruptly stopped, tearing her out of her thoughts.

"What is it?"

For a moment, neither of them answered. They looked at each other curiously, contemplating the feeling that had passed through them.

"I feel strange," Albert said.

"Yeah." Brandy looked back at Nicole, her brow furrowed in curious contemplation. "Strange."

"Sort of…" Albert was not sure how to put it.

"*Alone,*" Brandy said at last.

"Yeah." That was the word Albert had been looking for. "I feel very alone."

"What does it mean?" Nicole asked.

Albert shrugged. Once again, he had no idea.

They started walking again. Nicole's thoughts were now scattered. She had not felt a thing, but then again, she was not psychic like her friends apparently were. She considered what they told her about feeling very alone. Somehow that was extremely unsettling to her.

Chapter 39

Olivia felt it too, that deep, odd sense that she had suddenly been abandoned, as though something that had been with her, or perhaps inside her, was suddenly gone. She stared down at the floor, feeling somehow more vulnerable than before. She was suddenly and inexplicably sad.

Neither Wayne nor Andrea seemed to feel it. They both walked on in front of her, both of them looking straight into the darkness ahead of them. They appeared tired and a little apprehensive, but not at all distracted from the yellow line on the wall.

Perhaps it was nothing. Perhaps it was just some kind of mood swing, brought on by her weariness and the stress of these past two days. But her thoughts drifted back to the Sentinel Queen and the sad, weary song that she sang over her dying son…

They were approaching the end of the passage and some sort of chamber.

Wayne felt tense as they emerged into the open darkness. He expected to find more hounds, but instead he found himself looking out over some kind of artificial lake.

"Where are we?" Andrea asked.

Wayne's first thought was of the fountain where he, Albert, Brandy and Nicole first encountered the Sentinel Queen. This was likely a part of whatever served as plumbing here inside the Temple of the Blind.

Something splashed into the water nearby and the three of them froze.

"There's something in here!" Olivia whispered.

"This place just keeps getting better," Wayne groaned.

There was another splash, this one from a much greater distance, perhaps from the other side of the room.

Wayne glanced at the wall, at Albert's yellow line, and cautiously began to move in that direction.

Another splash. Then another.

He could be wrong, but Wayne did not think that a single creature was making all this noise. There seemed to be many of them.

If only he could light up the entire chamber somehow. What would he see?

"What do we do?" Andrea asked.

"We keep moving," Wayne decided, shining his light onto the wall and the chalk line that was drawn there. "That's why we're here."

As long as that line was still visible, he could remain confident that the others had managed to pass through here safely. Given that, there was no reason to jump to the conclusion that they were in any immediate danger.

Keeping as close to the wall and as far from the water as possible, the three of them hurriedly followed the line deeper into the room. More splashing rose from the water's edge as something struck the surface ahead of them again and again. But nothing approached them. Nothing attacked them.

Albert's line went past one passage after another, not bothering to flee from this chamber, which reinforced Wayne's hypothesis that Albert hadn't felt overly threatened when he was here.

Wayne wished he had some way of communicating with Albert. He'd give anything to know what he had learned about this place.

"I can't see them," Andrea whispered. "What are they?"

"Who knows," Wayne replied. "But they're running away from us." Just like Albert, he was reminded of frogs leaping into a pond well ahead of approaching feet. Whatever was in here with them, they appeared to be shy. And that was always a good thing.

"You think they'll leave us alone?"

"They might," replied Wayne. "Let's try not to get too close."

A stone bridge appeared from the darkness and led out over the water. As soon as they were abreast of it, Albert's yellow line abruptly ended.

"Where'd it go?" Andrea asked. She shined her flashlight around, frightened. In her mind's eye, she could see something lunging out of the water and snatching Albert away, chalk and all.

"Relax," Wayne assured her. "They probably crossed the bridge. I'm sure the yellow line continues on the other side."

But Andrea found it hard to relax. She looked out over the shadowy water and wondered what unthinkable horrors could dwell deep down in the depths.

"Come on," Wayne said and started toward the bridge. "Let's see what's over there."

Chapter 40

Almost an hour had passed since Albert, Brandy and Nicole left the reservoir and fled the unseen stalker. In that time, they had not heard a single hound. Nor did they return to their territory. In fact, they saw nothing but empty passageways stretching on and on into the darkness. They had not even seen their own chalk line in a long time. It was difficult to tell if they were gaining ground or losing it.

What they *had* found was more hills. Currently, they were descending, sinking deeper and deeper into the earth. They had no way of gauging how high or low they were, but Albert thought the hill must have taken them down at least four or five stories before finally leveling out. It was about halfway down this hill that the blue chalk ran out and Albert switched to purple.

That was another four sticks gone. He hoped the rest of the

chalk lasted long enough for them to reach the exit.

At the bottom of the hill, the tunnel merged with two others, all three joining into a single path, and the tunnel he chose led to yet another steep descent, taking them even lower into the labyrinth. There were no intersections, but unlike the other hills, this one began to turn as they descended, twisting to the right, so that they were spiraling down into the mysterious darkness. When they finally reached the bottom of the hill, the floor leveled off and they were greeted with another six-way intersection.

He chose the first passage to his left and began to follow it.

They had taken less than a dozen steps into this newest passage when the Caggo suddenly shrieked somewhere in the labyrinth, its terrible voice freezing them in their tracks.

It was closer than it was the first time they heard it. Albert tried to tell which direction it was coming from, but it was impossible to tell in these twisting corridors.

Brandy and Nicole had each grabbed onto Albert's arms when the shriek began, and they clung to him long after it had quieted.

"*God*, I hate that," Albert growled when he was able to catch his breath again. He wasn't sure how many more of those his poor heart could take.

"I really hope we find the way out soon," Nicole whimpered. "I really don't want to meet that thing."

"Definitely," agreed Brandy.

They pushed on, past one intersection and then another. He glanced down each of these other tunnels as they passed and in the second he spied a yellow line leading away into the darkness. They had crossed their own path again. And an old line, at that.

Hours ago, they had crossed that same intersection. He could have chosen to turn right instead of left, and he would have been in the same place he was now, after all the walking they had done.

The thought was terribly discouraging.

The tunnel forked ahead of them and Albert chose left as the Caggo's shriek filled the labyrinth once again, its voice seeming to drift right through the solid stone and into their very souls.

Chapter 41

Wayne stood frozen in the empty corridor as Olivia clung to his arm and Andrea forced down the scream that was struggling up from inside her.

"What the living hell was *that?*" Wayne stammered as the still silence of the labyrinth returned. The first time they heard it, they had been startled, frightened so badly they had been unable to push forward for a moment. It had sounded almost human, and Wayne was almost sick with the fear that it had been the voice of a woman, either Brandy or Nicole, suffering some unimaginable fate elsewhere in the tunnels, but this time he was certain that it was not them. No amount of pain or terror could make a human being sound like that.

"I'm scared, guys," Andrea said. She was scanning the tunnel behind them, half expecting the thing that had made the noise to come barreling out of the shadows after them.

"It'd probably be weird if you weren't," Wayne said, starting forward again. "That was terrifying."

Olivia followed reluctantly. "How much farther ahead do you think they are?" she asked.

"I don't know," Wayne confessed. "Probably a long ways."

Ahead of them, the passage broke off in three directions. Down one of them, the yellow line had been drawn on both walls, indicating a dead end. That was a little bit closer. And every little bit helped.

"I don't like this," Andrea groaned. She swung her light back and forth, afraid of the darkness on either side of her. "I feel like I'm going to puke."

"It'll be okay," Olivia assured her. "It can't be worse than what we've already been through."

"What *you've* already been through. Not me. If I see a zombie down here I'm going to pee myself."

Olivia gave her a reassuring smile. "That's okay," she said. "Me too."

Andrea giggled in spite of her fear.

"The zombies weren't so bad, really," Wayne said. "They were kind of fragile. It was the *horde* part that was freaking scary. It was like *Dawn of the Dead* out there."

Olivia shuddered at the memory. She wouldn't be surprised if she had nightmares every night for the rest of her life after that experience.

"You guys are like action heroes now. You know that, right?"

Wayne laughed. "I don't really remember it that way. I remember a lot of running and screaming."

"That's right," agreed Olivia. "I think I cried through the whole thing."

"I don't care," Andrea said. "I'm just glad you guys are with me."

Olivia reached out and squeezed her hand.

"Let's just hope we can find Albert before whatever made that noise finds us. If I have to fight another monster, I'd rather there be six of us instead of three."

They pushed on, ever deeper into the darkness, their lights swinging back and forth, paranoid that whatever made that dreadful noise would lunge from the shadows at any moment.

Albert's yellow line led them left and then right and then right again, the endless passages unfolding from the gloom ahead of them until at last they stepped out of the tunnel and onto a stone bridge. Around them, the same chasm they'd crossed before they reached the lake of mud stretched into a dark oblivion. More bridges crossed over and below them and on each side, each one identical to the next.

Andrea peered down into the infinite darkness beneath them. This place was so *big*.

"It's enormous," said Olivia. "Impossible. We'll never find our way through here."

Wayne was staring up at the bridges above him. "I wonder how many times the labyrinth crosses."

Olivia understood what he was thinking. "If we stay here long enough, do you think we'll see the others?"

"Maybe," Wayne said, looking out into the impossible darkness. "But we still wouldn't have any quick way of reaching them. We'd still have to follow the same chalk line to get to them." And there was also whatever made that scream. He didn't want to be here in plain sight if *that* should wander out into this chasm. "We'd be better off to keep moving, keep closing the gap."

Olivia nodded. He was right, of course. If they were ever going to catch them, they'd have to keep moving.

But looking around at the enormity of the Temple of the Blind, it was difficult to believe they would ever find their way out again.

Chapter 42

Albert chose right at what felt like the thousandth four-way intersection and led his companions down another steep hill that seemed to go on for half a mile before finally leveling off. A short while later, he finally heard the hounds again.

"I hate those things," Brandy grumbled.

Albert felt a pang in his heart for her. She was scared, and rightly so. The hounds had turned out to be significantly more deadly than he'd ever imagined. And he had a bad feeling about those terrifying shrieks they'd heard. If that was really the voice of the Caggo, and there was no reason to doubt that it was, what was the purpose of those shrieks? Was it a warning? A battle cry of some sort? A simple expression of rage or bloodlust? It wasn't a very stealthy thing to do, whatever it was. It must have known that such a cry would spook its prey. So why risk frightening them away?

Something wasn't right.

Ahead of them, the passage forked. Albert realized that the noise of the hounds was originating from somewhere down the right corridor. He still felt a strong compulsion to go toward the hounds, and he followed this feeling, hoping it would lead them out of here before the Caggo found them.

Neither Nicole nor Brandy argued with his decision. At least they had a plan. It was better than turning blindly down one passage after another until they stumbled across either the exit or the Caggo. (More likely it would be the latter.)

And besides, it wasn't as if the hounds were an immediate threat. Their sunken passageways kept them safely out of reach. And it didn't seem likely that this was something that would change.

The noise grew steadily louder as they walked, and soon they found themselves at another intersection. Again, the hounds were to the right. Albert continued to follow his ears and the noise continued to grow louder.

Now that he knew what the sound was, he could hardly help associating it with the sound of sharpening knives, making it seem all the more menacing.

At last, the tunnel ended and they found themselves on a wide ledge overlooking an enormous blackness. The noise of the hounds was coming from somewhere below them in the chamber.

Albert walked out toward the edge and shined his light down. He could just see the floor directly below them, but nothing more.

"What is this place?" asked Brandy.

There was a corner just visible on their right but the rest of the room was lost in the darkness. For all they knew, the room might have been as big as the City of the Blind, literally thousands of feet across the blackness.

"Let's see how far this ledge goes," Albert said, returning to the mouth of the passage they'd just exited and pressing the chalk to the wall again. They went left, keeping the purple line on that side as he had always done, and began to circle the room.

Another passageway led back into the labyrinth about forty feet beyond the one from which they had entered, and another about forty feet beyond that one. As they walked, they found dozens more. The room was as enormous as any other they had encountered, perhaps even as large as the City of the Blind, Albert thought, though it was impossible to know for sure. It had four corners, but whether it was square or rectangular, none of them could say. It was simply too big and their visibility was far too short to allow any real estimate.

Below them, the hounds droned on, the noise echoing across the room. There were many more here than there had been in the last room, dozens of them, by the sound of it, and all of them considerably more agitated than the others. It was distracting.

By the time they camc all the way around to their purple line again, Albert had begun to realize that there was something in the middle of the chamber, something big, something *significant.* He could not see it, but it was there. He could almost *feel* it.

"I think we need to get down there," he said, staring down into the darkness where the hounds made their eerie noise.

"How?" asked Nicole, peering over the ledge. It was too far down to jump.

He pressed the chalk to the wall and began a second line that led to the next passage. "Some of these led down," he recalled. "Maybe one of them will take us where we need to be."

Chapter 43

Wayne stopped as he approached the next intersection and stared at the walls of the adjoining tunnel. A chalk line had been drawn along the wall, just as before, but this line was purple instead of yellow.

"What does it mean?" asked Andrea.

"It means they ran out of the yellow chalk," replied Olivia.

Wayne turned and looked right. Facing this way, the blue line was on the left wall. If Albert had remained consistent, this meant that this was the direction they had gone. "It means that this path is fresher than the yellow path. Maybe a *lot* fresher."

"Do you think we're close?" asked Andrea.

"I hope so." Wayne turned and started down this tunnel, his pace quickened. With any luck, they would see flashlight beams before they saw whatever had made that terrible noise.

Chapter 44

Albert followed his ears. By the time they had reached the bottom of the slope that led away from the mysterious chamber, the roar of the hounds had diminished into a muffled hum. It was the sound of death, literally the sound of thousands of razor-like blades slashing together, perpetually ready to rend the flesh from his bones at any opportunity, a biological killing machine like nothing he had ever imagined before, but it was also the sound of their escape. The Keeper told them when they first entered the labyrinth that they would know what they were looking for when they saw it, and Albert felt that he had just seen it…although he had actually "seen" very little of anything in the inky darkness of that enormous chamber. It simply *felt* right somehow.

When they reached the first intersection, Albert peered

down each path with his flashlight, listening. Although it was difficult to tell, it seemed that the roar was a little louder from the left tunnel than from the right.

For several more minutes, he made his way toward the sound. The thin, purple line followed. He was already on his second stick of purple. If this wasn't the end, they would soon be marking the way with red. And red was the last color in the tube. After that was gone, they were out of luck.

Albert expected the tunnel to begin sloping upward again, taking them not onto the lower level, but right back up to where they were before, forcing them to start again. But luck was with them for the moment. When the tunnel ended, they found themselves looking into the same darkness, but from a lower perspective.

The layout of the lower level was similar to that of the one above. Spaced about forty feet apart were more passages leading back into the mysterious depths of the labyrinth. They were standing on a walkway that appeared to circle around the chamber, just like the one above it, but it was much wider. Albert walked out to the edge of this walkway and stared into the immense darkness. The hounds were concentrated some distance away, perhaps crowding around whatever awaited them at the center. Between here and there were large, square platforms arranged in a vast grid and connected by frightfully narrow beams of stone. These beams stretched between each platform and over the ominously scarred floor six feet below it. It was easy to see that once the hounds caught their scent and began to crowd the spaces beneath them, the consequences of a misstep would become considerably grim.

More and more, he grew certain that this was where they needed to be. Something profoundly significant awaited them out there. It was written in the very design of the room, in the courage required to cross those treacherous stone beams and risk falling to the hounds. But there was also that strange sensation he felt as he gazed out into the darkness. This room called to him, beckoned him, but not in the same way that the meadow called out to him. This was different somehow. It was far less menacing.

Without discussing it, he stepped out onto the first beam. It wasn't all that difficult a feat. The beam was a good twelve inches wide, plenty of room to plant both his feet and stand steady, but it was more than narrow enough to play with his head. And once the hounds found them, it would no doubt seem even narrower. It was like the difference between walking on a board that was lying on the ground and walking the same board suspended over a twenty-story drop. The fear of falling would work against them, making it harder to keep their balance. But the beam was plenty sturdy enough to hold his weight and it wasn't a great distance between each platform. As long as they remained cautious and calm, they would be perfectly safe.

Knowing this, however, would not necessarily make it any easier.

Brandy and Nicole followed silently, their flashlights and their eyes mostly fixed on the beam at their feet as they concentrated on keeping their balance, but they frequently glanced around them at the darkened room as well, constantly expecting something to lunge out at them.

Albert wondered what the hounds were so worked up about. Was there something about the labyrinth's exit that drew their attention? Did they feel some kind of desire to leave this dungeon of a world? He wouldn't blame them if they did.

But then again, he still had no proof that they were actually at the exit. For all he knew, this could be their mating grounds.

Yet he couldn't stop feeling that this place was extremely significant.

"What's even the point of this?" Brandy asked, practically shouting into his ear to be heard. "Why build something like this?"

Albert shrugged. "Maybe just to unnerve us," he suggested. "One last attempt to make us turn back."

"You'd think they'd give up on that by now."

"They *are* persistent."

They reached the first platform and crossed it to the next stone beam. As they made their way across to the second platform, a hound emerged from the darkness, charging toward them, snarling and snapping its jaws, its two tails slashing violently back and forth. It passed harmlessly beneath their feet, and yet each of them had frozen at the sight, half-sure that the fragile stone walkway on which they stood would suddenly crumble and drop them screaming to a bloody death. But the hound merely skidded to a halt a few yards away and whipped itself around, sniffing at the air in confusion.

As a second hound appeared from the same direction as the first, Albert stood watching them for a moment. He was still in awe of them. They were such *fascinating* creatures. Not even in movies had he ever seen anything to rival them. Their features were so different from that of any other animal that they could have been utterly alien. And in a way, he supposed they were.

Satisfied that they were safely above the reach of the hounds, Nicole crept forward and grasped Brandy's arm. She didn't like these things at all. They couldn't possibly be real, could they? At the very least they could not be natural. Had somebody actually bred these things? Where else could creatures like these have come from?

There were four of them now, crowding together and snarling at each other, and a fifth was creeping toward them from the far right, a smaller one. It moved slowly, noticeably cautious of the larger members of its pack, but every bit as lethal if it could only reach its prey.

"I've never seen anything like it," Nicole said, raising her voice to a yell to be heard over all the noise beneath them.

"I'll bet no one has," Albert returned. Then, without raising his voice enough to be heard, he added, "No one *alive*." He remembered the bone fragments he'd found in the room with the wounded sentinels the previous year, way back near the very beginning of all this. The Sentinel Queen said that people like Beverly Bridger and Wendell Gilbert had been drawn to the temple for centuries, people sensitive to psychic energies and lured by whatever called out to them from the far side of this labyrinth. Even though they could not possibly have understood what they were being drawn to, they came, and they all died for their trouble. Those bones were all that remained of at least one group of unfortunate adventurers. He shivered to think what they must have suffered when they discovered these monstrosities waiting for them in the temple's dark tunnels.

Brandy had begun to wish that she had never seen these things in the first place. They were terrifying, considerably worse than anything she had ever imagined. She hated to think what would happen if all these things ever found a way out of the labyrinth and back to Briar Hills. The carnage would be unthinkable.

Albert lifted his light and probed the darkness ahead of them. They were still not close enough to see what stood at the center of the chamber, but he was certain there was *something*. He could almost imagine that he saw a shadow in the blackness, a giant mass of some sort.

Nudged by Brandy, he forced his attention forward again and continued across the beam and over the hounds to the next platform and then on to the next beam. Together, the three of them made their way deeper into the chamber, marveling at the sheer scale of it. And just when it seemed that the room could not possibly be so big, that they must have made some kind of mistake, something materialized from the gloom.

At first, Albert thought it was the far wall, that he had crossed all the way to the other side without finding anything, but it was not the far wall. It was some kind of enormous structure.

The hounds were extremely agitated now. More and more rushed out of the darkness, snarling and brandishing their razor-sharp scales at each other. Albert lost count, but there were at least a dozen of them darting around the platforms and squabbling among themselves. And they were growing increasingly violent.

As he watched, two of the largest ones turned on each other and launched into a vicious brawl that carried them both back out into the darkness beyond his sight.

There were so many of them. What were they all doing here? Why were they drawn to this chamber of all places? It did not smell foul in here, neither of animal waste nor of the rotting carcasses of their prey. There was also no apparent water source.

A shape on the floor caught his attention and he held his flashlight on it for a few seconds before realizing that it was a dead hound, freshly killed and still bleeding. Several others were swarming over the carcass, tearing it apart, devouring it.

It was disturbingly easy to imagine one of their bodies in the unfortunate beast's place.

With a shudder, Albert tore his eyes from the ghastly scene below and shined his light up at the structure before them. The hounds were concentrated there. More deadly scuffles broke out beneath them. A spray of blood spurted upward as two of the creatures collided and the sight of the crimson spray, caught for a moment in his flashlight's beam, was chillingly surreal.

Several more carcasses littered the floor beneath the beams now. Each one was being slowly picked apart, cannibalized by their scavenging pack mates.

This was not typical behavior for these beasts. If it was, they would have killed themselves out long ago. And the lack of any smell of decay told him that the only carcasses in here were still very fresh. Something had them seriously worked up. Given that they didn't seem to notice the three intruders making their way toward the middle of the room until they were almost on top of them, he doubted it was them.

Something had arrived here before them, Albert realized, something that almost certainly crossed these same platforms on its way to the same mysterious structure. He stared up at it.

Anything could be up there, unseen, watching them.

He stepped onto the final platform and scanned the area in front of him with his light. One last stone beam waited to be crossed, beyond which was not a square platform, like the one on which he was standing, but a single, large segment of floor that stretched beyond his sight in both directions. Six feet beyond the end of the stone beam was a vertical rise, six feet tall, the same as the distance between them and the floor of the hounds' territory. Above that was another six-foot run leading to another six-foot rise and so on into the darkness, like giant steps.

Though he could not see the whole structure, it resembled an enormous pyramid standing in the middle of the room. It appeared that they would have to climb up each level to reach the top.

And while they were climbing, what manner of monster might descend on them?

He was increasingly certain that this was where they were supposed to be, but he was also increasingly certain that they were not alone down here.

"Hey!" Nicole cried suddenly. "What's that?"

Albert's light slashed the darkness all around him, expecting to see a terrifying form lunging from the shadows. "Where?"

"Up there!"

He turned and saw that she was looking back toward the outer corner of the room. There, in the darkness, one of the upper passageways was glowing.

"The Caggo?" asked Brandy.

Nicole stared up at the illuminated passageway. It was growing brighter. "With a light?"

"No," Albert replied. He turned and hurried back across the beams, away from the suspicious structure and toward that light. He could feel the skin prickling at the back of his neck. Nicole was correct. It wasn't the Caggo. It wasn't the Keeper or the Sentinel Queen or her blind son. It was somebody with a flashlight. And although it seemed impossible, only one living person even knew that they were down here.

Chapter 45

Wayne stepped into the enormous chamber and stared down at the three lights that were shining in the vast sea of darkness below. Albert, Brandy and Nicole. For a moment he couldn't believe that he'd actually caught up. It had been so long a journey.

"We found them!" Olivia exclaimed.

He realized suddenly that he was never completely sure that he'd actually be able to catch up. Hours behind them, he was never quite able to fully quash the thought that they might already be gone from the labyrinth and beyond his reach somehow.

They were moving across the bottom of the chamber, toward the perimeter of the room. He could see the square platforms and the narrow beams they crossed in the glow of their flashlights and wondered what this place was.

"Albert?" he called as they reached the walkway that circled the room and began running toward him.

"Wayne?" It was difficult to hear over the roar of those damned hounds, but it was definitely Albert's voice.

"Oh my God!" Nicole's voice now, bright, thrilled. "You came back!"

"Are you guys all right?" Wayne shouted down at them.

"We're fine," Albert replied, but his flashlight darted toward the middle of the chamber for a moment, as if he expected something to be there. "You?"

Wayne looked down at his bandaged leg and arms. Where would he even begin? "I'm a little worse for the wear, but I'm okay."

"Who's with you?" asked Brandy as she stopped and squinted up at his light. "Did you find Olivia?"

"I did. She's right here."

"I'm fine," Olivia called down. "Thanks to Wayne."

"Thank God! We thought we lost you!"

Wayne was relieved to find them all safe. But he still hadn't caught up with them. Not yet. He turned and searched the ledge on which he was standing. There were no steps within view. "How do we get down there?"

"Follow the purple line," Albert instructed. "Should be to your left. We'll meet you in the middle."

He turned and shined his light toward the wall to his left. There were not one, but two purple lines. On the other side of the passage was only one and he realized that they must have circled the room once before exiting. It was little things like that, he realized, that were the only reason he was ever able to catch up.

"Hurry," Albert said, and there was something in his voice that Wayne didn't like. Something was wrong.

"Come on," he said, turning away from the chamber.

The three of them hurried into the next passage, chasing the chalk line for the last time.

Below them, Albert, Brandy and Nicole hurried back into the dark corridors of the labyrinth to meet them.

Chapter 46

"I thought I'd never catch you guys," Wayne said as the two groups approached each other in the narrow passage.

"We didn't even know you were trying," Albert replied.

"We would've walked slower if we'd known," offered Nicole.

As they drew close enough to see more of each other than the blinding glare of their flashlights, Wayne realized that Brandy and Nicole were covering themselves, as though the sight of other people in the labyrinth had suddenly rekindled their modesty. The last time he saw them, they stood before him unflinchingly, as if standing naked in front of him was something they'd done every day of their lives, as natural as breathing. When he looked back at Olivia and Andrea he saw that they were doing the same and nearly laughed. He supposed he couldn't blame them. If he hadn't been through so much hell tonight, he might have done the same thing. But his nudity was the last thing he cared about right now.

"Glasses," Albert observed. "That must've made the emotion rooms easier."

"A little," Wayne admitted. "But I'm not quite as blind as your girlfriend."

"Well we can't *all* achieve perfection," quipped Brandy as she pressed her exposed body against Albert's back and took her first good look at Wayne from over his shoulder. "My god…" she sighed. "What *happened* to you?"

"I *told* you I was a little worse for the wear."

"'Worse for the wear'? You look like you escaped from an intensive care unit." She was staring at the bandages on his arms and leg. Both were stained black with dirt and blood. After a moment, her eyes turned to Olivia and she saw the bandages that were beginning to come loose from her shoulder and arm. "And you too?"

"We had a little trouble getting out of the Wood," Wayne explained.

"I'm glad you're in one piece," Nicole said. Then she added, "You *are* still in one piece, aren't you? You're not, like, holding your arm on with duct tape or anything, are you?"

Wayne chuckled. "No, I'm definitely still in one piece." Then he thought of the bite mark on his arm and the butchered flesh of his leg and added, "Well, actually, I might be missing a few *little* pieces here and there. But I'm pretty sure I've still got everything I *need*."

"What the fuck *happened* to you?" blurted Brandy.

"Long story," Wayne replied. He looked from Albert to Brandy to Nicole. "You guys don't look like you've taken a scratch."

"Well our feet are a little raw," Albert replied, "but otherwise we're fine."

"I sympathize."

Finally shrugging off her freshly renewed modesty, Nicole stepped around Albert and Brandy and hugged Wayne fiercely. "I'm just glad we found you," she told him. "We were worried." She turned her eyes to Olivia next. "And I really thought we'd lost *you*."

Olivia smiled shyly. "I'm a trooper."

"I'll say," Nicole laughed. "Seriously, what happened to you guys?"

"Which part?" Wayne asked. "The three-story corpse monster, the horde of zombies or the hound that almost took my leg off?"

"Jesus Christ!" Albert exclaimed.

"Corpse monster?" Brandy asked.

"Zombies?" stammered Nicole.

Olivia nodded. "He's *so* not joking."

"Okay, that's not fair!" Albert exclaimed. "You got to fight *zombies*? We've just been walking in circles all night."

Wayne shook his head and laughed.

It was now that Albert turned his light on the other girl, the one who had been standing behind Wayne as if hiding from them. For a moment he just stared at her, surprised. "Andrea?"

Andrea smiled shyly and lifted her hand in a small, shy wave that didn't reveal her covered breasts.

"You're the one who gave me the envelope."

She nodded and bit her lip.

"She was waiting for us when we got out of Gilbert House," Wayne explained. "Said a *mysterious voice* told her to wait for us and that she had to come along."

"A mysterious voice?" Albert asked, looking at her.

Andrea nodded again. She stood there without speaking, one arm across her small breasts, her other hand pressed between her thighs. Wayne could have laughed. She'd been unable to shut her mouth before and now she was like a shy little girl, too afraid to speak.

"She gave us a ride and got us some food and first aid," Wayne explained. We probably wouldn't have made it back here without her."

"Wow," Brandy said. "Your guardian angel?"

"I think so," Olivia replied.

Andrea blushed a little, but still could not seem to find any words.

"Olivia just refused to go home," Wayne added, looking down at her. "She insisted on coming. Threatened me if I tried to leave her behind, actually."

"I couldn't just go home," she said, as if that explained everything.

Albert's eyes fell on her and for a moment the realization of her nudity sent an odd sense of vertigo through him. It was like a reminder of how completely bizarre all this really was.

Wayne looked past Albert at the tunnels behind him. "Did you find anything?"

"We don't know," said Albert. Distracted by two more lovely naked bodies, he had to consciously focus himself to keep from becoming distracted. "I think so. That place back there feels pretty important. I think it *might* be the way out. Did the Keeper talk to you guys?"

Wayne looked at him, puzzled. "Keeper?"

"I'll take that as a no," Albert said, and then described their strange encounter with the hideous creature at the entrance to the labyrinth.

As he spoke, Brandy and Nicole sat down, resting their weary feet. Olivia and Andrea joined them, and then Wayne and Albert, realizing that they were the only ones standing, also sat.

"We didn't see anything like that," Wayne said when Albert had finished.

“That’s odd,” said Albert. “It seemed to want us to know what was down here.”

“Did you see the Caggo?” Olivia asked. The anxiousness in her voice was perfectly clear. She didn’t like the idea of finding more monsters down here. She had already seen far more than her share of murderous beasts for one night.

“We haven’t,” Albert replied. “But I think there may be something in that room. The hounds have been gathering in there. It might be waiting at the top of that tower.”

“Tower?” This came from Andrea, who was still hiding her naked body behind Wayne’s sizeable bulk.

Albert looked at her, confused. “Yeah. Or some kind of structure, anyway.” He wasn’t sure what made him call it a tower. He hadn’t seen enough of it to tell exactly what it was, but it had looked more like a pyramid than a tower. “Why?”

“The voice told me something,” she explained. She looked at Wayne, saw the understanding on his face, and then repeated what she told him in the car earlier, the part of the mysterious voice’s instructions that she hadn’t understood. “‘Atop the tower, the secret is blood.’ That’s what it said to me.”

“Oh good,” grumbled Nicole. “That doesn’t sound at all ominous.”

Albert ignored her. He stared at Andrea for a moment. It was still so surreal. She was the same girl who had appeared at his door so many hours ago, a manila envelope in her hand, but she looked so strange now, naked but for all the jewelry she wore, her pigtails now hanging dirty and limp over her shoulders. "Tell me about this voice," he said.

Andrea looked at Wayne for a moment, as if to ask if it was all right, and then began to tell her story, beginning with her leaving Albert and Brandy's apartment building that previous afternoon.

"So that was *you* in the woods," Albert marveled when she was done.

"You really didn't see me?" she asked.

"I didn't see anything. It just felt weird out there." He remembered standing there in the woods, resting his hand on the trunk of a tree. He'd felt as if something was there, but he'd been unable to see anything at all.

"That's so weird. You were almost standing on top of me."

"That *is* weird," Albert agreed.

"Maybe the Sentinel Queen did it," Nicole suggested. "She said that psychic minds are susceptible to suggestion. Maybe she hid her from you."

"She acted like she didn't know how Andrea got mixed up in all this, though," Wayne said.

"Maybe she was lying," Nicole speculated.

"Or maybe it was someone else," suggested Brandy. "Like the owner of that voice she was talking about. Maybe they were trying to protect her."

"But I wouldn't have hurt her," Albert said, looking at her, his eyes drawn to the rings in her eyebrow and nose. In the glow of the flashlights, her jewelry sparkled, catching his eye every time he glanced in her direction.

"Maybe it wasn't you she was being protected from," Wayne reasoned. "Maybe it was Gilbert House."

Albert looked at him for a moment, considering, then he turned his eyes on Andrea again. "That's a good point. If I'd seen her, I wouldn't have been mad or anything… I mean, I absolutely understand her curiosity. So I probably wouldn't have stopped her from coming with us."

Andrea stared back at Albert. If he'd seen her, would she have gone inside with them? Would she have died in there? A shiver ran through her body as she considered these terrible things.

"Or maybe she needed to stay put so she'd be there when we got out," offered Olivia. "I don't know what we'd have done without her."

Wayne nodded. "That's right."

"I'm sure there was some reason for it," Brandy decided. "And she's here now. She's one of us."

"I think so," Wayne agreed.

"Well, if Andrea's right, we need to get to the top of that tower," decided Albert. "And that might mean getting past the Caggo."

"Do you really think he's in there?" Brandy asked.

"I don't know. Like I said before, something had those hounds worked up before we even got there. They seemed particularly interested in the area around the tower. I'm thinking it's up there waiting for us. It even makes a little bit of sense why it never found us in the labyrinth in all the time we've been down here. Apparently, it decided to wait us out at the exit instead."

"Then what are we going to do?" Olivia asked. She did not like the idea of facing yet another monster.

"I honestly can't tell you," Albert confessed. "But we can't avoid it. We have to believe that there's a way. Why would the Sentinel Queen send us here if she knew we didn't stand a chance?"

"So, what?" asked Nicole. "We just keep our fingers crossed that we live through it?"

Albert shrugged. That was pretty much his plan. What else was there to do? Hadn't blind faith been a significant factor in getting them this far?

Wayne nodded. "I agree. We have to try it. But first I need to tell you something. I don't know what's going on here any more than you do, but I ran into someone who claimed the Sentinel Queen was lying to us all."

Albert nodded. "Sounds like something we should hear about."

"Tell us everything," Nicole pleaded. "I want to hear what

happened to you."

Albert agreed. "Any little detail could turn out to be important."

Chapter 47

Wayne told them his amazing story, beginning with his departure in the City of the Blind and his private conversation with the Sentinel Queen. He told them about the imaginary horrors of what she'd called "Road Beneath the Wood" and of the very *real* horrors that prowled the vast forest beyond the final seal of that tunnel. He told them of the mysterious old man and the disturbing accusations he made about the Sentinel Queen. He described to them how he found Olivia in the forest and how they fled for their lives from the towering corpse monster. He told them of their near-demise in the clutches of the dead and their harrowing escape through the dark hallways of Gilbert House. He told them of their journey back through the Temple of the Blind and the Sentinel Queen's response to the old man's words. Finally, he told them of his own trek through the labyrinth, following Albert's chalk lines and hoping he wasn't too late to help.

"That's incredible," Nicole marveled. She had visibly shuddered when he told them about the living corpses of the Wood and how they literally attempted to eat them alive. That would have been the end for her. In that situation, she would already have utterly lost her mind.

Brandy could find no words at all. She could not imagine surviving all those horrors. She was sure her heart would have burst long before reaching the safety of Gilbert House's cellar door.

"That old man," Albert said thoughtfully. He was still staring into the darkness that led back to the tower, still half expecting the Caggo to come rushing out at them, but he'd listened intently to every word of Wayne's story. "The devil?"

"I don't know," Wayne responded. "The Sentinel Queen seemed to think so, but I don't know if I believe her. It seemed pretty hard to swallow. *One* of them was obviously lying."

"Maybe both," Albert said, standing up. The others all took his lead and rose to their feet as well.

"Do you think we should turn back?" asked Brandy. "Just go home? What if that old man was telling the truth?"

"What if he wasn't?" Albert said. "I don't know if I can just turn back now. We've come so far."

Wayne shook his head. "I honestly don't know who to

trust. But I agree. We can't just turn back now. That Caggo probably won't let us out, first of all, and at least down here we're in the open. We've got room to fight."

Albert thought about the narrow path of platforms and stone beams leading out to the tower. He supposed it was still better than encountering the monster in a dead end corridor in the labyrinth where their backs were literally against a wall, but it was definitely not an *ideal* place to defend themselves.

"So what's the plan?" asked Brandy.

Albert began to walk. "The tower is in the middle of that room. We have to cross over the hounds. Then I guess we climb."

"*We* could go," Wayne told Albert as he walked beside him. "Just the two of us. They could wait for us here."

"No way!" Andrea exclaimed suddenly from behind them. "I want to go."

"We stay together," Brandy agreed.

"Definitely," insisted Nicole. "There's no way I'm staying behind."

"We're a team," added Andrea. "Remember?"

"Okay then," Wayne relented. "All together then."

Albert stared into the darkness ahead. "That tower is our way out of this damn labyrinth. I'm sure of it. I don't think it's a coincidence that you happened to find us when you did."

"You think someone intended for us to meet up in that

room?" Wayne asked. "Who? Seems like the Sentinel Queen would prefer to keep us apart."

"That old man, probably," Nicole guessed.

"Or the owner of Andrea's mysterious voice," Albert suggested. "She's the one with the key. That clue about the blood atop the tower… That'll probably be important."

The six of them emerged from the passage and Albert stared out into the black chamber, unable to stop wondering if the Caggo was really out there somewhere, watching them from the cover of the temple's perfect darkness. "We need to stay together, but we can obviously only go one at a time. I'll take the lead. Maybe you should take the rear."

Wayne nodded. "Agreed."

"Olivia doesn't have a flashlight," Albert observed. To her, he said, "You stay close to somebody; don't get separated without a light."

Immediately, Andrea seized Olivia's hand and held tight.

Albert turned back to face the darkness again, steeling himself against the fear he felt boiling up inside him. "Let's go."

He stepped out onto the nearest beam and cautiously inched his way across. Brandy and Nicole followed close behind him and Olivia and Andrea behind them.

Beneath them, the hounds immediately erupted into a furious frenzy as they caught their scent, drowning out all other sounds around them.

Not being able to hear bothered Albert. He paused repeatedly and looked around, half expecting the Caggo to lurch from the darkness at any moment and tear him apart just as the thing in Gilbert House had torn apart that poor girl on the third floor.

He wished he knew what the thing was, how to protect himself from it. It seemed like such a stupid thing to do, intentionally approaching the tower where he had ample reason to believe a dangerous monster was hiding. But he didn't know what else to do. The Keeper had warned them of the Caggo, had cautioned them to stay well away from it for their own safety, but the creepy little creature had neglected to tell them what they should do if they found it guarding the labyrinth's only exit.

Quickly, he moved from one platform to the next, growing more and more anxious with every step he took and trying desperately to see in every direction at once.

Below him, the hounds grew angrier. Fights broke out more frequently among them. At one point, two of the beasts hurled themselves at each other with such force that a spray of hot blood spurted upward and spattered across Nicole's bare legs, wrenching a startled scream from her which was terrifyingly unexpected to her companions.

"Sorry," Nicole squealed as she bit her lip against the grotesque feel of the hound blood on her skin and covered her naked breasts against the stark stare of the four flashlights that were suddenly bearing down on her.

A moment later, the others turned away and she was relieved that her nude body was no longer the target for every light in the room but her own. The feel of the hound blood trickling down her calves felt awful, but she dared not tempt losing her balance by trying to reach down on this narrow walkway to wipe at it. She left it and bore the awful feeling until they reached the next platform. Only then did she take the time to kneel on the cold stone and try to wipe it away, and by then it had already begun to grow tacky.

Hopefully there would be somewhere to wash off on the other side of wherever that tower led them. She stood up again and fell in line behind Brandy, who was already following Albert across the next beam.

The hounds continued their awful racket beneath their feet, the noise of their gnashing blades filling the silent chamber. Wayne hated the sound. He hated the creatures. He felt none of the intrigue that fascinated Albert. He did not care where they came from or how rare they might be. He did not care that he might be among the first people since ancient times to see them and live to tell about it. They were not animals to him. They were monsters. The endless pain in his leg was all the proof he needed. One wrong step and the beasts would happily devour any one of them. He couldn't help but think that if he had a gun, he would happily put a bullet into each of their snarling heads.

Albert walked on, his eyes on the path before him. He was no longer thinking about the hounds. He was far more concerned with the Caggo. Was it perched somewhere atop the tower right now, watching them, biding its time, waiting for the perfect opportunity to strike? He hated feeling so helpless. If only he knew a little more about this monster. Was it blind and deaf, like the hounds? Or did it have a full range of lethal senses? Or even an extra sense of some sort? How fast could it run? How big was it? Did it use claws to bring down its prey or teeth? And most importantly, was it merely a dangerous animal, or was it sentient? The Keeper told them that killing was its only joy. Did that mean that the creature enjoyed the hunt, like a cat stalking a mouse, or that it was actually the act of murder that pleased it? The thought of the beast consciously causing pain and death for its own twisted enjoyment was chilling.

The tower again came into view and Albert's eyes drifted up into the darkness, half expecting to see the sinister eyeshine of something staring back at him from high above. It still didn't look like a tower, though. It still looked more like a pyramid. But why had he called it a tower back there? The word had just slipped out of his mouth. And if it hadn't, Andrea might not have remembered her message. He wondered if someone had made him do that, the way the Sentinel Queen had made him leave his car door unlocked the night he found the box.

Albert made his way across the last of the stone beams,

resisting the urge to hurry, forcing himself to ignore the ravenous horde snarling beneath his feet. The closer he came to the center of the room, the longer each perilous crossing seemed to take and the more worried he became that he (or someone he cared about, or perhaps all of them at once) was going to topple off the beam and into the unthinkable nightmare below.

But he stepped off the beam and onto the relative safety beyond without incident, and so did everyone else, leaving the hounds to fight among themselves. And yet, he felt no real relief as he stared up into the darkness that awaited them. Somewhere up there, he was certain, was something far worse than a hound.

Albert didn't look for steps or a ramp. He doubted there would be anything like that here. After all, they had been climbing these six-foot rises all night. They were located throughout the temple, usually in conjunction with the territory of the hounds, although not always. Though inconvenient, these were not impassable barriers for them or they would not be here now. And convenience was obviously not a factor in the Temple of the Blind's design.

Without discussing it—they could barely hear each other anyway—he climbed the first rise and then stood and walked to the next. Beside him, the others did the same and soon all six of them were scaling the side of the structure, slowly making their way upward.

After climbing only the first two sections, Albert could

make out a high wall standing at the top of the pyramid. Two more, and he caught sight of a narrow set of steps ascending the outside of the wall from left to right and he realized that this was probably the tower Andrea had mentioned. The pyramid-like section was only the base.

Again, he wondered how it was that he happened to call it a tower while talking to Wayne. Was it only a coincidence? He climbed up another level and forced the thought away. It was unimportant. Right now he needed to be concerned with reaching the top safely.

"I see stairs," Wayne said as he paused to catch his breath. He was a level below Albert, moving much slower than everyone else. Between his screaming leg and his weary muscles, it was becoming difficult to lift himself up to each level. By comparison, Brandy, Nicole and Olivia were already on the level above Albert and Andrea was already waiting for them on the next level. He was not surprised, since she was easily more suited to this task than the rest of them. She was the youngest, the lightest and the most rested.

"I see them, too," Albert replied.

"Wonder how high it goes."

Albert could not even speculate. For all he knew, they were at the very bottom of the temple and preparing to climb to the very top. If the chasm they saw was any indication, this labyrinth was unimaginably enormous. He wouldn't be surprised if those steps went on for miles.

"And what about that Caggo thing? Do you have a plan for dealing with it? Because I remember we didn't do so hot taking on the thing in Gilbert House."

Albert definitely remembered that. It didn't seem like a terribly good sign of things to come. "I don't," he confessed. "I don't even know what the hell it is."

Wayne nodded. He'd expected as much. He didn't have any ideas, either. How could he, when he didn't even know what they were up against? He could only trust that they would be capable of handling whatever it was when the time came. "And what about the Sentinel Queen's doorway? Have you decided what you're going to do about that?"

Another very good question. According to the Sentinel Queen, they were here to open some kind of door. But according to the old man Wayne met on his frightening side-journey, that doorway would only lead to some kind of apocalyptic doom. "Hopefully I'll know when I get there."

"Hopefully," agreed Wayne. He could not say one way or the other what to do about the doorway. And it didn't seem that important right now anyway. Right now their only concern was climbing the tower and not getting their heads ripped off by the Caggo.

He swept the empty room behind him with his light and then glanced up at the others. Albert was still standing on the next level, preparing to climb to the next, but the others had all climbed one higher. He had to pick up his pace. If they spread out too much, he was sure the Caggo would waste no time dropping out of the darkness and seizing one of them. His eyes specifically rose to Andrea, who was higher up than everyone else and all by herself. She was vulnerable there. He wanted to yell up to her and tell her to stay with the others.

But *she* wasn't the one in the most danger.

At that moment, the beast shrieked again, its terrible voice filling the chamber and drowning out even the constant roar of the hounds. It went on and on, warbling like the mad screams of the tortured damned, a sound that chilled them each to their very bones.

And it came not down from the tower above them, but *up*.

The Caggo was below them.

Chapter 48

Albert stood frozen, his hands gripping the ledge above. If the Caggo was below them, then it wasn't the girls who were in the most danger. He turned and looked at Wayne, who was staring back at him from the lower level with wide, startled eyes.

"Hurry!" Albert urged, motioning for the others to climb ahead of him. "To the top!" Then he turned and knelt above Wayne, seizing both his arms and trying to help lift him.

"I'm not leaving you behind!" Brandy insisted.

"I'll be right behind you. Just go."

But Brandy turned and dropped back down to the previous step, unwilling to go without him.

"Just *go*," yelled Wayne.

"Just *come on*," Albert countered.

Andrea scurried up over the next wall and then turned and

looked back down at the others. Nicole and Olivia were climbing up to the level just below her, but Brandy was two levels below them, looking down at Albert and Wayne.

She glanced up above her and saw that the tower walls were only a few tiers away. She didn't dare race too far ahead. What if the Caggo got there first? She was certain she was no match for the monster alone. She was hardly a match for *anyone*.

Wayne managed to get his feet beneath him and stood up, hissing a little at the pain in his leg. "I'm good," he said, responding to the worried look on Albert's face. "Just get everyone to the top."

"I intend to," Albert said, his eyes scanning the darkness beneath them. There was no sign of the creature down there. But then again, what the hell was he even looking for? For all he knew, it could be invisible. Or it could fly. He glanced up the tower and saw that Brandy was still there, just above him, watching him. "Get moving," he snapped. "The faster we all get to the top of the tower, the sooner we can all get out of here."

"I'm not leaving you!"

Nicole helped Olivia up the next rise and then swung herself up after her, ignoring the aching in her arms and legs as Andrea nimbly climbed ahead of them. They were almost there. Only a couple more.

Albert knelt down and braced himself to give Wayne a boost, his eyes searching the darkness below him, watching for the inevitable flash of movement.

Brandy took a step back to give Wayne room as she scanned the space below them with her light. Still there was nothing. Why wasn't it attacking? What was it waiting for?

Albert had just stood up and grabbed the ledge to pull himself up to her when something large and pale darted by in the darkness below him, visible for only an instant and then gone.

"Albert!"

Recognizing the terror in her voice, Albert let go of the ledge and spun around, searching for whatever she had seen.

"Hurry up!" she cried.

His back against the wall, Albert scanned the darkness all around him. He could see nothing. All he could hear was the constant droning of the damn hounds.

Wayne, too, had turned and was looking for whatever had startled Brandy. But it was gone, vanished back into the shadows from which it had come.

Brandy was sure she hadn't imagined it. She found herself remembering the thing that attacked them inside Gilbert House. Big. Pale. Fleshy. Unrelenting. It had nearly killed Albert and Wayne and now here they were again, right in the Caggo's murderous path.

Nicole and Olivia climbed upward without stopping, urged along by Brandy's frightful shouts below.

Andrea paused each time, waiting for them to catch up

before ascending, staying one tier ahead of them and keeping her light on them as much as possible.

Only one more remained between her and the top of the tower's base. Then they could make a run for the steps.

"Hurry!" Brandy shouted. She shined her light left and right, worried now that the Caggo was circling around them, determined to attack them from the side or even from above.

Albert nodded. "Yeah. All right." He turned and gripped the ledge again. At the same instant, Wayne turned and nudged Brandy toward the wall, urging her to climb.

It was at that moment that the Caggo pounced. Brandy saw it as she began to move toward the wall, just before she could turn away. It bounded up the side of the tower's base in long, quick strides, like a jungle cat leaping from tree branch to tree branch.

Brandy screamed.

Wayne spun around, his flashlight raised, ready to bludgeon with it if needed. He saw it immediately, but he had no time to react. The thing was even faster than the monster in Gilbert House. It reached its target in the space of a few rapid heartbeats.

Albert never had a chance to see it coming. It hit him as he was pulling himself up. It did not sink claws into him, nor did it tear him with its teeth. Instead, it simply threw itself against him, mashing him violently against the stone. He felt a sharp pain as the box inside his backpack was shoved into his back. The very next second, the Caggo was off him and he fell hard onto the floor, gasping for breath as his flashlight skittered across the stone and out of his reach.

"*Everybody go!*" Wayne shouted. "*Get to the top!*"

Andrea quickly scurried up the last level and then bolted to the left, her eyes lifted to the stairs above her. Behind her, Olivia and Nicole hoisted themselves up as quickly as they could. But Brandy could not move. She stood there, staring down at Albert, one hand pressed to her mouth, too terrified to even cry out.

Albert knew he had to get up, knew he had to defend himself somehow before the monster came back, but he could barely move. He lifted his head to try and see his attacker, but before he could gain even a glimpse of what stood over him, the Caggo struck out with its foot, kicking him in the side of his face with enough force to roll him across the stone floor. A blinding flash of pain drove deep into his head and for a moment the world swirled out of control into a maelstrom of disoriented agony and confusion.

Brandy watched in terror as Albert flopped onto his belly and then lay there motionless, terrified that the monster had broken his neck. She couldn't even think about running. Her whole world seemed to be tethered to her lover's deathly still body and the horrible monster that stood over him.

Wayne dropped down behind the Caggo as it approached

Albert again and threw himself at the creature, determined to knock it off balance, but the beast was as clever as it was fast. It turned suddenly and caught him in the chest with its elbow, knocking him back. Without pausing, it lunged at him, striking him across his head with a large, meaty hand and sending him staggering back and over the ledge to land heavily on the step below.

Then, in the moment of stillness that followed, the monster turned its face toward Brandy.

She had pictured the Caggo as some horrible, alien thing, ten feet tall with wickedly sharp teeth, jaws dripping drool and huge claws designed to shred and tear. But this was nothing at all like she'd pictured. This thing was about the same size as Wayne, considerably smaller than the monster they encountered in Gilbert House, even. It was as pale as a corpse, with no hair and no eyes. Its brow was round and flawless, without even the faint impression of sockets, like those of the Sentinel Queen. It had no enormous jaws or teeth. Instead, its mouth was nothing more than a small slit. Alternately, its nose was large and flat. It had no visible claws, either, just two huge hands that looked like great bald paws, its fingers short and plump. Like the Keeper who greeted them at the beginning of the labyrinth, it had an abundance of flesh. But whereas the Keeper had appeared simply too small for its skin, this thing's hide was stretched out in odd places, as if parts of its body had been bloated at some point and then deflated. Loose flesh dangled from its meaty jowls and neck and hung in thick folds from its chest and waist. Its belly was swollen and fat and dangled like a jiggling mass of pale dough over its hips in a grotesque sort of loincloth. Its feet, like its hands, were short and round, but wide and heavy, looking almost elephantine, with its round toes poking out from under the folds of fatty flesh that pooled around its thick ankles.

It didn't look capable of moving with such speed and agility, but then again, Gilbert House's troll-like resident hadn't seemed capable of such speed either.

Wayne regained his feet and heaved himself back up to where the Caggo stood. He could hold this thing off. It wasn't so big. Not really. He was just as formidable as it was. He'd taken on much bigger monsters than this *tonight* already. He screamed at Brandy to run, to hurry up to the top of the tower.

But Brandy could not move. She could not tear her eyes away from the horrible monster that was now turning its strange face toward Wayne again.

Olivia reached the top of the base and dared a look back down just in time to see the monster lunge at Wayne. It knocked him back, sending both him and it over the ledge and slamming him hard onto the stone floor of the lower level once more. His flashlight spun away into the darkness and winked out of existence in the cacophony of the raging hounds below. She cried out for him and even moved toward the edge, wanting to go to him, to help him before the monster could kill him, but Nicole held her back.

"We have to keep going!" she said. "Hurry!"

Andrea reached the corner of the tower and ran around it, her eyes fixed on the steps above her as they drew closer and closer to her. A little farther and she would reach the bottom.

Wayne held up his arms, shielding himself as the Caggo straddled his body and battered him with its powerful paws. It was remarkably fast. He'd barely had time to brace himself before it shoved him over the ledge and dropped down on top of him. Now it was all he could do to squirm backward across the stone, trying to get out from under it before it beat him to death.

If he could only reach the next ledge…

Finally breaking her paralysis, Brandy dropped down and knelt over Albert. She had feared the worst, but he was already beginning to rise to his feet, his eyes fixed on the creature below him.

"Get to the top," he told her as he retrieved his dropped flashlight. "Find the way out."

"I won't!"

But Albert dropped to the lower level and began moving toward the Caggo.

Wayne pushed himself backward with his feet until he felt the floor disappear beneath his head and shoulders, then he twisted himself around and dropped down from beneath the monster's violent hands. As soon as he hit the hard floor, he rolled over and began to crawl across the stone as quickly as he could before it could drop down on top of him again.

He wished now that he had not brought his glasses. Though they had been valuable in helping him through the emotion rooms, they now were at risk of being broken and leaving him permanently blind down here in this deadly darkness.

Behind him, he heard the monster's bare feet slap against the stone and another of those fierce shrieks split the air at his back. He stood up as fast as he could manage and turned to face it.

Andrea reached the bottom of the stairs and began to climb, pausing only when she saw Nicole's light racing around the corner below her. She called out to them to hurry, but they needed no encouragement. They had both heard the murderous shriek of the monster.

"Just go!" Nicole shouted up to her. "Get to the top! We'll be right behind you!"

The Caggo lurched forward and struck Wayne in the chest, knocking him back.

Again, he threw his arms up, trying to protect himself, but the creature merely battered his bare arms, driving him farther back. He could not get any kind of advantage. He was like a child struggling against it. How could he ever have thought that he was any kind of match for this thing? It was like taking on a machine.

Suddenly, he found himself back in Gilbert House's courtyard, surrounded by the groping dead. This was practically the same situation. The only difference was that now there was only one monster. Just like then, it struck him that he might not survive this.

Albert dropped down behind the Caggo and rushed toward it, but again, the monster was too fast. It turned and knocked him up against the wall, sending a starburst of colorful dancing stars across his line of vision.

Wayne stumbled back a few more steps and then peered between his upraised arms just in time to catch one more blow from the monster. This time, its heavy fist sank hard into his gut, flushing the air violently from his lungs. He staggered backward, gasping for air, and slumped to the floor. The creature lurched forward once more and landed its massive fist against the side of his head, sending him sprawling.

It then turned and seized Albert's head in one huge hand and shoved him aside, almost lifting him off his feet with its massive strength.

Albert staggered a few steps and then stumbled and fell to the floor. He couldn't believe how strong this thing was. He had no chance of defending himself. He couldn't seem to harm it and yet it was tossing him around like a toy. He tried to get to his feet again, tried to get up so that he could get some distance between him and it, but the creature kicked him again, this time in his side, and he was knocked over the ledge with a painful yelp.

Brandy cried out for him and dropped down another step, desperate to help him. But she froze as the creature lifted its head up and sniffed at the air around it, the flesh of its jaws jiggling grotesquely. She didn't know what to do. She couldn't let it harm Albert again, but she was certain that she stood no chance against it. If Wayne was no match for it, she had no prayer of standing up to it alone.

Suddenly, the Caggo turned its hideous face toward her and her paralysis broke. She turned to run, grabbing the next ledge to pull herself up, but it was already too late. It leapt up at her. In the space of a single heartbeat, it had her in its huge paws.

Nicole and Olivia raced up the steps and around the corner in time to look down and see the Caggo lift Brandy up over its head, her feet kicking wildly, a shrill scream escaping her. Her flashlight fell from her hands as she searched for something to hold onto and landed at the Caggo's feet.

Albert leapt up, a hellish fireball of terror erupting from his heart. He tried to climb over the ledge, tried to reach the beast before it could harm her, but there was no time.

It was already too late.

Nicole lurched forward, screaming her best friend's name, terrified of what she knew was about to happen, and she would have fallen if Olivia had not stayed her.

The Caggo turned and threw Brandy out into the darkness.

Albert felt his heart stutter in his chest, threatening to stop utterly and drop him dead where he stood.

Nicole watched from above, helpless to do anything more. "Land safe!" she sighed, a fleeting prayer, a hopeless hope, as her best friend sailed through the air like a tossed doll. And the words rang over and over in her mind. *Please,* she thought. *Please land safe…*

Albert could think nothing at all.

For a moment Brandy was there, rotating end over end, shrieking with terror, and then she was swallowed by the darkness. An instant later, Brandy Rudman's scream was cut suddenly and sickeningly short and all that remained was the frenzied roar of the hounds.

Chapter 49

Albert stared down into the darkness that had just swallowed his girlfriend. He could hear the hounds as they swarmed the place where she landed. It was too easy to imagine the grizzly scene the darkness hid. He had tried to scream, but no sound would come. His voice seemed to have left him forever.

"*Come on!*" Olivia was tugging at Nicole's arm, urging her up the tower steps. Above them, Andrea had already circled around the tower once. "*We need you!*"

Nicole turned. She wanted to help. She wanted to go down and see if there was anything she could do, but she could do nothing down there. Olivia was right. They needed to get to the top of the tower. They were *all* going to die if they couldn't find the way out. Feeling as if she had been drugged, she turned and continued up the steps.

Albert heard the Caggo's stubby feet slap hard onto the stone. It had leapt down to the level just above him. He turned toward it, numb with shock, and found himself looking right into the creature's repulsive face.

It was now that Albert realized that the Caggo was not a mere beast like the hounds or even the monster in Gilbert House. It was much more than that. The Caggo was a reasoning creature, far more intelligent than a mere predator. It had the chance to grab him and toss him to the hounds just as it had done to poor Brandy, but it didn't. It didn't attack him at all. It was bent over, with its fat hands planted on its knees, intentionally positioning itself right in his face, smelling him.

The creature would kill him. That was definitely on its list of things to do, but not yet. First, it had to see what its prey was *feeling*. It had to see what sort of *anguish* it had inflicted. It was actually taking pleasure in his pain.

Albert stared into the thing's ugly face for a moment, his anger growing. The thing was actually arrogant, he realized. It actually believed that they had no chance. That was why it never attacked them inside the labyrinth. That was why it let them begin climbing the tower before showing itself, why it was not at all concerned about Andrea, Nicole and Olivia reaching the top. It never believed for a moment that they had any chance of escaping. It intended to take its time and enjoy every second of their agony.

The very idea enraged him.

His flashlight was lying at his feet where he dropped it when he realized that Brandy was in trouble. Almost without thinking, he bent and picked it up. Then he smashed the handle of it into the Caggo's flat nose with all his strength.

The beast staggered backward, its huge paws plastered to its bleeding face.

"*THERE!*" Albert screamed at it. He heaved himself up to the next level and slammed the flashlight down onto its exposed toes, wrenching from it a second howl of pain.

Now Wayne was on his feet, too. Circling around the monster, he snatched up Brandy's flashlight from the floor of the next tier. Holding it in both of his fists, he slammed it as hard as he could between the monster's shoulder blades. When it turned to face this new attacker, Wayne thrust his knee up under the beast's flabby belly and into the hot flesh of its huge scrotum. "*HOW DOES* THAT *FEEL, FUCKER?*"

As the Caggo took two staggering steps backward, still howling, its great paws dropping from its bloody face to its wounded groin, Albert brought the flashlight down again, this time onto the back of the Caggo's fat neck.

The monster shrieked again and threw both its paws out, catching Wayne in his chest and throat, hurling him backward. Again, he fell over the ledge and landed hard on the floor, taking the brunt of the fall on his right shoulder and knocking off his glasses. Brandy's flashlight left his hand and clattered all the way to the bottom, vanishing forever into the darkness just as his own had done…and just as poor Brandy herself had done.

The Caggo then turned to Albert, only to take another blow to the face from the flashlight. It staggered back, still howling.

"*BASTARD!*" he screamed. A red rage had risen in him. It was like nothing he had ever felt before, like some powerful energy that threatened to burst from his skin like air from an over-inflated balloon. His mind was empty of all other emotions. All he wanted was to cause pain to this thing that had torn apart his life.

High above them, Nicole was racing up the steps, forcing back the tears in her eyes. Poor Brandy. She wanted so badly to go back down, to find where she landed, to see if she could possibly still be with them, but she could not. She had to keep going, had to reach the top of the tower. It was the only thing to do. It was the only way out.

Up and up she climbed, with Olivia right behind her, trying hard not to notice how high they were. There was no rail, and a terrifying drop onto bone-shattering stone lay mere inches from her feet. A single misstep and she would plunge to her death. Sickened by the thought, she lifted her face upward instead and wondered how far ahead of them Andrea was.

She didn't wonder for long. She turned the corner and spotted her. She was standing in a doorway at the top of the steps, shouting for them to hurry.

They were almost there.

Albert swung the flashlight again. It had seemed that he was winning, that he might even kill this horrible creature, but this time the Caggo ducked the flashlight and grabbed him. Just as it had done with Brandy, it lifted him up over its head and then hurled him off the tower and out into the darkness.

For a moment, he was suspended in the air, his body slowly turning in a constant summersault. He had time to realize what was happening, more than enough time to panic, but no time to prevent the tragedy he knew was fast approaching. He struck one of the stone beams on his right side, the corner of the stone burying into the meat of his right arm just below the shoulder. The pain was sudden and excruciating, like a bolt of lightning along his nervous system. He heard the hollow crack as the bone snapped. Then he struck the floor and landed squarely atop the box inside his backpack.

The entire world became a sea of blinding pain.

High above, the doorway through which Andrea had vanished led to another set of steps leading farther up within the tower. Nicole and Olivia hurried up them, both of them panting, their legs burning.

Andrea was waiting for them inside a small room at the top of the stairs, staring at a large, stone box in the middle of the floor.

"What do you make of it?" Andrea asked.

Nicole shook her head, still trying to catch her breath. The sides of the box were smooth stone. The top was a sort of funnel, dipping down into it. From the center of this funnel rose a large, stone spike, just like the ones that had killed Beverly Bridger. "I don't know," she replied. She was hardly able to think. She could not get the image of her best friend falling into that darkness out of her head. "What does it mean?"

"It looks like some kind of sacrificial altar," Olivia observed between labored breaths. "Like something you're supposed to spear a sheep on…to catch its blood or something."

Nicole shivered. "Let's not go with that idea," she said. "We don't have any sheep." But she could not take her eyes off the stone spike. It reminded her too much of what happened to Beverly.

Albert tried to sit up, but his arm screamed at him. *Broken*, he thought, remembering that sick snapping noise he'd heard when he hit the platform, and a wave of vertigo washed over him. He had to get up. He was down with the hounds. If he didn't get up he would be shredded like leftovers in a garbage disposal.

No, he thought. *Not yet.*

He wasn't sure why it was so important for him to get up. What did it matter, now that Brandy was gone?

But he couldn't surrender just yet. Perhaps later, but not yet.

Summoning all his strength and will, he rolled onto his left side and then somehow rose to his feet, clutching at his arm. His whole body was trembling now. The edge of the beam had not merely broken his arm but split the flesh, hacking him open like the blade of a dull axe. Blood was running down his arm and dripping from his fingertips.

His flashlight had left his hand at some point during his fall and must have come to rest atop the ledge behind him, because he found that he could see a little. He was standing with his back against the tower's base, blinking back tears of pain, with no sign of the hounds, though he could still hear them somewhere close by.

Now what? He couldn't climb back onto the tower in this condition.

Then the Caggo was there. It landed on the platform in front of him and crouched there. He could just see it in the dim light. Though eyeless, it seemed to be glaring at him. A low growl rolled from its throat. It was angry now. It was going to make him pay for causing it such pain.

Albert had no prayer now. With his arm broken, he was as good as dead to this monster. He backed away from it, sliding along the wall of the tower. Nearby, the noises of the hounds were growing louder. They were coming his way and wasting no time. Perhaps they had smelled the blood.

"Come on then," he growled at the beast.

As if answering his challenge, the Caggo jumped down into the pit with him and stalked closer. There was blood trickling from its nose and Albert had that much satisfaction at least. Perhaps it would get infected and the bastard would die down here. Not that it would do him any good now, but it was something to wish on this vile creature, and about as much as he had the power to do in his condition.

It took a moment for Albert to register what happened next. Perhaps it was the irony that was too much for his mind to handle, or perhaps the sheer stupidity of the beast, the way its arrogance and rage became its fatal undoing.

Its right leg vanished into a violent spray of blood. It howled, an awful, agonizing sound, and a hound appeared from the crimson starburst, gnashing its jaws and its razor-lined hide. Snarling, it skidded to a stop and then twisted around for another pass. A second hound appeared from the side, plowing through the monster's other leg while it still teetered from the loss of its first.

With a massive shriek, the Caggo fell onto the hounds as two more arrived, shredding the helpless creature in a spray of crimson gore. Hot blood splattered across Albert's legs and belly, even onto his face.

Albert turned away from the bloodbath that was taking place in front of him and tried to climb up onto the ledge even as he continued to feel hot, thick droplets of the Caggo's blood fall upon his shoulders like nightmarish rain. He had a brief moment of opportunity while the hounds were distracted by their prey, a mere second or two to climb out of their reach before they caught his scent and came for him as well…but it was no good. With his good arm broken, he could hardly lift his feet off the ground.

Behind him, the gnashing of the hounds grew closer and he turned to see two of them converging on him. He closed his eyes against the sight and braced himself for cold, bloody death.

But this was not Albert's time to die.

Suddenly, his backpack was seized and he was dragged up and out of reach of the nasty creatures a bare heartbeat before they slammed against the stone base of the tower below him.

"I don't get it," Nicole said. She was growing frantic. With no way of knowing that the Caggo was dead, she was still trying to find the meaning of this odd box. She could no longer hear Albert or Wayne. Only another of those horrible screams from the Caggo. *Please, God,* she thought, *don't let it kill them. Please.*

The box did not open and the spike did not move. The funnel was too narrow for any of them to reach into. There was nothing else up here that could possibly mean anything. The room was otherwise completely empty. In fact, it was barely a room at all. It was more like the frame of a room. A large, window-like opening took up most of each wall, staring out at the same utter darkness that had enveloped them since they first descended beneath the city so many hours before. There was no ceiling and nowhere to go but back the way they came. The solution could be nothing else but this strangely ominous stone box.

"'Atop the tower, the secret is blood,'" Andrea said, repeating the words the voice had spoken to her in the forest.

Nicole stared at the spike, considering what Olivia had said about it looking like a sacrificial altar.

Albert lay upon the cold stone for a moment, looking up at Wayne, unable to believe that he was still alive.

"Jesus Christ," Wayne said, staring at the carnage that was taking place nearby. His voice was too low to be heard over the racket of the hounds, but Albert read the words on his lips.

Albert nodded and then tried to sit up. He was extremely lucky to be alive. Had Wayne taken just one more second getting to him, the hounds would have turned him to pulp.

"Careful!" Wayne shouted. "My God… That has to hurt like hell."

"It does." He looked up at Wayne, his eyes pitiful, "Brandy…"

Wayne shook his head. "I don't know. She's over there." He shined the remaining flashlight out over the swarming hounds. Brandy was lying on one of the stone platforms, one leg dangling over the edge, just inches above their reach.

Albert scrambled to his feet, ignoring the intense pain from his arm, and ran across the stone beam to her side.

She had not fallen to the hounds. Thank God for that. But she was so still, so motionless. She'd fallen a long way. He knelt beside her and lifted her head into his good arm. "Brandy?" His eyes were already filling with tears. "Brandy? Baby?"

She did not respond. Her glasses had not fallen off, but were askew. With his broken arm, he reached out, wincing terribly at the pain, and shakily straightened them for her.

He lifted her higher, cradling her. He did not want to check for a pulse. He did not want to feel the emptiness in her veins. He did not want to feel her poor body without life in it. "Brandy?" he said again. His voice was failing him, so he pressed his lips to her ear. "Wake up, Baby. We have to go."

Wayne stood on the other side of the beam. He could not stand to watch. It was heartbreaking. He turned his eyes down, studying the flashlight. It was Albert's, the one he dropped when the Caggo grabbed him. It was the only one the three of them had been carrying that survived.

"Please," Albert begged. "Please…"

Nicole closed her eyes. She thought about Albert. Albert was the clever one, the mystery solver. He would know what to do. And he would have the courage to do whatever it was. But Albert wasn't here. Now it was her turn. She'd have to think like him. In the darkness behind her eyelids she could still see her best friend falling into that darkness, could still hear the hounds swarming below them. Albert always had faith. He always had courage. So could she.

"Fuck it," she said. She opened her eyes and brought her hand down hard on the stone spike.

Olivia and Andrea gasped.

She stood there, wincing at the pain, hardly believing she had been able to do such a thing. A small piece of the spike was protruding from the top of her hand. She'd speared herself completely through.

"*What are you doing?*" Andrea screamed, her voice shrill.

"The only think I can think of," Nicole replied through clenched teeth.

As her blood ran down the spike and into the stone box, Albert lowered his head and wept. This was the woman he was supposed to spend his life with. He'd decided that long ago, within days after they made their first trip into the temple. It wasn't supposed to be this way. This wasn't supposed to be where the Temple of the Blind led them. Why had he come here? Why had he insisted on this damned adventure? *He* should have been the one to take that fall, not Brandy.

It was his fault.

He would not make the trip without her. Wayne and the girls could go on without him. That was all there was to it. He was useless to them without Brandy. He was useless even to himself without her.

Chapter 50

Brandy reached up and touched Albert's arm. In an instant, all his fears were shoved aside and gleaming hope muscled its way up from the dark depths of his screaming heart. She was looking up at him. Those brilliant, blue eyes that he loved so dearly were not dim, like the eyes of the dying, but as bright as they had ever been in life. They were tired, sleepy, but *alive.* Slowly, she shook her head. "Don't do that," she said to him, her voice inaudible over the roar of the hounds.

"Oh, God," he gasped. "I thought…" But he could not bear to say what he had thought.

Brandy closed her eyes. "Hurts."

He didn't need to hear her. He read her lips. "Where?"

"My head."

"Anywhere else?"

She shook her head again. She didn't know. Everywhere. She hurt all over. Her body was one solid mass of pain.

Wayne glanced back up at Albert and thought that he must be imagining things. Brandy's body was no longer limp, no longer still. She had her hand on his shoulder. Her lips were moving. She was speaking to him.

"You're okay," Albert sighed, pressing his mouth to her ear so that she would hear him. "You can't ever leave me. I love you too much."

She smiled at him. "I have a headache," she said. Then her eyes widened suddenly as she remembered how she'd come to be where she was. She tried to lift her head, but the pain stopped her. Her head was pounding. "The Caggo…!"

"Dead," Albert assured her.

She relaxed again, relieved.

Albert looked over at Wayne, caught his smile and returned it. He couldn't believe it. She was still with him. She was still alive. She was still his.

It was a miracle.

High above them, atop the tower, Nicole's blood disappeared into the stone box.

The three of them stood silently around the altar, waiting.

"Nothing happened," said Olivia.

"Okay. So what do we do now?" Nicole asked through gritted teeth. Her hand trembled upon the spike as the pain began to spread.

Andrea shook her head. "I don't know, but *I'm* not doing that."

She was sure this had something to do with blood. It was a sharp spike mounted over a funnel-shaped basin. What *else* could it be? It wasn't like they were expected to juice a lemon up here. And Andrea's mysterious voice said the secret was *blood.* It all fit together.

Inside the stone box, her blood trickled down the spike and into the rounded bottom of the basin below it. From there, it ran to a small hole, from which it fell in thick droplets through a huge, black emptiness. Like crimson rain, it plunged through the hollow core of the tower, down and down into a great black depth, where it at last crashed into the still surface of the liquid far below.

"I don't think that's what you were supposed to do," Olivia said.

Nicole was opening her mouth to respond when a ball of fire suddenly erupted from the box, burning her hand and sending all three of them sprawling to the floor.

Outside the tower, the sudden "whoosh" of flames was startling. Wayne jumped and turned toward the sound, staring at the brilliant flames that blossomed from the darkness and revealed what the shadows had been hiding. For a moment he was transfixed by the sight. The entire chamber was illuminated, its massiveness unveiled to them for the first time. Giant stone beams appeared overhead, crisscrossing like the enormous fibers of some incredibly vast spider's web, bathing the ceiling above them in deep, undulating shadows. In the center, the tower stood like a grand monument, much taller than he expected, a great, stone monolith, at least six stories tall with steps spiraling around and up its four sides. There were several openings in the walls of the tower, narrow slits, like windows, but located in odd places, as if haphazardly strewn across its smooth surface. Each one revealed a sliver of the inferno that had been ignited within, glowing like the wicked eyes of devils in the gloom.

Brandy cried out for Nicole. She was up there somewhere, with Olivia and Andrea, and now the whole tower was burning. Were they burning too? The thought was more than she could bear.

Something began to rumble deep in the stone beneath their feet and Wayne lowered his eyes to the floor. What was going on? Was this supposed to be happening? "What did they do?" he wondered, but his voice was lost in the chaos of the hounds below and the inferno above.

Nicole, Olivia and Andrea gained their feet and fled down the stone steps to the open doorway at the top of the outer stairs. Far below them, deep within the tower, another chamber erupted, intensifying the blaze. The box into which Nicole's blood had vanished exploded in a great billowing fireball, engulfing the top of the tower in flames and hurling chunks of smoking stone to rain down like hellish hail.

A column of fire raced up between the massive stone beams to the dome-shaped ceiling above and vanished into a large, chimney-like hole that had been impossible to see for the shadows until now.

Nicole emerged from the tower and hurriedly began to descend the narrow stairway, her hands pressed to the wall beside her for support, her eyes drawn to the dizzying drop that waited mere inches to her left. If she should stumble and fall, she would meet the stone floor below at a brutal speed.

Behind her, Olivia's heart thumped harder as the flames illuminated the floor far below, but she dared not linger. Whatever they had set in motion would not be stopped, and she had a strong feeling that they should put as much distance as possible between them and the little room at the top of the tower.

Andrea was last to leave the tower and was barely out of the way when flames belched violently from the doorway behind her. She screamed, terrified, as the heat pounded against her bare shoulders and back, threatening to burn her alive.

Another shudder raced up the tower as yet another chamber erupted into flame. This time, the entire labyrinth began to quake, threatening to shake them off the narrow steps and send them plunging to certain death.

Wayne saw them as they rounded the corner of the tower and hurried down the steps. Relieved that they were still okay, if only for the moment, he turned and crossed the stone beam as quickly as he dared to Albert's side.

"I think that's our cue," he declared. He handed Albert back his flashlight and then bent and scooped Brandy up into his arms. His eyes returned to the tower, where the girls were still descending the steps as fast as their weary legs would carry them, racing the expanding conflagration that had already engulfed the top of the tower above them.

"What the hell did they do?" Albert asked.

Wayne shook his head. "Whatever it was, I hope they did it right."

There was an enormous concussion from somewhere far below their feet, like a thunderclap. The very stone reverberated beneath them with the force. A second later, a large section of the tower's base fell in with a resounding boom. It did not collapse, but rather shifted, as though whatever chaos was taking place below this chamber had knocked away some hidden support and allowed the stones on this part of the tower to drop ten feet straight down, neatly revealing the exit for which they had been searching.

"*That's it!*" Wayne yelled. He made his way back across the beam, still cradling Brandy in his arms. He wobbled frightfully beneath her extra weight, but maintained his balance. It was easier without the hounds stalking his every movement. They were now running away, rapidly fleeing this chamber and the pandemonium that had erupted from it.

Nicole looked over her shoulder. They had descended nearly half the steps by now, but still she could feel the heat. The flames were growing, engulfing more and more of the tower above them. If the inferno kept growing at this rate, they wouldn't make it. And yet she did not dare go any faster. She was already afraid that she would trip and fall, or sprain an ankle and go sprawling over the side, but the thought of being burned alive was equally unthinkable.

Wayne rushed over to the newly revealed exit, still cradling Brandy in his arms, and peered down at the waiting tunnel. It led away from the tower, beneath the floor from which the hounds were quickly vanishing.

Brandy did not look at the new passage. She was staring up at the tower, watching, holding her breath as she waited for Nicole and Olivia and Andrea to round the corner of the steps and come back into view. She clung to Wayne's neck, hardly feeling his body against her, her hands clenched into nervous fists behind him. "Come on…" she breathed. "Come on, Nikki… Please…"

Below them, the ground shook as yet another chamber ignited in the deep, blazing belly of the tower and the inferno lurched upward with a resounding roar, sending more chunks of stone, some as big as the hounds, raining down around the tower.

"My God..." Wayne breathed, squinting up into the blaze. It was swelling, creeping ever farther down the tower walls, engulfing it little by little. It was too bright to look directly into. He could feel the intense heat from where he stood and could only imagine how hot it must be upon that narrow stairway.

Seconds passed like minutes as debris rained down around them. Albert watched with a combination of terror and awe. It was like standing at the base of an erupting volcano (or at least how he *imagined* standing at the base of an erupting volcano would be like). Smoking streamers sailed down through the air. Large chunks of stone crashed against the tower's base. It was overwhelmingly frightening, and yet he could not look away. His heart hammered in his chest. He could barely feel the throbbing of his broken arm as he waited breathlessly for his friends to appear.

When they finally came around the corner and back into view, each of them breathed a tentative sigh of relief. Now, they had only to cross the nearest face and turn one more corner. Then they would be nearly to the bottom.

But they were still in terrible danger. Smoking bits of rubble were falling down around them and the intense heat from the flames was only growing stronger.

A large hunk of stone, nearly the size of a man, dropped

from the top of the tower, trailing a tail of smoke and flames behind it and missing Andrea by only a few naked feet. Her scream was clear and shrill, even over all the noise, but she did not stop. She covered her head and pushed on, one step at a time.

"Hurry!" cried Nicole, her eyes fixed on the corner of the tower ahead of them. They were almost there. They wouldn't even have to go all the way to the bottom step; they could simply jump over the side when they were close enough to the floor to land safely.

But another loud concussion filled the chamber, shaking the entire labyrinth, and Olivia teetered for a moment, her balance thrown. She threw her arms out, her heart catching in her throat, unable to even scream. And then Andrea had her, seizing her shoulder and pulling her back so that they both sat down hard on the steps.

"*Oh god!*" Olivia panted. "*Oh god!*"

"It's okay," Andrea promised, still clutching her.

"Come on!" Nicole called back as she reached the corner. Other, smaller concussions were shaking the floor beneath them, each one stronger than the previous. The last big explosion had set off some sort of chain reaction and she was sure they didn't want to still be on this tower when it reached its apex.

"What is that?" Albert asked, his eyes sweeping the stone at his feet.

"Nothing good," Wayne knew. And within seconds the rumbling worked its way up into the tower and a massive fireball erupted from the top with a terrible, thunderous boom.

Nicole did not dare glance up. She jumped down from the steps as a wave of heat washed down over them. Her bare skin prickled with its intensity. Any hotter and her flesh would begin to burn. She scanned the dark room around her, trying to gain her bearings, her heart racing. "Where are they?" she asked. "Where do we go?"

"This way!" Andrea shouted. Finally off of the treacherous steps, she grabbed Olivia's hand and led them around the side of the tower. Once around the corner, they could see the others standing at the bottom of the base, waiting for them.

There was no sign of the Caggo, but they had little time to consider their luck. As if reminding them of the peril they still faced, a fireball the size of a pickup truck slammed into the tower's base directly in front of them and cracked in half, spilling flames and debris down the side in a fiery cascade.

Screaming, they darted between the flaming boulder and the tower wall and began their final descent as more fire and stone rained down from above.

Their backs and shoulders were hot, as though they had lain too long on their bellies under a hot summer sun. Something stung Nicole's left shoulder. A stone the size of a bowling ball bounced over their heads, narrowly missing Olivia. Andrea staggered briefly as her bare foot came down on a broken chunk of stone, but managed to keep her balance. Something sizzled through the air between Nicole and Olivia. They expected to be struck dead at any moment, and yet somehow they kept going.

They dropped down one level after another, as quickly as they dared, their feet aching with the effort, and soon they were nearing the bottom.

"Just a little farther," Wayne said, speaking softly, as though willing his thoughts to them. He could almost imagine the entire tower exploding into one final fireball, swallowing the three of them in a great, flaming hell, incinerating them just when they thought they'd escaped. His heart thundered against his ribs and he felt as if his blood was rapidly draining from his body. "Come on…"

He was also gripping Brandy far too tightly in his arms, but she barely noticed. She, too, was staring up at them, praying for them, hoping desperately that she wasn't about to watch any of them die.

"Go!" Albert screamed as the three neared the bottom of the base, and Wayne turned and looked at him, distracted. "*Now!*"

Wayne looked up at the approaching girls once more and then turned and dropped into the hole with Brandy still in his arms.

"Hurry!" Albert screamed at the others. "This way!"

Nicole and Olivia reached the bottom and ran to where Albert was standing. They hesitated only a moment before following Wayne into the mysterious new tunnel.

Andrea paused at Albert's side and turned to look back up at what they'd been running from. Flames were shooting upward with such intensity that it made her eyes water to look upon them.

"Go!" Albert yelled, screaming with all his breath to be heard over the noise.

There was another crash, much softer than any of the others, and high above them a piece of fire seemed to step out of the inferno. Andrea stared up at it, her face hot even from this distance. A piece of stone, easily the size of a railway car, fell outward and crashed against the stairs, breaking in two. These two halves, still in flames, plummeted toward them.

For a few frantic heartbeats, she couldn't move. She stood there, staring at these two great hunks of fire and stone as they raced toward her.

"*Go!*" With his good arm, Albert grabbed her and shoved her toward the exit, almost knocking her into the hole, but it was enough for her to regain her composure. She jumped down and vanished into the tunnel after the others.

Albert jumped in behind her, and when he landed, his arm sent a jolt of agony through his body, freezing him for a moment. Above him, one of the stones struck dangerously close to the hole and like an electric shock it set him in motion. He sprinted into the tunnel as a storm of smoking stones rained down around him.

Wayne had not stopped until he was almost fifty yards into the tunnel, and he did not relax until he watched the last of his friends enter the passage behind him.

"*Oh God!*" Olivia sobbed. She stopped walking and dropped onto her knees on the hard stone. "That was *so* scary!"

"That was…probably the coolest thing…I've ever done," Andrea panted. She leaned against the tunnel wall, ignoring the bewildered looks Nicole and Olivia gave her.

"Where's the Caggo?" Olivia asked.

"Caggo's dead," Wayne assured them all. "Albert fed him to the hounds."

"Sweet!" exclaimed Andrea between breaths. "Albert rocks."

"*Wayne* rocks," Albert corrected her as he approached. "I would've ended up just like the Caggo if he hadn't hauled me out of there."

Brandy looked up at Wayne, her eyes shimmering. He had saved Albert's life?

"I should've been there sooner," Wayne lamented. "Took me too long to find where that thing knocked my glasses to."

"Took you just long enough, I'd say," Albert said, remembering the two hounds that were speeding toward him in those final, critical seconds.

Nicole did not care about the Caggo. She did not care about the hounds. She did not care about her injured hand or the uncomfortable heat that was radiating from her naked back and shoulders. She went straight to Brandy and took her hand, her eyes already filled with tears. "Oh my God," she said between breaths. "Are you okay?"

Brandy nodded. "I think so. I just hit my head." She looked up at Wayne. "You can put me down now. I think I'll be okay."

Wayne looked down at her, distracted. In all the excitement, he'd hardly realized he was still holding her. Gently, as though she were the most fragile thing in the world, he put her down on her own feet.

"I thought you were gone," Nicole sobbed as she embraced her best friend.

"I did too." Now she could feel the pain in the rest of her body. Her whole back ached, and especially her bottom. It was a miracle she hadn't broken her back or cracked open her skull.

Wayne's eyes drifted up to the ceiling of the tunnel. There was a noise, he realized, very faint under the roar of the flames above them.

Olivia caught sight of Albert and gasped. "Oh God!"

"It's okay," Albert assured her. "It's mostly the Caggo's blood." But even as he said this he saw her eyes fall on the gash in his arm

"It doesn't look okay."

Nicole and Brandy turned now to look at him. Neither of them had realized that he was injured.

"It's broke," Albert confessed. "Snapped it when the Caggo threw me to the hounds."

"*Oh my god!*" cried Brandy. She pulled away from Nicole and held her arms out to him. She wanted to do something, but she was afraid that if she embraced him she would hurt him.

"Guys," Wayne interrupted, his voice urgent. "I think we should get out of here."

"What is it?" Albert asked, but now he heard it too. It was sort of a creak and a groan at the same time, as though the walls of the labyrinth were slowly pulling apart. They all turned and looked back down the tunnel toward the glowing entrance. They could still hear the roar of the flames above them, but the light was fading. There was something eerie in this growing darkness, something *bad.*

Albert felt his heart sink with dread. "The curse," he said, suddenly remembering what the Keeper had said. It had warned them not to linger, but here they were, just standing here, waiting for whatever they'd unleashed to walk right up to them.

"I think you're right," replied Wayne. He took the flashlight from Albert and nudged him forward. "Go! Everyone run!"

The six of them turned and raced down the tunnel, away from the dark thing that was moving toward them through the labyrinth.

Chapter 51

Brandy's head was pounding. Never in her life had she experienced such a throbbing headache. All she wanted to do was lie down and sleep until the agony went away, but she pushed on, running as fast as she could, reminding herself that Albert must be hurting far worse than she right now. He was running beside her, clutching his broken arm. Even at a glance she could see the way he locked his jaw tight against the pain, as if forcing down a scream of agony. She had merely bumped her head. Even given the likeliness of a concussion, he would still be hurting long after she recovered.

Assuming any of them lived that long.

Andrea again took the lead. She could still feel the heat of the flames on her skin. It felt as if she had a sunburn covering most of her back. But even given this and the pain she felt in her feet and legs from climbing and then descending all those stairs, she was in better shape than anyone else down here.

Olivia and Nicole were running almost side-by-side, trying to keep up with their lither companion. Nicole's hand still hurt, but she dared not look at it. She did not want to know how bad it was, especially not now, not when she could do nothing about it anyway. She glanced over at Olivia instead and saw clearly the fear in her eyes. The poor girl had been running or hiding from some dire peril after another for days. How did she manage to keep going through all this?

Wayne hung back at the rear of the group, remaining behind Albert and Brandy, trying to coax them along in spite of the considerable pain he knew they must have felt. They both needed a doctor. For that matter, he probably needed one too. In addition to the zombie bite, his shredded leg and all the other injuries he'd sustained over the course of the night, he was now aching from head to foot from the battering he took at the hands of the Caggo. A faint taste of blood told him it had bloodied his nose at least a little and it felt like his lip was split. He also suspected that one or two of his ribs might be cracked, but he wasn't sure. His shoulder hurt like hell, too, where he landed on it. But this was hardly the time to be inventorying battle scars.

He chanced a look back the way they came and immediately wished he hadn't. Behind them, the tunnel had grown unnaturally dark, as though something were absorbing the light, or perhaps radiating darkness. He wasn't sure if that was possible, but until tonight he hadn't believed in monsters at all, so what the hell did he know? The walls seemed to simultaneously expand and contract. And at the very center of it was a queer void that for some reason filled his heart with mortal dread to look upon. He turned his face forward again, freshly panicked. "*Hurry!*"

Up ahead, the tunnel began to rise steeply and soon they were laboring up a massive hill.

Wayne wanted to look back again, wanted to be sure the darkness behind them was not closing in too quickly, but he dared not. He could hear that sound, as though the whole place were pulling apart, widening to make room for whatever it was that was coming for them, and he felt a sort of terror that he had not even felt when he believed the Caggo was going to kill him.

This, he realized, was the *real* guardian of the labyrinth. The Caggo had only been a pathetic sentry, a childish, sadistic beast, but toothless in the greater scheme of things.

Andrea caught sight of a narrow opening ahead, about chest high. "I see something!" she cried. "We're almost there!" She did not know that this was the end. She knew absolutely nothing about the labyrinth, but it was a start. It was a goal, something to focus on besides the rapidly approaching doom behind them.

Perhaps they would be safe on the other side of the opening. Perhaps whatever was chasing them was too big to fit through it.

She ran faster, pushing herself, her eyes fixed on that one chance of escape.

"Get in there!" Wayne shouted. "Don't stop for anything!"

Andrea reached the wall at the end of the tunnel and poked her head through the opening, quickly examining it. It was fairly narrow and would probably be a tight fit for Wayne. Probably uncomfortable as hell for poor Albert, too, with his broken arm. But the rest of them should have little trouble. Beyond this hole, another tunnel stretched onward. It was identical to the one on this side, but there seemed to be something different about it, something she felt immediately, but that she could not quite grasp in her rush.

She crawled through the hole and tumbled ungracefully onto the hard floor on the other side.

Olivia and Nicole reached the opening next and turned to wait for Albert and Brandy.

"Go!" Albert told them.

"Not until you're through!" Nicole insisted.

Albert saw the way she was holding her arm against her chest and his heart gave a pitiful cry. Not her, too. Would none of them survive this night unscathed?

Brandy reached the hole and leaned in. From the other side, Andrea took her hand and guided her forward. Olivia and Nicole each took one thigh and gently, but quickly pushed her forward.

As she tumbled out of the other side of the hole, Andrea did her best to keep her from hurting herself any more than she already was, but it was an awkward task.

"Hurry," Nicole told Albert, who hesitated only once. He wanted Nicole to go in first. He wanted her to be safe. He wanted Olivia and Wayne to be safe as well. He would rather have stayed and gone through last, but he knew Nicole well enough to be sure that she would not let that happen, not when he was hurt.

He bent and looked through the hole. There were markings on all four surfaces, just like the ones that covered the stone leading into the entrance of the labyrinth. Even through the pain of his fractured arm and the terror he felt from whatever was bearing down on them, he was able to notice this small detail.

Andrea and Brandy reached through from the other side and seized his good hand. Behind him, Olivia and Nicole pushed him through by his legs. They tried to be gentle, but his injured arm screamed with freshly awakened pain. He cried out in agony as he was fed through the hole, the backpack threatening to catch and slow them down. He wondered once if he would have to back out and take it off, but it slid through the opening without much trouble.

Although they tried to catch him, Andrea and Brandy were not quite able to keep him from tumbling to the floor and jarring a bolt of agony from his broken bone that made the whole world waver out of focus for a moment.

Wayne had stopped and was looking back the way they'd come. The tunnel had grown not just dark but utterly black. The noise had risen into a roar, as though there were a freight train coming down the tunnel straight at them. And that probably wasn't such an exaggeration. Whatever was moving toward them was much more massive than anything he'd ever seen before, much more massive than anything that should be able to squeeze through this small tunnel. "Go!" he told them. "*Hurry*!"

"Not without you!" Olivia screamed.

"I'm right behind you! Go!"

Nicole grabbed her by the arm and urged her forward.

Olivia wanted to argue, but she knew that would do nothing but waste valuable time. She squirmed into the hole with the same ease that Andrea had shown and tumbled into the waiting arms of the girls who'd gone before her.

Wayne watched the darkness in front of him. He actually saw it move, as though it were folding in on itself. The very sight seemed to unlock new realms of terror inside his head. Entire chambers of his mind he'd never known were there seemed to be opening wide to him, revealing deep, abysmal wells of terror that none of this night's other horrors had been frightening enough to expose.

Once Olivia was clear of the tunnel, Nicole glanced back at Wayne, who was finally beginning to back toward the wall.

"Come on!" she screamed over the strange roaring. "We're all through!" Then she turned and pushed her head and arms into the hole. Immediately, her wrists were seized from the other side and she was pulled out of the labyrinth.

As Nicole tumbled to the floor, the opening through which she'd just crawled suddenly swelled. Like a blossoming flower, it spread open to the unnatural darkness behind it, spewing strange, gaseous shadows like foul, black smoke. Then something shot through it, narrowly missing her kicking feet as she rolled out of the way.

It reached out at them, wickedly fast, a long, sinuous shape of slithering darkness that sailed over Brandy's head and snatched at Andrea's face, who threw herself to the ground to avoid it.

For a single second it remained there, wavering in the air, a thing that was like nothing at all, only a thin, snake-like void, a blackness that seemed darker than any shade of black they had ever seen. And then it vanished, fading like a ghost before their eyes, taking the unnatural darkness with it.

But they did not linger on the mysterious black thing. They didn't wonder why it had simply vanished and ceased its pursuit. They didn't worry that it would return. The only thought in each of their heads was that Wayne had not emerged from the tunnel.

"Wayne?" Olivia called, her voice already broken with dread. "Wayne!"

Albert had been standing to the side of the opening when the thing reached out for them. Now he turned and peered through it. Wayne was there, standing on the other side with his back to him. His light was still on. Albert could see the shape of his body, his strong, broad back, his thick arms. He could also see the ragged, two-inch hole just to the right of his spine, the hole that had been torn straight through his torso when the snake-like thing came through the opening. It had passed right through him like a bullet. "*Oh God!*" he cried. "*Wayne!*"

Olivia had approached behind him. At the sound of Albert's startled voice, her panic rose like an explosion. "*Wayne!*"

Nicole, Brandy and Andrea looked at one another, terrified.

Slowly, Wayne turned and bent forward, looking through the opening. For a moment he said nothing, only stared at Albert through the lenses of his glasses, and then he held the flashlight out to him. "Take it," he said, his voice soft, weak. "I…don't need it anymore."

"The hell you don't!" Albert forgot about his broken arm. He reached in with his left hand and seized Wayne's wrist. With more strength than he knew he possessed, he pulled his wounded companion through the hole, dragging him from the labyrinth.

Wayne slid heavily out of the hole and fell with a limp thud onto the ground.

"*Oh God!*" Olivia cried, staring at the bloody hole in his

back.

"I should have made him go first," Nicole said. She was staring at him, not believing what she was seeing. Behind her, Andrea was kneeling on the floor, her hands clasped to her bosom, her pretty eyes wide and afraid.

Albert rolled Wayne onto his back. His belly had the same ragged, blood-filled hole. He was bleeding, but not as much as he should have been. The hole had been singed by the passing entity, cauterized, as if he'd been run through with a white-hot sword. "Come on," he said lamely. "Get up. It's not that bad."

"Liar," returned Wayne.

Albert looked back up at the opening through which they'd just pulled Wayne. The thing had come through and then just disappeared. Why hadn't it come after the rest of them? Did it have something to do with those markings? The Keeper had told them that the curse was bound to the labyrinth. Perhaps it had struck whatever strange force kept it sealed and was repelled.

Olivia knelt beside him and took his hand. "No," she whimpered. "You can't leave us." She reached up and straightened his glasses for him. He wouldn't want to lose them on the journey ahead.

He shook his head. "Not my choice now." He held the flashlight out to her. "Take it."

"No," she said. "I won't."

"You'll need it. You…only have the three now."

"*You'll* need it," Olivia insisted. "You're coming with us."

Wayne turned to Albert. "I'm just dead weight. Take them. Go…*wherever* the hell it was we've been trying to go…take care of them."

"*No!*" Olivia was sobbing now. "*Don't you dare!*"

"Listen," Wayne said to Albert, ignoring Olivia. "No one knows where I went last night." He drew a long, shuddering breath. It was getting hard to speak. "Don't tell anyone you were with me. There's…nothing you can do for me…and those people up there…" he swallowed hard, as if trying to swallow the pain itself, "…they'll just make it hard on you…might even try to blame you…so just keep it to yourselves, okay? If not for you then for me."

"Wayne no!" Tears streamed down Olivia's face. She could not stand to hear him say such things. How could they not tell the world what happened to him? How could they let his family wonder that way? What about his mother? It was wrong.

"Come on," Albert said. "Don't give up."

"I want you to go," Wayne told him. "Right now. I don't want you to watch me die."

Albert shook his head. Wayne was right. He was leaving them. They couldn't take him with them any more than they could have taken Beverly with them, but he still did not want to leave him. Wayne had done so much for them. He'd saved both his and Olivia's lives. He'd probably saved all of their lives at least once tonight. "I can't do that," he said.

"You can. You will. Please."

Albert stared at him, hurt.

"You can't," Andrea said, still kneeling on the hard floor behind Brandy and Nicole. "You can't go like this."

"I…wasn't a good person."

"The hell you *weren't!*" Albert snapped.

Wayne shook his head. "No. I could have been a lot better. I made a lot of mistakes." He stared up at Albert for a moment and then turned his eyes to Olivia. "But I think I ended good enough."

Albert shook his head, still wanting to argue.

"I can be satisfied with this. Really."

"Oh, Wayne!" Olivia was sobbing too hard to speak anything more.

Wayne closed his eyes. "Please go."

Albert took the flashlight from him and stood up. "If that's what you really want."

"It is."

For a moment Albert stood there, more unhappy than he had ever been in his life. "Thank you," he said. "For saving my life. For taking care of us."

Wayne gazed up at him. "Thanks for letting me come along."

Albert handed the flashlight to Olivia and then turned and

walked away so that the others could say their goodbyes.

Brandy stood up and approached Wayne. "Thank you," she said. "So very much."

Nicole stepped up behind Brandy and put an arm around her. "It was very nice to meet you, Wayne." It sounded lame, but there was nothing else she could say. Tears streaked down her cheeks and her breath hitched in her chest.

Wayne smiled at them both and watched them walk away.

Andrea came next. She knelt down and hugged him gently, then kissed him on the cheek. "I…" she choked on her emotions and had to stop and sob into her hand. "I don't know what to say," she continued after a moment. "Maybe if I hadn't come with you…"

Wayne shook his head. "Thank you," he said to her. "For coming. It was…" He thought about what Nicole had just said and found the words fitting. "It was nice to meet you."

She kissed him again, the tears no longer letting her talk, and then stood up and hurried away from him, unable to take any more. Nicole and Brandy met her a short distance away and put their arms around her.

Olivia stared down at Wayne, her tears streaming down her face. This was her hero, the one who risked everything to come after her, even though she was only a stranger to him. What did you say to your dying hero?

"It was worth every minute," Wayne told her. "I feel good.

I hurt, but I feel so good. I really do."

She smiled at him, then bent and tenderly kissed his parched lips. "Thank you," she said simply. She took a deep, shuddering breath, trying to calm the sobs that threatened to bubble up her throat at any moment. "Thank you for my life. Thank you for taking care of me. Thank you for being a wonderful—" Her voice cracked and she was unable to go on.

Wayne smiled back up at her. "You're welcome," he told her. "It was my pleasure."

Olivia stood up, sobbing, and walked away.

Wayne closed his eyes for a moment. The pain seemed to be fading and that was good. He had not been lying when he said that he had ended well. He had saved two lives tonight. That was much more than twice the worth of his own, as far as he was concerned. When he opened his eyes again, the light had faded. They were walking away, leaving him, just as he had asked.

He stared up at the dark ceiling above him and let himself think of Gail Porbin. To his surprise, he realized that he didn't really miss her anymore. He finally felt at peace with that part of himself. Instead, it was Olivia who occupied his thoughts. She was such a lovely girl. He was sure he had made the world a better place by making sure she was still a part of it. And that made him happy. His only regret in these final moments of consciousness was that he would never see her again.

As the darkness swallowed him completely, so did his

weariness. He closed his eyes and slowly drifted away.

Chapter 52

The five of them moved on without speaking. Albert lingered behind a few steps, his heart heavy. He regretted terribly that he could not do more. It felt wrong leaving Wayne there in the darkness like that. But what more could they do? They had no way to save him.

He felt so useless.

He lifted his eyes and gazed at the four young women who walked ahead of him. He could feel the overwhelming burden as he wondered how he could possibly hope to keep them all safe through whatever trials still awaited them when he could not even save Wayne. He was only one man, and a man with a busted arm at that.

Brandy, Nicole and Olivia walked close together in front of Albert, holding hands and comforting one another. It was difficult to believe that Wayne was gone. Of all of them, he should still be here. After all he'd been through, after all he'd accomplished…

But this was the very nature of the Temple of the Blind. It took without warning, without mercy, without sympathy. It claimed Wayne as quickly and as certainly as it had claimed poor Beverly.

And it could claim any one of them just as swiftly. It could claim all of them, if it so wished. And perhaps it would do just that before it was all over. Perhaps that was simply their fate.

Olivia, in particular, felt hollow inside. She'd gotten herself into a lot of trouble these past few days, and it was only thanks to Wayne that she was not dead now. He was her hero, her shining knight. He rode to her not once, but twice, bursting from the darkness to carry her back to the light like any girl's favorite fantasy. And how many times had he saved her since then? He braved the fear room alone to spare her and Andrea its terrors. He pushed her out of reach of the hound that chewed up his leg. In fact, he made sure he was the last one to leave the labyrinth… just so that if one of them didn't make it…

She shuddered beneath the weight of her tears and Brandy and Nicole squeezed her hands. She still had *them*. She still had Albert. She still had sweet Andrea. She was not alone here in this cruel darkness. And yet, she couldn't begin to imagine continuing on without *him*.

Andrea walked ahead of everyone, her eyes fixed blankly on the darkness into which they were journeying. If she stopped walking, she would begin to cry. She was sure of it. And she was also sure that if she began to cry, she would not be able to stop.

It wasn't right. Wayne didn't deserve to die that way.

But he was gone.

Forever.

As she pushed forward, one step at a time, Andrea suddenly realized what was different about this tunnel. It was the air. She no longer felt that too-familiar, closed-in feeling that had pervaded those narrow passageways for the past several hours.

They were no longer in the labyrinth. They were somewhere else now.

But she was far too weary and too sad to even wonder about where they were.

Tears fell onto the cold, stone floor as the five of them walked on into the unfeeling darkness.

ABOUT THE AUTHOR

Brian Harmon grew up in rural Missouri and now lives in Southern Wisconsin with his wife, Guinevere, and their two children.

For more about Brian Harmon and his work, visit
www.HarmonUniverse.com

Made in the USA
Middletown, DE
26 August 2019